25'

Baldwinsville Public Library
33 E. Genesee St.
Baldwinsville, NY 13027

DEC 3 0 2019

WITHDRAWN

P9-DGG-372

PRAISE FOR AMBER COWIE

"*Rapid Falls* is an ingenious thriller cleverly disguised as a straightforward story about two sisters coping with the aftermath of a tragedy. Just when I'd thought I'd figured it out, the novel twisted into something entirely different, leading to an ending worthy of Alfred Hitchcock. You aren't going to want to miss this remarkable novel."

—Karen McQuestion, bestselling author of *Hello Love*

"*Rapid Falls* flips the script of the family saga of tough love and simmering resentments so hard and fast I think I got vertigo. Dark, delicious, and utterly subversive . . . I leave you with a warning: this one packs a wallop."

—Emily Carpenter, author of *Every Single Secret*

"Blood is thicker than water, but in *Rapid Falls*, both are fraught with danger. Sibling rivalry, obsessive first love, and a tragedy that haunts a family: the suspense had me hooked, desperate to see what secrets would surface. But that's the trouble with sisters—how can you hide a dark heart from the person who knows you best?"

—Jo Furniss, bestselling author of *All the Little Children* and *The Trailing Spouse*

"In this smart, riveting thriller reminiscent of Patricia Highsmith's works, a dark alchemy of family secrets and sibling rivalry spins ever more wildly toward a shocking, diabolical ending. I couldn't put it down!"

—A. J. Banner, *USA Today* bestselling author of *The Twilight Wife*

"In *Rapid Falls*, two sisters are haunted by a prom night tragedy. One's life is spiraling out of control and one seems intact. But appearances can be deceiving. Cowie brings her readers to the edge of a cliff and then dares them to dive off—right into the rough and tumble that is Rapid Falls. Twisty and gripping."

—Catherine McKenzie, bestselling author of *Fractured* and *The Good Liar*

"In *Rapid Falls*, everyone is the good guy in their own story. Like a spider spinning a web, Ms. Cowie skillfully takes this notion and elevates it to a fantastically dark and dizzying place. Say goodbye to any preconceived ideas about sisterhood, the power of grudges, or happily ever after, because this book will sweep them away and leave you gasping for more."

—Eliza Maxwell, bestselling author of *The Unremembered Girl*

"Hypnotic and darkly twisted, *Rapid Falls* is the true definition of a page-turner. It's so compelling that you will not want to put it down. Cowie's smart storytelling and mesmerizing prose paints a stunning debut, making it one of my favorite psychological thrillers of the year."

—Kerry Lonsdale, Amazon Charts and *Wall Street Journal* bestselling author of *Everything We Keep*

"*Rapid Falls* is a deeply seductive psychological thriller about two sisters and the secrets they struggle to keep as their lives—and their lies—begin to unravel."

—Sheena Kamal, bestselling author of *The Lost Ones*

"Amber Cowie conjures up the pressures of living in a small town where everyone thinks they know your business so evocatively that I kept turning round to see who was watching me. A great read."

—Imogen Clark, author of *Postcards From a Stranger*

"Years after a tragic car accident, a young woman's 'perfect' life unravels one stunning revelation at a time as the events of that fateful night come back to haunt her. Amber Cowie's gut-wrenching thriller sends you reeling through drunken bonfires, small-town intrigues, and family secrets as a single betrayal alters the course for everyone involved. A page-turner from start to finish; you can't look away until the jaw-dropping conclusion."

—D. M. Pulley, bestselling author of *The Buried Book*

RAVEN LANE

OTHER TITLES BY AMBER COWIE

Rapid Falls

Baldwinsville Public Library

WITHDRAWN

RAVEN LANE

A NOVEL

AMBER COWIE

LAKE UNION
PUBLISHING

This is a work of fiction. Names, characters, organizations, places, events, and incidents are either products of the author's imagination or are used fictitiously.

Text copyright © 2019 by Amber Cowie
All rights reserved.

DEC 3 0 2019

No part of this book may be reproduced, or stored in a retrieval system, or transmitted in any form or by any means, electronic, mechanical, photocopying, recording, or otherwise, without express written permission of the publisher.

Published by Lake Union Publishing, Seattle

www.apub.com

Amazon, the Amazon logo, and Lake Union Publishing are trademarks of Amazon.com, Inc., or its affiliates.

ISBN-13: 9781542003728 (hardcover)
ISBN-10: 1542003725 (hardcover)
ISBN-13: 9781542091206 (paperback)
ISBN-10: 1542091209 (paperback)

Cover design by Shasti O'Leary Soudant

Printed in the United States of America

First edition

*To Joan Jacobsen, who has always been my biggest fan.
Thank you for teaching me that stories are best told
under a cozy blanket by someone you love.
(Sorry for working blue.)*

PART ONE

When the call came, those who could hear it were changed forever. For some, it was a scream of unbearable agony. For others, it was the song of a siren: an invitation that they could not resist. In fact, they had been waiting for it all their lives.

—*Torn Grace,* The Call

CHAPTER ONE

She knew she should be happier. It was the second weekend of September, the perfect moment when summer leans lazily into fall, and the evening air was sweet with the scent of her neighbor's roses. A bird sang softly high in the trees as Esme watched condensation form on the wine bottle. Each bead seemed compelled to gather the weight of the others, causing them all to fall. She blinked when her husband, Benedict, disturbed the progress of the drops by lifting the bottle to pour the last inch of wine into his glass, leaving hers empty.

"Should we go in?" he asked, gesturing to the sliding glass door of the kitchen behind them. "Are you hungry?"

"Not yet," Esme said. "It's still early."

Benedict smiled, shrugged, and raised his glass. Esme returned the smile, relieved at how natural it felt. She wished suddenly that the glow on their back deck from the slow touch of sunset could last forever, that time would stop now, in this moment. She began to speak, only to find him distracted by a burst of music from another house on Raven Lane. He craned his neck toward the source of the sound: the home of Kitty Dagostino. Esme's words died on her lips.

Benedict shifted in his seat as if the beat was making him anxious for more excitement. She knew it was difficult for him to have an audience of only her, especially on a night like this, when he was celebrating his own success. One of his modeling clients had just been asked to walk in a major designer's show at Paris Fashion Week. Benedict would want to share the news with as many people as possible. She knew that soon he would start making plans for an impromptu gathering of their friends on Raven Lane. The best and worst part about their close-knit neighborhood was that there was always someone around to confide in. It often seemed as if nothing could stay private.

She needed a little more time before she was ready to let this moment end.

"When does Ranvir leave for Paris?" she asked.

Benedict turned to her with wide eyes, as if startled that she was still there. As she had guessed, his mind had drifted far away. "I'm not sure. We didn't get into details. I've got a call on Monday to finalize things."

"Oh."

His glassy eyes made her wonder if the news about his client's achievements had been entirely welcome. Perhaps he was lost in thoughts of his past failings, not his current success. Eighteen years ago, Benedict's own modeling career had stalled and then sputtered out completely. Tonight, when he'd arrived home from work bursting with pride, Esme had been happy that her husband was not holding on to the decades-old disappointment. It was the perfect occasion to open a bottle of wine she had been saving. After a couple of glasses, however, her husband's pride had cycled to a mood that seemed slightly frantic. He tossed back the last of his wine, then let his eyes skim the bare skin of her shoulders and chest.

"What should we do this evening? Zoe's away for the weekend. We have the house to ourselves."

Esme smiled at the mention of their daughter, who was currently attending a science conference, the first of her senior year extracur-ricular activities. Zoe had been in school for only a week, and already her calendar was filling up. Benedict leaned toward her and ran his fingers up the inside of her leg to the hem of her light jersey dress. As his hand inched even higher, she fought the urge to leap from her seat. She shifted her knee instead.

"We could invite people over?" Esme said.

Benedict stood up, and Esme winced as the metal legs of his chair scraped the cedar deck. She couldn't tell if he felt rebuffed or if the thought of being social had replaced his desire for sex, but it didn't matter. Her husband had moved on.

"Why don't you see if Sophie and Ray want to stop by? You're right. This is a night for celebrating my success, after all. We are going to par-tay."

He exaggerated his faint German accent on the last word to make Esme laugh, and she responded dutifully. She could tell that inviting their two closest friends over was only the beginning of the raucous evening Benedict was envisioning. Sophie Bernard and Ray Peters had lived next to them for years; it was Sophie's beautiful roses that kept their backyard perfumed during the short summer season in Fraser City. Benedict rocked his hips from side to side in time to the muted pop music still floating on the breeze.

"Party, huh?" Esme said.

"Why not? It's Friday. I've just had a huge breakthrough. Summer's almost over. Zoe's out. Let's enjoy each other, my beautiful wife."

"Okay, okay," Esme agreed before pausing. "Wait, I think Sophie is away this weekend. Should we ask Kitty instead?"

"Whatever you wish. My darling, Esme, dance with me?"

He extended his tanned arm toward her, and she tilted her head playfully without reaching to meet it.

"But I don't even know this song. It sounds more like something Zoe would be into."

"The music is just the backdrop, Ez. The mood is what we make it!"

She smiled but stayed seated while he gyrated in front of her. His long body blocked the sunset and cast Esme in and out of shadow as he moved in time with the beat. The changing light lifted an old memory from her mind. Seventeen years ago, she used to coax newborn Zoe to sleep by rocking her in and out of the beam of the streetlight that faced her bedroom window. Her daughter's butterscotch-brown eyes would droop closed in the dark, then open again in the light, filling with wonder each time she caught sight of her mother. No one looked at Esme like that anymore. Zoe was a teenager now, focused on her own pursuits. Just this afternoon, Zoe had raced out the door as soon as her friend arrived, before Esme could so much as say goodbye.

"Well, then I'll call Ray and Kitty. Are you going to invite José?"

Benedict's eyebrows knit together at the mention of his longtime friend and co-owner of his modeling agency.

"No. José is . . . busy tonight."

"Wasn't he at the party at the agency?"

"So many questions, my darling! The time for talking is done! The time for living is now!"

An infectious smile lit up his green eyes, making the brown flaw in the corner of the left one flicker. Benedict broke into even more enthusiastic, exaggerated movements with both hands raised, weaving them through his thick blond hair. Esme could see the long sinews running up his forearms. With the setting sun behind him, he looked even more handsome than he had the night she'd met him nineteen years ago in a crowded nightclub.

"Tell them to come over in half an hour. I'll run out and stock up on supplies."

She glanced at her cell phone.

"Sure. Probably a couple bottles of each, red and white."

"Your wish is my command."

He loped across the deck, through the kitchen, and down the hall to the front foyer, where they kept their shoes and coats. Esme trailed him, noticing the prettiness of her copper pots glinting in the low setting sun that burst through the windows. Even the hallway, which was shadowed for most of the day, gleamed with beams of light. Benedict's hair shone golden as he stopped just shy of the front door.

"Drive carefully," she said.

Benedict reached for his sneakers and jammed them on his feet. As usual, they were lying haphazardly on the floor mat rather than placed carefully on the shoe rack like hers and Zoe's. Benedict often acted more like a child than Zoe did. He flung open the front door, and Esme followed him as far as the step, admiring the way the pink sunset painted the space between the Dagostino and Stein houses across the street.

Raven Lane was a cul-de-sac with five detached homes arranged in a U shape, tucked into an area just two blocks away from one of Fraser City's busiest commercial areas, where Esme's restaurant was located. The lane had little traffic beyond the residents coming and going— a series of one-way streets made it difficult to access unintentionally. Though Raven Lane was empty, Esme could hear the murmur of cars and conversation from the patios on Main Street. Out of habit, she hoped Dix-Neuf was experiencing the usual rush of after-work drinkers and diners.

Kitty's pearl-colored SUV was parked in her driveway diagonally across the street, but Miriam and Levi Steins' electric car was nowhere to be seen in the driveway in front of her. Esme was relieved not to have to invite that couple over tonight. The Steins' reserved nature resulted in them socializing very little with the rest of Raven Lane's residents, and when they did, Esme found the forced conversation tiring.

As Benedict walked to the car, she looked to her left to check if Ray was home, straining her eyes to see past the hedge that demarcated the property line between their homes. Depending on how close to the house Ray parked, she could sometimes make out the shape of his vehicle in the driveway through the tiny gaps between the branches twisted around each other in the hedge. She still remembered when the trees had been planted a dozen years ago by the people who had owned the house before Sophie and Ray. Back then, the hedge was an unobtrusive line of foot-high cedars. *A natural barrier between the houses*, their neighbor had said, and Esme had agreed, telling him that she loved the way the green fingers of the trees brought a bit of nature to their city street. Neither of them had anticipated that the cedars would thrive so well in the Pacific Northwest conditions. The branches had knit together quickly, forming a hedge that had grown higher than their first-story windows. Ray needed a stepladder to trim it, on the few occasions that he did.

Tonight, the shadows from the setting sun obscured her view through the cedar trees. It was 7:00 p.m., but Ray's job as a sportswriter often meant late nights, so he might not be home yet. She couldn't see a car in the drive, though a blur of movement down the street caught her eye. The sharp rattle of the motor of their own compact SUV brought her attention back to her husband. Through the two-inch gap of the unrolled window, Esme could hear the heavy, excited consonants of German broadcasters announcing a European football match. Benedict winked at her through the windshield, tapping his hands on the steering wheel of the BMW before giving her a wolfish grin. In a heady rush of wine, she leaned forward and pulled down the stretchy fabric of her dress, revealing an intricately laced bra. Her unusual daring captured Benedict completely, and he kept his eyes locked on her, even as he reversed quickly down the driveway.

Esme heard the crunch of impact, the sickening sound of his car hitting something.

Someone.

The thick thud of a vehicle striking muscle and bone was both unfathomable and immediately familiar. It had the same obscene thwack as Esme tenderizing meat in her restaurant kitchen.

In an instant, Benedict's expression changed from lust to terror. Esme sprinted down the slight slope of the driveway, past her stunned husband, who had already opened the SUV door and exited. She rounded the vehicle and saw the lean body of Torn Grace, their

8

neighbor from two doors down, sprawled out with the back of his head against the pavement. As her feet rushed to close the distance to his body, her mind made sense of the accident in staccato bursts, like a camera freezing still shots of the scene so she could process it one tiny piece at a time. Torn's bicycle was twisted beneath Benedict's back tire. He must have been thrown from it by the impact of the crash.

When she reached Torn's body, she saw his blue eyes staring up at the deep-pink and purple sky. A day's worth of black stubble dotted his jawline. Her stomach heaved as her hearing amplified. Benedict's breath was heavy and uneven behind her. She turned to look at her husband, who was still standing by the driver's side, as if frozen in place. Her gaze darted away from him and back to the bike lodged underneath the car, its wheel spinning. The catch of the rough edges of the tire's rim against the bent fender ticked like a cicada in the quiet summer air.

Torn had grown up in the city. He'd never learned how to drive. It was something people in the neighborhood good-naturedly teased him about: typical eccentric writer couldn't drive a car like everyone else; he even had to opt for a hipster mode of transportation. Only now she couldn't find any humor in the gruesome scene splayed out before her.

None of that matters, she told herself as she once again focused on the broken man at her feet. She forced herself to ignore the evening sounds as she knelt beside Torn's lifeless body.

A halo of blood had formed around Torn's head. She looked around for his black helmet, which she had never seen him ride without. She wondered if he had been hit hard enough to throw it from his head, then realized that was impossible. Helmets were made to withstand impact. He must have left the house without it.

The concrete beneath her knees was still warm from the late afternoon sun, though she couldn't shake the feeling that it had been heated by the life leaving Torn's body. She touched the skin on his neck, feeling frantically for a pulse. She had to resist a sudden, deep urge to gather him in her arms and weep when she failed to find the steady rhythm of his heartbeat. Instead, she unbuttoned his shirt and began CPR. She couldn't tell if she was imagining it, but Torn's body felt cooler with each compression on his chest. No breath came from him as she fit her mouth onto his. Had Benedict been going fast enough to kill him? A chill flooded through her when she realized that she could be touching a body and not a human. Her dark thoughts nearly broke her rhythm, but she pushed them away until she felt nothing.

Footsteps and people. Voices thumped hollowly against her, like heavy-bodied moths pummeling a glass door. She lifted her head after a breath to see Kitty Dagostino's long, tanned legs in a pristine linen suit. Kitty's face was pale under a heavy layer of makeup. *She must have had a showing today*, Esme thought absurdly as she pumped up and down on Torn's chest. Esme's panic ratcheted up when she saw the fear in Kitty's mascara-framed blue eyes. A sharp spike of adrenaline stabbed the middle of her forehead as she turned back to Torn. The dull roar of sound formed into language when Kitty spoke.

"I saw the whole thing from my window!" Kitty cried, gesturing to the bright-yellow door on her place across the street as if Esme had forgotten where she lived. "It was an accident. It was an accident!"

Kitty's voice became choked as her flurry of words changed to sobs. Esme jerked her head toward the car, where Benedict still stood. He hadn't moved an inch since climbing out of the driver's seat.

Ray rushed around the corner of the hedge toward them. *He was home all along*, Esme thought. She dismissed the unnecessary observation as quickly as it had come, forcing her mind to stop grasping for the mundane to escape the horror that lay before her. Ray's unshaven face was red with exertion, and he sounded out of breath as he stopped in front of Esme and Torn. His eyes were full of raw pain, and Esme remembered that his brother had been killed in a car crash in his teens. Kitty's and Ray's reactions proved that this was not a nightmare. This was really happening. She administered another breath as Ray spoke in a voice close to a shout.

"Esme! Benedict! Is Torn okay? What happened?"

Esme raised her head as she continued pressing hard on Torn's chest, motioning toward Benedict. Ray understood immediately and went to join her husband. Suddenly, Esme heard the repetitive tone signaling the open car door, as if she had just tuned in to the frequency. She looked down at the man she was desperately trying to bring back to life. Esme counted her compressions and delivered another breath before speaking.

"Kitty, call 9-1-1. We need an ambulance."

Kitty's phone was already in her hand.

"Where's Aaron?" Ray asked, looking frantically for Torn's husband.

Esme looked up. "He went back to Syria last week."

Ray didn't respond. A muted burst of laughter from a Main Street bar was the only sound besides Kitty's hurried request to the dispatcher. Esme kept pressing Torn's chest up and down, however futile the effort. Between breaths, she stared behind her husband to the pale-purple streaks across the summer sky. The wind was in her favor. She could still smell Sophie's evening roses. She breathed in and out, trying to focus on the sweet scent for one last moment before her life changed forever.

CHAPTER TWO

At some point, Ray touched her shoulder and told her he could take over. Esme couldn't tell exactly how long she had been trying to revive Torn, as her time was measured in the seconds between chest compressions, but the evening was still light enough to see the scars from cuts and burns on the backs of her hands after sixteen years of running a restaurant. Her skin was too old now to erase what life had done to her. She stood up, rubbing her forearms to relieve the ache of the intermittent pressure, as she watched Ray's corded arms smoothly assume working on Torn's still chest.

The ambulance arrived shortly after Ray began. When the dark-suited medic motioned Ray aside to efficiently minister to Torn, the other paramedic herded Esme to the side of the driveway where Kitty and Benedict had gathered, thanking Esme quietly before returning to her partner. Esme nodded dumbly. They watched Torn's body being loaded onto a stretcher in rapt silence, like they were attending a macabre piece of street theater. The crack of the ambulance door closing seemed to echo down the empty street. Despite expecting it, Esme startled as the siren blared. She hoped that the paramedics' sense of urgency was a good sign. *Torn can't be dead*, she told herself. She must be wrong about how far gone he was. After all, she was a chef, not a doctor.

A police car pulled up, blocking their driveway. The officer who stepped out of the driver's side pressed her lips in a stern line, regarding the small group of Raven Lane residents. Esme tried not to wince as the woman's eyes fixed on her. The officer's coffee-brown skin had deep brackets around her mouth, suggesting the frown was as well worn as the creases left on an unfolded paper airplane. In contrast, her younger partner smiled kindly at them when he exited the passenger's side. His sandy-brown eyes were warm with compassion as he surveyed the scene, pulling out a notepad almost immediately. *Good cop, bad cop*, she reminded herself, trying to tamp down her natural instinct to cling to kindness in the face of trauma. The younger officer was the first to speak.

"Hello, I'm Officer Cole. We have a report of a person struck by a vehicle. Who was the driver?"

Benedict stepped forward. "I was driving." His voice shook slightly, and Esme dared another glance at the frowning female officer, who had walked around the side of the car to join her partner. The older woman's eyebrows knit together as she looked Benedict up and down. Her partner stepped forward.

"Thank you, sir," Officer Cole said. "Can you come this way?"

As the officer waved Benedict into the back of their car for questioning, Esme wondered if he would have to sleep at the station that night. She knew the police had the right to take him in and determine the charge after questioning.

"We need contact information for the victim's next of kin. Is he married?" The older officer's voice was surprisingly soft and melodic, with a faint trace of an accent. Esme's tongue felt too thick for her mouth as she tried to answer. Kitty turned her head in Esme's direction, then back to the officer. During the glance, Esme noticed that Kitty's makeup had smeared into black smudges below her eyes, uncharacteristically marring her usual flawless appearance. Kitty took a deep breath.

"Yes, but his husband is away. He works out of the country."

Esme searched the officer's face for a flinch at the mention that Torn was married to a man, but the scowl remained unchanged. Esme's close attention did not go unnoticed, however. The officer squared her shoulders and looked directly at her.

"Do you have contact information for him, ma'am?"

The question sent a pulse of pain to Esme's forehead, and she rubbed it.

"Esme. Didn't you look after their dog last time they were away?" Kitty prompted.

"Yes, I did." She tried to ignore her stab of panic at the thought of Aaron and Torn's loyal Saint Bernard, Professor. Aaron traveled so much for work. *Who will take care of Professor if Torn is . . . dead?*

The older woman's dark eyes seemed to get colder. "Do you have the telephone number?"

"It's on my phone."

"Okay."

The woman took out a battered notepad, then looked at Esme expectantly. Esme felt uncertain about what she was supposed to do next.

"My phone is in the house."

"Uh-huh. Do you live here?"

The officer looked toward the white house behind Esme, who followed her gaze, as if needing to verify that the home she had lived in for seventeen years was, in fact, her own. Raven Lane looked surreal in the growing darkness, lit only by the red-and-blue flashes of police lights. Esme was nearly overcome at the strangeness that surrounded her, as if nothing she said were real, as if she were in a dream. She wondered if she was in shock. She pinched the skin on her arm to remind herself that this was not make-believe. It all mattered, perhaps more than anything ever had.

"I do."

"Are you related to the driver?"

"He's my husband."

The officer scanned her from head to toe. Esme realized that she had suddenly become more interesting to the police.

"Stay here for now. You can go inside after a few more questions. Name?"

"Esme L—" Esme stumbled over her words before cutting herself off to collect her thoughts. For some reason, she had almost blurted out her maiden name, which she hadn't used in nearly two decades. "I'm Esme Werner."

"Husband's name."

"Benedict Werner."

"What is your name, Officer?" Kitty interrupted.

Esme was grateful for the reprieve, though she worried Kitty's sharp tone might make the officer even more aggressive.

"Officer Singh." The woman kept her eyes locked on Esme as she answered Kitty's question. The band of tension across Esme's forehead cranked tighter.

"Benedict was not responsible for this," Kitty said emphatically.

Singh regarded the tall blonde, pausing before addressing her again. Esme couldn't tell if she was being respectful or reproving of Kitty's outburst.

"Did you witness what happened, ma'am?"

Kitty's mouth twitched at the last word, but she nodded vigorously. "I saw the whole thing from my front window. I live there."

She pointed diagonally across the street. Even in the dimming light, Esme could see the bright pop of Kitty's yellow door and the carefully pruned branches of the rhododendron bushes that buttressed it. As always, Kitty's lawn was immaculate; she instructed her gardener to trim errant blades of grass by hand after its twice-monthly mowing. Kitty loved flowers that could be regulated, and from May to September, blossoms burst forward in an exacting sequence. Daffodils were succeeded by tulips, which were followed by light-pink cherry blossoms on the two trees planted on the front corners of the yard. Each year, the red rhododendrons started blooming days before the cherry tree dropped its flowers, as if Kitty's force of will could command nature. Esme shook her head. She was distracting herself again. She needed to hear what Kitty was saying to the police.

"It was an accident. Benedict was carefully backing out of his driveway when Torn cycled past. There was no intent to harm or injure. We are all friends here. My name is Katherine Dagostino, by the way. I am a close friend of Mr. Werner, and I can tell you that he would never hurt a fly."

Kitty's voice turned silky as she introduced herself. Before becoming a real estate agent, Kitty had been a news anchor for a local station. She had never been able to fully discard her love of a good story. In fact, the only thing Kitty loved more than relaying information was being a part of the action.

Ray cleared his throat, and Esme was reminded and reassured by his solid presence beside her. Ray was only five inches taller than her own five feet, but his body was strong as a result of his years spent on his father's fishing boat on the East Coast. He spoke levelly, his deep voice both deferent and firm.

"I saw the accident too. I was on my porch, right there."

Ray pointed to his house next door and they all turned, though no one could see through the thick hedge. Esme knew that behind the branches was an explosion of life and color. Red Japanese maples clashed with purple hydrangeas and dangling wisteria. Sophie, Ray's wife and Esme's best friend, loved flowers as much as Kitty did, but her garden was as chaotic as Kitty's was controlled. Sophie never worried about the timing of blossoms or the placement of blooms, and she wouldn't dream of hiring a gardener to wrangle its wildness into submission. *It's part of the reason the hedge has become so unruly*, thought Esme disloyally. She swallowed hard to dispel any blame. The crash had not been a result of Sophie's landscaping decisions.

"It was terrible timing but completely unintentional," Ray said.

"And you are?"

"Raymond Peters."

"The victim is Torn Grace. The author," Kitty said.

"Uh-huh," Singh said without affect as she made a note. Kitty widened her eyes toward Esme, seemingly to bemoan the officer's lack of awe at the fact that they had one of the literary world's sweethearts as a neighbor, but Esme kept her face blank.

"I sold him and Aaron their house," Kitty continued.

The officer ignored her. Instead, she pointed to the house directly across the street from them, which neighbored Kitty's. The windows were dark, and there was still no car in the driveway.

"Who lives over there?"

"Miriam and Levi Stein." Kitty spelled out the names for Singh. "They aren't home a lot. They play in the city orchestra."

Once again, Kitty paused to see if Singh was impressed, but the officer remained unfazed as she jotted down the names.

"Okay." She looked around at Esme, Kitty, and Ray. "I'll need full statements from all of you."

Kitty agreed readily and began to detail her exact position at the time of the crash. Esme let herself be lulled by her neighbor's flowing words until she heard Benedict's voice rise sharply. Kitty heard it too and stopped speaking abruptly. She, Esme, Ray, and the officer looked in the direction of the police car. The back door on the passenger side was open, and Benedict was sitting sideways, his long legs stretched out onto the ground. Officer Cole leaned against the back of the car, writing notes. Despite his relaxed demeanor, Esme guessed it was no coincidence that he had put himself in a position where he could block Benedict's exit from the car if her husband decided to move suddenly. Benedict seemed distraught. He was speaking quickly, gesturing wildly, and seemed to be struggling to maintain control of himself. Esme concentrated on the police car's flashing lights to stifle her own panic at her husband's rising tone.

"I told you I don't know how fast I was going. I need to get out of this car."

Benedict tried to stand, but, just as Esme had guessed, the police officer put a hand on top of his shoulder. It was a simple gesture made much more menacing by the gun hanging off his belt.

"Please sit down, sir."

Benedict sat, defeated, and buried his head in his hands. Once again, his ragged breath was loud enough for Esme to hear.

"Ma'am?"

Esme turned back to Singh.

From the look on the officer's face, it was not the first time she had asked for Esme's attention.

"I'm sorry, what did you say?"

"I need you to focus on my questions. Did you see the incident?"

Esme fought the urge to respond to the officer's condescension with the haughtiness her French grandmother and namesake had always employed when challenged by a stranger. For her sake and for Benedict's, she tried to borrow her mother's personality instead: calm, rational, and measured.

"I did. I was standing right there."

She waved toward the front of their house, then felt her face grow red as she remembered what she had done. The possibility of Ray or Kitty having seen her flash her husband caused her stomach to flip.

"My husband was making a quick trip to the store on Main Street. He was coming right back." She looked past the officer and back to the police car.

Benedict was speaking more quietly now, but his body flailed as he punctuated his story with movement. He jabbed in the direction where Torn had fallen, leaning close toward Cole. Esme wondered if the officer could smell the alcohol on his breath. Kitty tensed beside Esme, as if she was also straining to hear Benedict's confession. Singh spoke again.

"What is your husband's relationship to Mr. Grace?"

Esme noticed that the officer didn't have to look at her notes to jog her memory about Torn's last name. Maybe she did know who he was after all. *Or maybe she is just really good at her job*, Esme worried.

"They were—" Esme was surprised at the catch in her voice. "Friends. They were friends. We all were. Are."

"Okay. Look, I'm going to need a place to sit down with each of you. Could we use one of your homes?"

Kitty practically leaped forward. "Of course. Please, my home is just across the street."

"Good. I need to speak with my partner; then I'll be calling you in for your statements one at a time. This shouldn't take long."

Singh cast one last lingering look at Esme before joining her partner at the car. He turned his back on Benedict, who was now staring at the ground in defeat. The two police officers spoke in low voices. The flashing lights seemed to get brighter as the night darkened around them. Benedict's face was alternately lit with red and blue, making him look angry, then ill.

"Where is Aaron, exactly?" Kitty asked.

Her gaze was fixed on Esme, but Esme was still watching Benedict, tracing his lips and movements with her eyes. After a moment, Ray answered.

"Syria." His voice was tight, as it usually was when he spoke with Kitty. Their relationship had been strained since last September, after Kitty discovered that he had given her teenage daughter a cigarette.

"I know! But where in Syria? It's a big country, Ray." Kitty's voice was short.

Ray didn't rise to the bait as he replied calmly, "The east, I think."

He rubbed his hands over his face, and Esme heard the rasp of his palm against graying whiskers.

"It's so awful to think of him getting that phone call," Ray said.

Esme nodded dully. Aaron was employed by an international medical aid agency as a frontline physician. Torn could rarely get through to him when he was on assignment, and even when he could, Esme knew their conversations were too staticky and full of delays to be worth the attempt. How would the police deliver news like that over a breaking connection? She wondered whether Singh or Cole would be the one to tell Aaron that he needed to come home right away. She sent a silent plea that it would be the latter, more compassionate, officer. The two police officers finished conferring, and Singh walked back up the driveway, keeping her eyes locked on Esme as she approached the group.

"Mrs. Werner? I'd like to speak with you first."

Kitty touched Esme's arm reassuringly before taking a step back. "I'll show you the way," she said.

"Officer?" Esme rushed to ask. Ray glanced at her when she stammered slightly on the word. "Will you be the one to deliver the news to Aaron?"

"Yes, I will." Her voice became impatient. "Mrs. Werner, need I remind you that we are investigating a serious motor vehicle collision? The sooner you can speak with us, the faster we can get back to the station with your husband. And the sooner we can let Mr. Grace's husband know what happened."

"You're taking Benedict in? But it was an accident. We all told you that."

"Mrs. Werner. Please."

She felt Kitty's and Ray's gazes from both sides. Esme realized they were waiting for her to start walking, so she did. She rubbed her hands together as their group closed the distance between them and the squad car. Night had fallen, and the warm air was starting to cool. Benedict's head jerked up, and their eyes met. Closer up, the combined light of the interior of the car and the flashing bulbs on top turned Benedict's pallor a sickly shade of gray. Esme didn't smile or reach her hand out to her husband as Kitty led them around the hood of the car and across the street. She kept her eyes on her feet rather than looking toward the house that sat between Kitty's home and Ray and Sophie's residence. The house that belonged to Torn and Aaron.

Less than a year ago, Torn and Aaron had moved into the largest home on Raven Lane, the cornerstone of the street, as Kitty had described it in the listing. Now Torn was hurt, maybe even dead, and Aaron would soon learn that even though he spent so much of his life in a place where death occurred nearly every day, it had hit the hardest at home. Worse yet, Esme's own family was responsible.

CHAPTER THREE

Given Raven Lane's small size, homeowners were encouraged to sell their houses by invitation through a private sale with Kitty's realty firm rather than on the open market. Because of her gentle but insistent persuasion, Kitty had been the real estate agent listed for every sale on Raven Lane for the last twenty years, allowing her a chance to screen potential residents to ensure they were "a good fit." The euphemism meant people who were in the creative fields, the more famous the better. Despite the brevity and banality of Kitty's stint as a local news anchor, she had never let go of the belief that she was part of a special elite artistic community, and, as such, she wanted to ensure that her neighborhood reflected her status.

Esme had felt nervous as the polished, pretty woman with the perfectly rounded pregnant belly the same size as hers stressed this point to her and Benedict seventeen years ago. The director of Esme's second film had invited them to view the home as some twisted olive branch after Esme had been forced to quit. During the showing, she had been uncertain that Kitty would find their status as a former actress and a former model appealing, so she was thrilled to get the call that the sale had been approved. Kitty told her in a conspiratorial tone that it was their shared pregnancies that had swayed her decision, despite the couple's current hiatus from their creative fields. Esme had been too nervous to tell Kitty that the hiatus was permanent. Benedict had recently lost his contract with one of the most well-known modeling agents in the city, and she never wanted to return to acting. Not after what had happened.

Only four months pregnant, Esme had just started to show and wasn't used to strangers assuming the life-changing event was a topic for casual conversation. Even so, she laughed along with the real estate agent, basking in relief that she would get to raise her child in such a safe, esteemed neighborhood. The place on Raven Lane was everything she had been hoping for, and she didn't want to lose it.

Hours after their moving van had been emptied, Kitty knocked on their door and invited them to her annual Valentine's Day party. At the time, it had been a deep comfort to Esme to learn that her neighbors worked hard to be a part of each other's lives. It was only later that she realized that intimacy couldn't exist without intrusion. By becoming part of the neighborhood, she had unwittingly agreed to both.

Last August, when the costume designer for the city ballet who owned the home at the top of the lane had been offered a job out of state, Esme had been excited at the prospect of new neighbors. It had not taken Kitty long to find the right candidates. Two weeks after the house was listed, it was sold to Torn and Aaron Grace. Esme had been stunned to hear the name of an author whose third book, *The Call*, had recently launched him to national fame.

Their arrival coincided with Kitty's back-to-school barbecue, held annually on the second weekend of September. Kitty had hosted the event each year since their daughters, Julia and Zoe, began kindergarten. Things had changed since Kitty's first party. Julia's father was long gone after an acrimonious divorce, and though Julia and Zoe were both entering their junior years of high school, they had little else in common despite their close friendship as small children. As time had passed, Zoe's interests had turned to her studies while Julia immersed herself in fashion, makeup, and dating. Still, the annual party continued, and, like all events that Kitty hosted, it was considered mandatory attendance for the residents of Raven Lane unless they were out of town or deathly ill.

Miriam and Levi had skipped it during their first year on the block, and Kitty had sent them a note espousing the value of community.

At last year's party, which Esme knew was much more about Kitty meeting the new neighbors than celebrating the start of the school year, Esme had been running late after a long lunch rush at Dix-Neuf. She texted Benedict and Zoe and asked them to go ahead without her so that she could grab a quick shower. After she stepped out of the water, she stared in the mirror at the high cheekbones and fiercely soft brown eyes she had inherited from her grandmother, wishing her features were not so undermined by the fine lines and discoloration of her forty years. She pulled on a summer dress and swiped on lipstick before leaving the house, happy to see the warm sun bathing the nearly identical houses of Raven Lane.

The two-floor stucco rectangles, with their small front lawns and larger backyards, had been built in the early 1980s, prior to the new Pacific Northwest aesthetic of raw wood and cedar shingles that now dominated developments. Esme liked the dated uniformity that defined the street. It made her feel like she was part of a club that was so exclusive nonmembers didn't even know it existed. As the warm wind blew gently on her face, Esme could hear laughter and the rising notes of Mariah Carey, whom Kitty insisted was still relevant. She crossed the street, then walked through the narrow lane between the houses.

Kitty's recently rebuilt deck was larger than any other on Raven Lane. Esme saw Ray and Sophie, Benedict and Zoe, and Julia standing on the golden cedar planks. There was no sign of Kitty or Torn and Aaron Grace. Or Miriam and Levi, but that was no surprise. Since Kitty's scolding, the couple had begun to plan weekends away that lined up with the date of the annual gathering. *Bad timing*, Miriam had muttered the week before, fingering the cross around her neck nervously. Esme noticed her cheeks tinge pink with the lie.

"Esme!" Sophie had spotted her first.

Esme smiled as she walked to Sophie's side and brushed her cheek with a kiss. Her best friend looked effortlessly pretty, as usual. Sophie's nearly white-blonde hair was swept into a casual bun, with loose strands escaping to frame her face. The summer sunshine had coaxed a light spray of freckles across the bridge of her nose, and she looked stylish, though slightly too thin, in a light denim sundress. Esme often left her care packages, joking that without her, Sophie would die of organ failure as a result of negligent eating. She had always reminded Esme of an elegant Parisian version of Betty, the girl next door who Archie pursued endlessly in the comics she used to read as a child. Unlike Benedict's German accent, which had dulled over time, Sophie's French affectations seemed to grow stronger every year.

It had been Esme who had proposed Sophie and Ray as residents of Raven Lane ten years ago. When her former next-door neighbors had been offered jobs in Toronto, Esme had encouraged Kitty to reach out to Sophie and Ray as the next possible buyers. *An artist and a writer*, Esme had said. Kitty's eyes had lit up, so Esme decided not to mention that Ray's novel was still unfinished.

"It's my gorgeous wife!" Benedict cried, turning away from a conversation with Ray. He swept Esme up in a hug. He was over a foot taller than her, and her feet dangled off the ground, making her laugh. "You look beautiful," he whispered in her ear.

She felt his words vibrate through her whole body, and she told herself to wear lipstick more often as he set her down gently. She couldn't remember the last time he had made her feel that way.

"Thank you," she murmured as the others gathered around her.

"What did you bring, Mom? I'm so hungry." Zoe dove for the covered platter in Esme's hands. Esme darted it out of her reach, then looked at Benedict for direction.

"How long until we eat?"

"Kitty is giving the grand tour to our newest neighbors." Benedict grinned, and Sophie laughed softly. Kitty loved to point out the improvements she had made to her house over the years, particularly those that had come after she had been awarded a hefty settlement in her divorce proceedings. "She said I should put the steaks on after they all come out to join us."

"Sounds good."

Julia approached them with a small wave to Esme. She was named after her mother's favorite actress and had grown into a stunning young woman, as if Kitty's choice had been enough to will her daughter's beauty into existence. In many ways, Esme felt like Julia's second mother. She remembered five-year-old Julia leaving a trail of glitter through the Werner house every time she visited. Esme had swept up the endless sparkling piles, wondering out loud in loving exasperation if she shed it like a snake's skin. Now her cropped black T-shirt skimmed over a round chest before ending abruptly at the top of her visible rib cage. An inch of tanned skin was exposed between the hem of her shirt and the top of a light-pink cigarette skirt. Her hair, a natural lemony blonde, had been bleached a grayish white and dip-dyed lavender at the ends. She was still slender, but her small frame served to exaggerate the curve of her hips.

"I'll help you, Benedict. The barbecue can be, like, tricky some-times. Sort of like Dustin's pants."

Benedict chuckled at the inside joke as he stepped to the side to let Julia turn the dial. Over the last year, Julia had grown six inches and asked Benedict to sign her with his modeling agency. The two of them had always been comfortable with each other, but their new daily con-tact had established a shorthand that Esme had never witnessed between Benedict and Zoe. Esme was unimpressed that Julia still insisted on speaking in the robotic monotone she had adopted since becoming part of Benedict's agency. Teenage girls seemed to want to appear as if nothing mattered to them, which both puzzled and annoyed Esme. She was glad Zoe still spoke like herself. Esme met Sophie's eye, and her friend smiled.

"Please can I eat something, Mom? I'm not going to last much longer," Zoe said, reaching again for the dish in her mother's hand. This time, Esme relinquished it.

"Me neither," Ray grumbled into his cocktail. "I don't understand why it always takes so long for Kitty to serve food when the whole point of us being here is to eat."

"Okay, just one."

Her daughter lifted the wrap and Ray grabbed a cookie. Before Zoe could take a pastel-colored treat for herself, Benedict swooped in with the barbecue tongs and plucked one up, offering it to Julia.

"A cookie, Ms. Roberts?"

Julia giggled at the nickname he had coined for her when she was a toddler before arranging her face once again in a blank expression. Julia had never been able to resist Benedict's sense of humor. The week after her father left Kitty for another woman, Julia had closed herself up in her tree house, telling her mother that she refused to return to their home until her father came back. Only Benedict's handmade puppet and accompanying silly voice had coaxed her out.

"Okay," Julia replied. She drawled out the word, as if she cared nothing for cookies, but she couldn't hide the way her eyes shone as she bit into it.

Zoe shot a glance at her, then at Esme, who tried not to laugh at her daughter's disdain for Julia's posturing. So far, they had been lucky that Zoe had not been sucked into the stupidity of teenage angst. Esme hoped they could avoid it altogether. Zoe was a serious student who was already planning to pursue a physics degree after graduation. Nothing was going to get in her way. *High school is just what you have to do before your life actually begins*, she had told Esme, who had agreed. She remembered feeling the exact same way, though for her, it had been acting and not science that she saw in her future.

Benedict snapped his tongs above his head like a merengue dancer. He seized another cookie in the tool's grip and turned to Zoe, who had already jammed one into her mouth. "And, my lady, may I also present you with a token of my undying service?" Zoe smiled through pink crumbs as he dropped it on her flat palm with a ceremonious bow.

"Can you put the rest on the table over there, Zo?" Esme watched her deliver the platter, palming several more cookies before she headed toward a deck chair to read without being bothered. She felt a strange sense of sorrow for the day her daughter would be at college and no longer reading in the corner at their parties.

"Seriously, can we try and hurry Kitty along a little?" Ray's ice cubes clinked in the empty glass as he finished its contents.

"Right? I don't really think that my mom realizes I won't be staying here, like, all night," Julia said.

"You have plans for later, Julia?" Sophie asked.

Before she could answer, the sliding glass door opened.

"Finally," Ray said darkly. Esme looked at Sophie again, and she shrugged.

"He just got another rejection," she whispered. Esme raised her eyebrows sympathetically at her friend as she heard Kitty's high heels tapping toward them. After more than a decade, Ray's novel remained unpublished, which Kitty still held against Esme.

"And here are your new neighbors!" Kitty called.

Benedict waved, then extended his hand to the two men who stepped onto the deck behind Kitty. Esme drew in her breath as Torn Grace looked directly at her. Days after Kitty had told her about the Graces purchasing the largest house on Raven Lane, Esme had bought a copy of his most recent book, though she hadn't gotten further than the dust jacket. His picture hadn't captured the intense blue of his eyes.

Ray and Sophie moved forward to the couple and introduced themselves, but Benedict's rich voice cut through their pleasantries.

"Benedict Werner. I'm the man who's about to feed you."

The man beside Torn laughed and reached to shake Benedict's hand.

"Aaron Grace. Nice to meet you."

Aaron's brown eyes were warm behind black-framed glasses. He was short, only an inch or so taller than Ray, and his reddish-brown hair was cropped tightly. Freckles danced across his cheekbones. He looked serious but kind. Esme had no trouble imagining him abroad, in a canvas tent, making life-and-death decisions. Kitty had been impressed with Aaron's devotion to the medical charity that employed him. She was willing to make exceptions to the creative clause on Raven Lane for a man like that, she had said. *He was just as unique as a storyteller*, she said. *Perhaps more so*. Aaron touched Torn's back, bringing him into the circle of people who had gathered around them.

"This is my husband, Torn."

"Hello." Torn's perfect smile lit up his eyes. His coloring was striking: his hair was nearly as dark as Esme's, but his eyes were lighter than Sophie's denim dress. Esme guessed he couldn't be more than thirty-five, though the straight, strong line of his jaw gave him the unassailable perfection of someone younger. He shook Benedict's hand just as Julia spoke impatiently from the far side of the deck.

"Mom, seriously? Can we eat, like, today?"

Kitty's smile was tight. "Julia, hon? Please don't be rude to our guests. Introduce yourself."

"I'm Julia," she said. Her tone made it seem like an insult. The cords on Kitty's neck stood out.

"And this is our resident bookworm," Benedict laughed, pointing toward their daughter.

"Zoe." She looked up from her electronic reader, then looked down again, but not before Esme caught her double take at Torn. She had never seen the expression of fascination that flitted across Zoe's face.

Benedict turned toward Kitty, who was staring at Julia, now preoccupied by the screen of her phone. "Yeah, Kitty. Let's start the grill. Don't worry. I made sure to get the gluten-free buns for you."

"Thanks, Benedict. That was very thoughtful." Kitty squeezed his forearm before she turned to the rest of the group to issue orders.

Esme tried not to be annoyed at her husband for failing to introduce her or at her neighbor for flirting with her husband. Kitty was being Kitty, and Benedict basked in the attention. It was just the way they functioned together.

"Sophie, Aaron, would you mind helping me carry out the food?"

Ray walked furtively toward the path between the houses, likely to smoke a cigarette without Kitty scolding him. Esme watched in bemusement as Julia glanced at her mother's back, then followed. She hoped Ray would have the good sense to turn her down if she asked him for one.

Torn was still standing by the door, looking at her as if waiting for her to join him. As she moved toward him, she suddenly felt self-conscious about each step, like she had forgotten how to walk. She extended her hand.

"I'm sorry, I got lost in thought. We haven't been introduced. I'm Esme."

"You don't have to introduce yourself to me. I know exactly who you are. You're Esme Lee."

Esme was surprised at the mention of her screen name. No one had recognized her in years. She thought the lines on her face had erased Esme Lee altogether. The sliding glass door opened again and Sophie emerged, salad bowl first.

"Esme, can you unfold that table on the side for me?"

"Of course. Excuse me."

Torn smiled, but she felt too confused to return it. As she wrestled with the squeaky back leg of the table, Benedict called Torn over to the grill. Her shoulders slumped with released tension once Torn's back was to her.

Sophie set the salad down on the table. "He's cute, non?"

"Is he?" Esme said absently. She ignored her friend's skeptical expression as the rest of the party joined them. Ray and Julia walked back from the side of the house, smelling strongly of mint gum, overly sweet perfume, and cigarettes. Esme realized that Julia had doused herself in Kitty's signature scent, likely guessing that given her mother's daily use of it, it would disguise the smell of smoke without arousing suspicions. Kitty was talking too animatedly to Aaron to notice, only pausing long enough to admonish Sophie for not laying out the tablecloth. Esme volunteered to find it, grateful for a quiet moment to collect her thoughts while the rest of the party hummed outside. When she returned, Benedict was carrying a steaming platter of steak and ribs to the table. The group loaded up plates, then settled on the deck chairs arranged in two different conversational groups.

Kitty nearly sprinted for the seat beside their newest neighbors, with Julia in tow. Meanwhile, Esme waited until Torn and Aaron had seated themselves before she selected her spot in the other collection of chairs occupied by Ray, Sophie, and Benedict. She felt unsettled by the memories of her past life that Torn had stirred up and wanted to avoid them, and by default him, for as long as possible. She affectionately shoved Zoe's feet off the long deck chair to make space for herself.

"I thought you were hungry," she said, handing her daughter the plate she had made up for her. Zoe began eating before Esme could pass her cutlery.

"Thanks, Mom!" Zoe grinned through a mouthful of cornbread.

"Good book?" Sophie asked.

Ray grunted, as if the question pained him. As Zoe began to respond, Benedict spoke over her.

"Torn seems like a good guy. Interesting," Benedict said, looking over at Kitty holding court with the two men. Esme saw Zoe look at Torn again. The curiosity in her eyes made Esme swallow hard.

"It's nice to have new neighbors," Sophie said, and Zoe mumbled agreement before focusing her attention back on her plate.

"Yes, it is," Esme agreed, grateful for the opportunity to say something light about Torn while reminding herself that he hadn't intended anything untoward by referencing her past. Maybe he even thought she was recognized often. And Zoe's interest was nothing more than an adolescent girl's recognition of a handsome man. Nothing to worry about. She took a bite of Caesar salad to try and push down the lump in her throat.

"You like him?" Benedict asked.

"He seems nice enough," she said.

"Good. I just asked him to come for Monday night dinner."

"Oh, great idea." She took a sip of her lemonade to help calm her mind, which had begun to race. Zoe had a study date planned, Sophie and Ray were heading out of town for the week, and Kitty had a late showing. She had been about to cancel the weekly dinner party altogether. Instead, she and her husband would now be spending the evening with the man who had just reminded her of the person she wanted to forget she ever was.

CHAPTER FOUR

For ten years, Esme had hosted the weekly dinner at her house on Raven Lane. The tradition had started by accident the day Ray and Sophie moved next door. Esme invited them for a meal so that they wouldn't have to rummage through their still-packed boxes for pots or pans. Kitty phoned Esme in annoyance minutes later, telling her that she had planned to host the new couple. Esme sighed, then told her to come along, which she had, with Julia. When Kitty called two days later to ask her to host the dinner again the following week, Esme was happy to agree. She loved having a chance to experiment with food in a way she couldn't at Dix-Neuf. Monday night dinners were fun. She had never been at a loss as to what to prepare. Until the night she knew Torn would be there.

One week after Kitty's barbecue, six hours before Torn and Aaron were scheduled to arrive, Esme told herself to stop being silly as she perched on a barstool at their kitchen island, flipping through cookbooks that hadn't seen the light of day in more than a decade. *Why does this matter so much?* she asked herself as she rejected dish after dish. She was a celebrated chef; her restaurant had become a pillar of Fraser City's casually elegant dining scene, winning awards throughout its decade and a half in existence. Besides, judging by the way Torn had dug into Kitty's store-bought potato salad and coleslaw at her back-to-school party, he was hardly a discerning critic. And it was really Benedict's party.

Though he had invited them over for dinner, she knew his motivation wasn't food related. Her husband was starved for new conversations and new faces in their social circle. Benedict loved the security and status that owning a home on the coveted Raven Lane offered him in his wider social circles, but he had been bored of the repetitive social gatherings for years. Of course, that didn't stop him from enthusiastically accepting every one of Kitty's invitations. Even a dull party was better than no party in Benedict's mind. Having two new people on the street could be a salve for her restless husband. This dinner was about Benedict, not her or the woman she had once been. Even as she told herself to stop worrying about what Torn had said at Kitty's party, her mind drifted back to her past.

Torn had seen the version of her that she had worked so hard to bury. The Esme Lee that she created after she had landed her first film role while waiting tables at a dive bar. When the scruffy guy in a flannel shirt handed her his card after paying for a pitcher of draft beer, she thought he was hitting on her. *Give me a call if you're interested in starring in a movie*, he said with a shy smile. He looked like a fading hockey jock in his early thirties, slowly going to seed, but she had heard of people being discovered in unusual circumstances. It was the reason she had taken the job at the rundown bar so close to the two major studios in the city, attending acting classes on the few evenings she had off. There was nothing she wanted more than a part in a real film. She called as soon as her shift ended from a greasy landline in the corner of the kitchen because she was eighteen and the world still seemed full of possibilities. She had been right to trust her instincts. His name was Brian Smith, and he invited her to read for the main role in the indie rom-com film and cast her minutes after she finished speaking the last line.

They had shot the entirety of *Seeking Mercy* in five months. The role had changed her life. But now she was a chef and restaurant owner. People no longer looked at her the way Torn Grace had, and until that moment, she had been grateful to have been forgotten. Even Kitty didn't seem to remember that Esme was once an actress on the rise. Despite the fact that her fame had contributed to Kitty's approval on the house, she now viewed Esme as the neighbor most likely to cater a dinner party at a moment's notice.

She told herself to focus, pulled out her phone, and opened her internet browser with the intention of checking out a few food blogs. Instead of opening the bookmarked pages, however, she typed "Torn Grace" into the search field. The first hit was a video link: an interview between Torn and a reporter with the BBC. The lines that described it were brief. **Meet Torn Grace, whose recent bestseller, The Call, retells H. P. Lovecraft's most famous work. The book has sold over 100,000 copies in its first six months.**

She had looked around nervously before hitting play, as if Zoe or Benedict were about to walk in on her, even though they were in the middle of their school and work days. On the screen of her phone, Torn was seated across from the interviewer in a dramatically lit studio. Only the two men and the desk between them were bathed in light; the rest of the room was black, as if the interview were taking place inside a cave.

"What prompted you to revisit H. P. Lovecraft? What about his work inspired you to write your own version of his world?" The interviewer had his back to the camera, drawing the viewer's gaze to Torn's face. In the stark lighting, his blue eyes were the same color as the lapis ring that Esme's grandmother had worn every day of her life.

Torn had taken a breath and raised one eyebrow. He looked cocky but somehow grateful at the same time, as if the reporter had finally asked him the right question. The endearing expression made Esme feel a rush of heat, and she shifted in her seat as the video continued.

"Lovecraft was terrorized in many ways by the monstrous world he believed surrounded him and surrounded all humans. You can see it in his writing, the dread that we are all just one small move away from unleashing the beasts and demons of hell: monsters that are worse than our current imaginings. I read Lovecraft when I was a kid. You know, just to make sure that I could have the worst nightmares possible." Torn paused and grinned at the interviewer's chuckles. Esme sucked in her breath. Then his face turned serious.

"When I read Lovecraft, I got scared, but it took me years to figure out what was really frightening me. Even as a kid, I believed that Lovecraft was only partially right. I think that monsters do exist, but not in another dimension or a far-flung place that no one has explored yet. I think that each of us has a monster inside of us that we spend our lives trying to contain."

The interviewer paused, shuffling his notes.

"But you made it a love story," he said.

"Love stories are the most monstrous of all." Torn grinned. "It's the time when the monster inside everyone is released."

"Are you in love, Mr. Grace?" the interviewer asked.

Torn looked right into the camera. Esme felt as if he were staring at her.

"Yes."

The interviewer spoke softly. "So then how do you control the monster inside of you, Mr. Grace?"

His eyes seemed to sparkle with something in between joy and malice. "Who says I do?"

The clip ended there. Esme lifted her gaze from the screen of the laptop and looked at the book she had purchased weeks ago lying on the counter in front of her. The clean white letters on the black spine seemed to beckon her. She slipped off the stool and took it in her hand, flipping it to the first page.

> After the earthquake, they began to go mad. At first, there were explanations. The media attributed the well-known director driving his car directly into a crowded café in Paris to drunk driving. Rumors spread of an illicit, highly mind-altering new drug that was sweeping through

Hollywood when the celebrated actor barked gibberish during her speech to the United Nations. It wasn't until the entire cast of an esteemed television show joined hands to jump off a cliff together in Iceland that people began calling it what it was: madness embedded in the minds of tens of thousands of people, the world over.

It lasted five days, in the month of March. Then it was over. During that time, the afflicted were unreachable. Writers, artists, and performers were imprisoned in their own minds, unable to speak or seemingly hear anything in the world around them. Some reached for weapons. Hundreds died by their own hand, and no one could do anything to stop them. It ended just as suddenly as it began. We thought it was over. We didn't realize that something had been embedded in us. Something that was waiting for its chance to emerge.

Torn's words were disturbingly inspiring. A menu idea came to her in a flash, and she placed the book down. Pâté de canard en croûte: deboned duck stuffed in a pastry crust. A dish that looks like one thing but is something else entirely.

She'd gotten so swept up in the hours required for the preparation of the complicated dish that she was surprised when Zoe returned home from school. Benedict arrived shortly after and helped her set the table. At 7:00 p.m., the doorbell rang, and the sound felt like an electric buzzer against her skin. She busied herself tearing lettuce for the salad as Benedict went to the front door to greet their two guests, but she couldn't deny the fact that her hands were shaking.

"Now I'm really glad I told you to bring the wine." Benedict's voice preceded him as the three men walked down the hallway and entered the kitchen. Benedict flashed the labels of the two bottles toward Esme as he reached for a corkscrew. Esme recognized both varieties as ones that she kept in stock at her own restaurant. They sold for more than fifty dollars apiece. No wonder Benedict was impressed.

"Welcome to Monday night dinner!" she said warmly, kissing Aaron's smooth cheek and Torn's stubbled one as they said their hellos. "I've got bread and tapenade on the back deck."

"That sounds great," Torn said, already moving to the sliding glass door with ease. Every house on Raven Lane had the same layout. The front door opened into a foyer with stairs leading up to the three bedrooms. A doorway to the right opened into a large living room. The living room, spacious and bright, took up most of the front of the house; the kitchen and dining room were in the back. Esme assumed that his comfort with their home stemmed in part from the identical floor plan, but his confidence both impressed and unnerved her. She thought back to his elegant words and wondered what he saw when he looked at the cheerful, wild prints that she and Benedict had hung on their walls.

"Do you need a hand?" Aaron asked.

"No, go ahead. I'll be right out." Esme smiled at Aaron, who followed the other two men. She dressed the salad and then joined them.

Once outside, Esme breathed in the scent of warm earth. Unlike Kitty's and Sophie's, Esme's backyard contained little in the way of flowers, except for an astonishingly successful French lavender plant that resided in the sunniest corner near the back fence, blooming purple for most of the summer and then fading to silver during the cooler nights of fall. Instead of flowers, their yard overflowed with food. She had spent days digging up the grass root left behind by the previous owner to create four large raised beds, bringing in yards of soil to create rich growing spaces for fresh vegetables. Esme felt proud as she realized that Aaron was gazing at the ripening tomatoes, kale fronds, and feathery carrot heads with wonder. The September harvest looked lush and spectacular.

"It's incredible back here," Aaron said as he stepped off the two raised steps of the deck to walk between the planked beds. "This is exactly what I want to do with our yard, Torn," he called over his shoulder.

Torn took a deep sip of wine. Benedict motioned for him to sit down on a large outdoor couch, which he did. Esme walked to Aaron's side, eager to support his excitement about her hard work.

"How wonderful!" Esme felt her nerves dissolving as he smiled widely at her. "You garden?"

"Does murdering houseplants count?" Torn called from the deck.

Benedict laughed before he responded. "That's how I garden too."

The two men clinked glasses. Esme moved closer to Aaron, whose gaze was fixed on his partner with an unreadable expression.

"I don't do well with houseplants either. Too precious," she said. Aaron turned back to her with a smile. "I like things that can take care of themselves. Garden plants are bred to survive, as long as no one takes away their basic needs."

Aaron looked down sheepishly. "I think I fail in the basic needs department. Torn's not wrong about my lack of a green thumb. The gardening might be a bit of a reach for me. I travel a lot. My plants usually die of dehydration."

Esme wondered why Torn couldn't water the plants, but she kept it to herself. She knew Benedict would also let her garden go to seed if she left him with it. "Well, there's always drip irrigation. I'd be happy to get you set up."

"That would be fantastic."

"Kitty mentioned you work for an aid agency?"

"I'm a doctor with Aid Beyond Boundaries. I've been working in Syria for the past few years." Aaron reached over to touch a cherry tomato that was gleaming in the orange sunset. His gentle gesture made Esme note again how quietly handsome he was.

"Please, help yourself," Esme said, and Aaron plucked it from the vine. His eyes widened with pleasure as he popped it in his mouth.

"It's still warm from the sun. That has got to be the most delicious thing I've ever tasted."

"Just wait until you try dinner," Benedict called as they turned to make their way back onto the deck. "Esme is a phenomenal cook, and she's been slaving away for you." His smile was wide as he handed both of them glasses. "To new friends!"

Esme touched her glass to the others, hoping the light from the late setting sun would hide the flush that had swept over her cheeks. She felt embarrassed that Benedict had noticed how hard she had worked on dinner and irritated at his demeaning description of her profession.

"It does smell incredible," Aaron said.

"The proof will be in the pudding, I suppose," Esme said. "But thank you. How often do you travel?"

"The contracts are usually a month there and a month or so back. I'll leave again in two weeks."

Esme gasped. "Oh, wow. That's such a commitment. It must be hard to be away so much."

"It is," Aaron agreed.

"Hard on me, you mean," Torn said.

"Difficult for you both," she replied, her eyes still on Aaron. Deep sadness creased his face, and she wondered if it had been triggered by his husband's comments or his memories of the things he had seen. She felt the weight of his work pass between them, and she nearly reached out to touch him. Then his face changed again, and he flashed his perfect smile. Esme was struck by how much it transformed his serious expression.

"If Torn's writing, he barely notices I'm there anyway. Ask Professor. Our poor dog loses ten pounds every time Torn starts a new project. Now that he's a bestselling author, I fear for his survival," Aaron said.

She laughed, helping him lighten the mood.

"That's not true." Torn batted Aaron's shoulder, and Aaron tilted his head doubtfully. "Okay, maybe it is. I do tend to get a bit, um, involved with my work."

"It must be hard not to, right? Art requires sacrifice. Discipline," Benedict said. Esme thought fleetingly of Benedict's late nights and missed appointments while modeling, but she smiled agreeably toward him as Torn responded.

"For sure. But also, am I going to be the guy who tells his husband not to volunteer his incredible skills in the most horrible situations in the world? My husband is a hero. I married a man who performs miracles. I can't tell him to take off his cape just so that he doesn't miss movie night."

Aaron laughed, and Torn leaned in to give him a kiss. Esme smiled again, noting the way that Torn had claimed Aaron's heroics for himself. Kitty had told her that the two men had been married for only six months, though they had dated for several years. They'd met when Torn was a journalist and interviewed Aaron for an article on aid agencies. Esme had been amused at Kitty's infallible ability to glean information from her clients but couldn't help being interested in their relationship as well. It was nice to have newlyweds on Raven Lane, a marriage that had not yet been dulled by years of small slights and discordant pursuits.

"Well, you can always bring the movie to our house when Aaron is away," Benedict said, bringing Esme back to the conversation.

Aaron groaned. "Benedict, if you only knew what you were inviting upon yourself. Torn only watches monster movies. The older, the better."

Esme laughed. "Oh God. No calls from Cthulhu, please. Benedict's dreary Herzog films are bad enough."

"Esme. For someone who claims to not be a fan, that was amazing pronunciation of the mythic beast," Torn said.

Esme felt her cheeks color again. Aaron saved her from another embarrassment by pushing Torn affectionately on the shoulder.

"Don't try to persuade her into watching your weird movies, Torn. She's with me, bud. Rom-coms and Oscar winners, right?"

Esme paused for a beat to figure out if Aaron was making a dig at her, but his smile was sweet, not cruel.

"Absolutely. After a long day at the restaurant, romantic comedies are about all I can handle."

Aaron paused. "Do you ever compare them to *Seeking Mercy*? It must be a bit weird to have starred in such a cult classic."

Esme felt the blood rush from her face. "I . . . don't really think about it like that. It was such a long time ago."

"No one recognizes Esme anymore," Benedict said. "Even I almost forget who she used to be."

Esme stared at her husband, who was too busy finishing his glass of wine to notice her eyes on him. If only she had the same powers of amnesia.

Torn looked directly at her. "I don't hate romantic comedies. They just have to cast the right lead. Someone who makes me feel like I would do anything to kiss him. Or her . . ."

"Like Tom Hardy?" Aaron said. His joke drew attention away from her past life so effortlessly that Esme wondered if the man was even more empathetic than she had realized. Benedict laughed at Aaron's teasing, and Esme did her best to join in, trying not to read too much into Torn's pronouns. The timer beeped loudly.

She stood. "I'll be right back."

"That didn't come from inside," Torn said, pointing at the small black bird perched on the fence post. "Do you keep your kitchen windows open often?"

Esme looked up at the raven, who called again. Its imitation of the oven timer was pitch-perfect. "All the time."

"Ravens are notorious for their warped sense of humor. It's what has made them a trickster figure in myths around the world," Torn said. "I had one on our old street that used to mimic a car alarm. It drove our neighbors crazy, but I thought it was hilarious. When I saw the name of this street in the listing, it seemed too good to be true. Ravens are my kindred spirits," he said as the bird flew off. Esme couldn't tell if he was joking.

"Do you have a warped sense of humor?" she asked.

"No," Torn said, leaning forward and locking Esme in his gaze. "But mimicry is an art I know well. Not everyone is what they appear to be. We all play roles, don't we?"

Esme felt her breath catch in her throat at Torn's insinuation and how closely it aligned with what she had just read in his book. On Raven Lane, she was the perfect neighbor, the successful chef, and the loving wife and mother, but it seemed as if Torn could see the person she thought she had hidden nearly twenty years ago. He looked at her as if she was still all there. She glanced at Benedict, whose attention was fixed on opening the second bottle.

Aaron smiled at his husband. "And this is Torn, playing the role of the haunted, mysterious author."

Esme laughed, grateful once again for Aaron's quick wit to distract her.

"Well, if that's my role tonight, I should probably have more wine," Torn said, holding his empty glass toward Benedict.

"Fine idea," Benedict said, lifting the bottle to refill his glass. "I, on the other hand, am not clever enough to pretend to be anything but what I am. What you see is what you get."

An electronic melody began, and Esme turned toward the door.

"Unless that bird has found a way into the kitchen to trick me again, that is my cue," she said. As she pulled the golden pastry-covered duck out of the oven, she felt relieved to see its perfect unbroken surface.

CHAPTER FIVE

At 5:00 a.m. the day after the crash, Esme sat alone in her dark, empty house. It was hard to believe that their first dinner together had occurred only a year ago. Now Torn was in a hospital, Aaron was an ocean away, and Benedict was in police custody. The fates of the three men had jerked her in and out of wakeful sleep all night, prompting her to reach for Benedict only to find his side of the bed empty. Finally, she twisted out of her sheets to try to answer the questions reverberating in her mind. Was Benedict being charged with a crime? Was Torn dead? Would Aaron hate them both?

She despised the way Benedict's absence could still make her uneasy, but they had been married for seventeen years, together for nineteen. She had spent too much time as his wife to suddenly be without him. They had been apart only a handful of nights during their early marriage and when she was pregnant. After Zoe was born, it had always been the three of them. Now she was disconcerted, almost afraid, to be in an empty house with no husband, no daughter. At the same time, it was a relief to know that Zoe would be sequestered at the space conference, where all outside media was banned, for nearly two more days. As per the conference guidelines, Zoe hadn't brought her phone and wasn't due to arrive home until the next day around dinnertime. Esme was grateful her daughter had been far from Raven Lane last night. She wasn't sure how she was going to tell Zoe about the crash and Benedict's incarceration. She needed more time to gather facts.

As she padded down the hall to the kitchen, she felt cold, as if the warmth that had leached from Torn's body as she pushed on his chest had been drained from her as well. In the blackness of the not quite morning, Esme prepared her coffee, then dialed the number on the card Officer Singh had given her the night before. A switchboard operator picked up and relayed sparse details to her in a bored drone that reminded Esme of Julia.

"Benedict Werner. Individual was questioned and detained. Investigation remains open."

"So he's still there?"

"No more information is available at this time."

Silence. Esme felt her hands prickle in irritation.

"When will he be released?"

"Ma'am. As I said, I have given you all the information I have."

"I'm his wife. I need to know. I need to know if he's coming home. I have to . . . know what to do next." Her voice broke with emotion, but her outburst elicited no sympathy.

"That is all the information that is available."

A headache began to take root as Esme disconnected the call. She had made a note to herself to tell Zoe everything the police told her and now realized that she had no new information to convey. She glanced at the clock on the stove. It was too early to think about calling a law office. Or was it? Maybe Torn was sitting up in bed right now, asking for something to eat besides a fruit cup. She dialed the hospital where Torn had been taken. The nurse she was transferred to was as terse as the police. *Information is for relatives only.* Panic tightened Esme's throat as she hung up. No one was going to tell her if Torn was dead or alive, or if her husband needed a lawyer. She couldn't even call Aaron for an update. She was no longer a part of the world she used to live in, the one where there were answers.

Gnawing uncertainty compelled her to exit the shadowy, quiet kitchen. She left her half-empty cup of coffee on the counter and exited the dark room. As she stepped up the stairs, every creak on the floorboards reminded her of Benedict, of what they used to be like together, tiptoeing downstairs after finally getting baby Zoe to sleep.

Esme turned the shower faucet to a temperature that was almost unbearably hot and stepped in, letting the scalding water pelt her body. In the first weeks of Zoe's life, Benedict had been so loving with the colicky newborn, crooning German lullabies for hours as Esme fought to feel any joy through the weighted blanket of hopelessness, exhaustion, and pain that smothered her. He was the only one who could soothe Zoe in the middle of the night. Esme had often remained in bed in the darkened hours, listening to her husband care for the baby.

When she stepped out of the shower, she forced the memories down. She had to think straight. She still had so much to figure out. She left the steamy bathroom to pull on a black T-shirt and a pair of fitted jeans. The sky began to blur into gray around the edges of her reflection in the full-length mirror as she smoothed down her shirt. She decided to walk to Dix-Neuf. There was always something for her to do there, and Esme thought best when her hands were busy.

Last night, it had been nearly 10:00 p.m. by the time Officer Singh finished taking her statement and released Esme to stumble across the street, grateful for the darkness hiding the spot where Torn had been hit. This morning, she walked purposefully, keeping her eyes averted from the sidewalk. She couldn't bear to see the blood mottling its gray surface.

Despite the chill in the air, her head still felt foggy as she walked the familiar route to her restaurant. Main Street was quiet in the dim early morning, with only scattered cigarette butts on the sidewalk recalling the action from the night before. Her sleepless night made her movements clumsy as she unlocked the front door of Dix-Neuf. The restaurant smelled like burnt sugar. *Crème brûlée must have been on special last night*, she thought. It had been her grandmother's favorite dessert.

"La nourriture, c'est l'amour," her grandmother used to say as they rolled out pastry on the butcher block that stood in the center of her stone kitchen in the northwest corner of France. *Food is love.* Esme had spent every summer in France with her grandmother from the age of three to thirteen so her mother could track black-footed ferrets as a research biologist. Her grandmother's kitchen had been warmed only by the fire they used to cook with. The triumph of nursing a bed of red embers to create the precise conditions for making bread had been a beloved daily ritual for Esme. She felt magical when she learned how to transform sacks of flour into delicious loaves of bread.

Her grandmother treated her as if nothing else mattered, unlike her mother, whose practical parenting often veered into impatience. It was only in the quiet kitchen, with her grandmother's soft humming accompanied by the licking of the fire, that she was able to ignore her worries about her mother forgetting her entirely. As much as she loved her grandmother, she hated her mother's long absences each year. When her mother remembered to call, Esme promised that all her favorite foods would be waiting when she came to pick Esme up. If food were love, Esme had thought, it would be powerful enough to bring her mother back to her. And it had, year after year.

As she made her way through the dark dining room by feel, Esme remembered three-year-old Zoe devouring five chocolate croissants in one sitting on a stool at the bar to the cheers of her kitchen crew. She had always hoped that food would also be powerful enough to ensure that her daughter never felt as unwanted as she had as a child. She had opened Dix-Neuf when Zoe was tiny and, unlike her mother, had kept her daughter at her side through every step of the way.

Esme paused to turn on the light only after she pushed through the swinging door between the dining room and the kitchen. Usually, she scanned the front of the house for any glassware or plates that her servers might have left behind, but not today. She wanted to stay in the darkness as long as she could. The view of the dining room would only bring back more memories, and she didn't want to think about Torn, sitting in his favorite booth by the window, typing rapidly on his laptop, or remember the way he used to sheepishly prop his bike outside the window, within his sight line, when he forgot to bring his lock. Aaron had been right. When Torn was writing, nothing else mattered. Including basic security and safety.

Esme glanced at the clock above the door. It was 6:00 a.m. Dix-Neuf didn't open until 11:00 a.m. on Saturdays for the late brunch and lunch crowd, so her head chef, Anthony King, wouldn't be here for three hours. She would have Dix-Neuf to herself: plenty of time to work out the tension that had set into her jaw, hopefully before it coiled its way into a migraine. She hoped to find a moment of peace this morning surrounded by the familiar, beloved walls of her restaurant.

Sixteen years since she had come to view the space with Zoe strapped to her chest, and she loved it even more now than she had then. If the house on Raven Lane had been her safe haven after the disastrous end to her acting career, Dix-Neuf had been her lifeline out of the sadness. Owning and operating a restaurant was simple and honest, exactly the kind of work she needed. She cooked, she set the price, people ate. It was a clear-cut transaction. And though she poured her soul into her creations, that wasn't what her customers sought to claim.

~

They had been living on Raven Lane for nearly a year when Esme realized what she needed to do next. The transition from modeling to agenting hadn't been easy for Benedict, but after several months, he had adjusted to his role at the Padillo-Werner Modeling Agency. It wasn't the same as working the runways, he said, but it felt good to be respected by the young hopefuls who flocked to the studio after their parents forked over the five-figure fee for headshots, wardrobe, and introductions, even if there were only a few of them. Neither José Padillo, his best friend and business partner, nor Benedict seemed worried that the agency was running at a loss each month. Benedict had withdrawn significant chunks from their savings to furnish the office opulently, telling her that no one would pay a premium for their services if the place looked like a second-rate operation.

Despite her hesitation at spending so much of their capital, Esme had been envious as he described his new clients and their hunger to succeed. There seemed to be nothing left for her to hope for now that her acting career was over. Her transition from starlet to new mother had been challenging. She had never felt so purposeless, often filling the house with daytime television that she barely absorbed, staring wordlessly at Zoe's features as the baby fed endlessly from her body, then frantically showering minutes before Benedict arrived home so he wouldn't realize she had stayed in her pajamas all day long. She knew her attempts to be cheerful weren't convincing.

Days before his birthday in June, when Zoe was five months old, Benedict had come home with a tin of cupcakes that a client had baked for him. The icing was buttery soft, and the cake melted deliciously on her tongue. Seeing Benedict's eyes light up at the taste of someone else's baking reminded her of how good it felt to have someone fall in love with her food. She knew she could give him just as much pleasure as his client had, if not more. After all, she had done it before.

When she was nineteen, she had only ever baked for her grandmother and her mother. Though Grand-mère Esme fawned over her granddaughter's cooking, they both knew Esme's versions of her grandmother's recipes paled in comparison. Her mother never expressed an opinion about food. She was just as happy with a peanut butter sandwich as a croque monsieur. So Esme felt nervous as she placed her offering on a huge folding table in the center of the wrap party for

Seeking Mercy. The party was a potluck, and Esme had prepared her grandmother's most exquisite recipe. Her stomach dropped when Brian, the director of the film, reached for one of her creations.

"Did you make these?" he asked.

Esme nodded as he popped a plump madeleine in his mouth. His eyes closed, and Esme was relieved to see delight pull up the corners of his mouth. After working with him for months, long days that often bled into the next morning, she had finally managed to capture his every sense. When he looked at her again, his eyes contained only joy. Esme had been thrilled at her own abilities.

She baked cookies for her next audition to help the next director remember her as well. It worked. Within a month of the wrap party, just days after her twentieth birthday, she landed another lead role, financed by the world-famous producer Jed Matheson at MirrorMirror Productions. It was her big break. Esme felt as if nothing could stop her trajectory toward fame. She was wrong.

After quitting acting, she had let her sadness drag her down, her drive to be seen replaced by an overpowering need to stay hidden. Benedict's client's cupcakes made her realize that there was another way for her to be celebrated, without ever being noticed. The next day, after Benedict had left the house for the agency, she decided not to turn on the mindless chatter of television she had been using to keep the house alive. She put Zoe down for a nap, then dug through a stack of boxes in their basement, mostly nonessentials that she hardly remembered owning, until she found the leather-bound book that her grandmother had kept on the shelf by the flour she milled herself. Her recipes.

Benedict had come home that night to a meal of a freshly baked baguette, chateaubriand, and glazed beets. Every bite was delicious. Esme's sorrow had given her cooking a depth she had never managed to achieve when her grandmother was alive.

"Esme, how did you do this? You are a genius!" His words were garbled by a mouthful of bread, but the wonder in his eyes was unmistakable.

That week, she enrolled in an evening culinary arts program in a boxlike building that overlooked Slow Creek. For the next six months, she had a reason to fight through her fatigue and get dressed, brush her hair, and go out in the evening. As she held Zoe in her arms throughout the day, she thought longingly of the kitchen where her chef whites hung. Each night, when she stepped into the shining, brightly lit stainless-steel room, she felt strong and safe. The dusting of flour on her hands again felt almost as good as the translucent powder that makeup artists used to brush on her cheeks. Shortly after her graduation, she contacted Kitty to find her a commercial space.

The moment Kitty unlocked the glass door of 19 Main Street and stepped aside to let her, with one-year-old Zoe strapped to her chest, into the dim space that had recently housed a Lebanese restaurant, Esme saw Dix-Neuf come to life before her eyes. The scent of cumin still lingered in the air, the tiled floor was peeling in the entryway, and the walls shimmered with lingering grease, but none of it mattered. In her mind, Esme tore out the scarred leather banquettes and Formica tables, demolished the hulking service station, and ripped the musty institutional carpet from the floor. She imagined herself whitewashing the wooden floor and walls and building shallow curio shelves from floor to ceiling to display art. She envisioned the charcuterie sharing boards her black-clad servers would bring to tables, full of handmade sausage, fresh pastries, and preserved fruit and vegetables. She felt the steam coming off the open mouths of the ginger and lemongrass mussels as they traveled from kitchen to table. She saw the individual casserole dishes, warm and bubbling with cassoulet, soups, and meat. Most importantly, she felt surrounded by a beautiful blur of people worshipping her creations without ever seeing her face.

"This is perfect," Esme whispered, stroking Zoe's soft hair. Her daughter's weight reminded Esme that she had to become strong enough to support her for the rest of her life. No matter how conflicted she had been after Zoe's birth, she loved her daughter now. Dix-Neuf was for both of them.

Kitty admonished her. "You haven't even seen the kitchen yet."

Though she had already made up her mind, she humored her neighbor. "Show me."

As soon as she stepped into the kitchen, Esme didn't hesitate.

"I'll take it," she said to Kitty, who beamed and slid a clipboard loaded with the lease application into her hands.

"No, no," Esme said. "I don't want to rent this space. I want to buy it."

Kitty had asked, first subtly, then overtly, how Esme could manage to swing both the down payment for their house on Raven Lane and the outright purchase of a commercial property at such a young age, but Esme had never shared the secret with Kitty or anyone else. Even Benedict didn't know the whole truth. Just because it had led to something good didn't make the way she had acquired the money any less awful.

~

No one would recognize the spotless kitchen as the filthy space Kitty had shown her years ago. True to her vision, in the first month of ownership, she had replaced the dingy counter and greasy grill with six-inch-thick solid-wood butcher block counters and spotless stainless-steel fixtures. Everything was kept sparkling clean at Esme's insistence, and she found something close to peace in the pristine room as she looked around.

Her pastry chef had already come and gone; he baked at several restaurants in town and started his shift at 3:00 a.m. to complete the orders in time. The counters were piled with freshly baked loaves and rolls, and the kitchen smelled like warm bread. She breathed it in, grateful for the comfort.

She stepped to her station and pulled down spices to make a rub for a side of beef that her newly appointed head chef, Anthony King, would finish later. She had trained Anthony at her side for over a decade, starting when he was still in high school, obsessed with Dungeons & Dragons, and barely able to keep his pants up due to the unnecessarily thick chain that he used to connect his ratty belt to his wallet. Slowly, he had grown from a quiet, acne-plagued teenager to a serious, committed young man, enrolling in the same culinary program she had graduated from. He was her most loyal and dedicated employee, the only member of her kitchen staff who had lasted more than a handful of years before leaving for other opportunities. She had promoted him steadily from dishwasher to sous chef. Five weeks ago, on her fortieth birthday, she had stepped aside to give him the highest position available to allow her to pursue the next great phase of her restaurant. He had accepted immediately, his eyes full of awe.

"Of course the answer is yes. I feel like I've just been knighted by the queen," Anthony said.

"Hardly," Esme had scoffed, though the idea made heat rise into her cheeks.

"I can't believe you want a lowly dishwasher running your kitchen," he joked. "I guess I finally figured out what you meant by no wasted steps."

Esme had laughed as she remembered drilling the idea of efficient movement into Anthony when his aimless paths from sink to bus tray twelve years ago had nearly driven her to distraction.

"You certainly did," she said.

"I won't waste this opportunity either," he said, turning grave. The weight of his voice had been heavy enough to push down her doubts about leaving her kitchen in the hands of another, no matter how excited she was about what was to come.

"Good luck, Chef," she answered.

Anthony had transitioned into the role almost seamlessly. For the first week, she thought that her new project, a renovation of the special events space into a proper French patisserie, would require all her time, but she hadn't understood the slow pace of bureaucracy. Now, four weeks after filing the permits, a task she had considered a simple formality, her application was still being reviewed. Esme found herself a chef with no kitchen.

She fingered the soft, flat leaves of sage to release the almost medicinal smell. Her grandmother used to walk her through the long rows of dark earth and scented air of her herb garden, teaching her what each plant could do. *Sage is clarifying and unifying,* Grand-mère Esme used to say. *If used correctly, it lets other flavors sing without speaking too loudly itself.* Esme sharpened her knife and began to chop the leaves, trying to focus on what had to happen next.

She was startled to hear the bell on the door jingle. She cursed herself for forgetting to lock it behind her.

"I'm sorry, we are closed," she called through the open window between the kitchen and the dark restaurant.

"Oh, chérie. You are always open for us, non?"

"Sophie! Oh, thank God. Come on back. I don't want to turn the lights on."

Sophie entered the kitchen first, followed by Ray, and wrapped her arms tightly around Esme.

"I am so sorry. This is tragique." Tears sprang to Esme's eyes. Sophie stepped back and stared in her face. "You must be exhausted."

"I didn't sleep much last night. But you? When did you get back?"

Esme knew that Sophie had been in New York meeting with a gallery that was interested in showing her work. In the ten years since Sophie had installed her wall of miniatures in the curio shelves at Dix-Neuf, her work had become increasingly sought after by collectors. Esme wasn't surprised. She often found customers marveling over the tiny scenes Sophie had created out of white stone: the apple being given to Snow White, the White Witch's tempting Turkish delight, Persephone eating the pomegranate seed with her agonized mother in the background. Each piece was too delicate to be handled, but all the more devastating for their untouchable, miniscule expressions of guilelessness, greed, and sorrow.

Sophie blew her long bangs out of her eyes. "Oui. It feels like nearly lunchtime for me. I flew in this morning, expecting to take a taxi, when who should appear before me but Ray. I was so happy to see him. Until I heard the news." Sophie turned to look at her husband.

In the bright light of the kitchen, Ray's face looked drawn and pale. He was a night owl, staying up late to write both for work and pleasure, and Esme wondered if he had slept at all. If there was a late-night game he had to cover, Ray would often be awake well after midnight to ensure he still had time to work on his novel. He had told Esme that if he ended his day with his sportswriting, he had dreams he was drowning in a closed room slowly filling up with men's body spray. She had laughed. He had not.

"Have you heard from Benedict?" he asked.

"No." The three of them were silent. Esme knew she should tell them about the fruitless phone call to the police, but she was overwhelmed by exhaustion. Her knees weakened, and she realized that without a task to perform, she might collapse. She pulled a loaf of French bread from the pile and began slicing it, placing it on a large wooden sharing board. She added a round of ripe Brie, breaded in toasted almonds, then drizzled it with a golden thread of maple syrup. As Ray reached for the cheese knife, Esme's phone rang. Sophie and Ray stared at her as she pulled it out of her pocket and looked at the screen.

"It's the police." Sophie's eyes were full of anticipation as Esme tapped the screen. "Hello?"

"Esme, it's me."

The sound of Benedict's voice made her lean against the counter hard enough to bang her hip.

"Benedict. Are you okay?"

Sophie's eyes grew wider.

Benedict sighed. "Nobody beat me up, if that's what you mean. They are going to let me go after a few more questions."

Esme's stomach sank. "They're still questioning you? You've been there all night already. It was an accident. What else could they possibly need to know? Are you being charged?"

"No. They have to wait for the district attorney or something."

"That's good."

"It's not good."

"Why?"

"Esme, I need a lawyer."

"What do you mean? What is going on?"

Her husband's voice sounded thick, as if he were fighting tears. "Torn's dead."

"No. God, no." She closed her eyes against the sickeningly bright halo that now shone around the light in the kitchen. The migraine she had been hoping to avoid was on its way. She gripped the edge of the counter with her free hand, nearly gagging at the thought of Torn's cold lips against hers. She had been right. Benedict's voice buzzed in her ear.

"I can't believe I killed him. I can't believe he's dead." Benedict cleared his throat, and Esme winced as the ugly sound amplified through the phone. "We need to talk to someone, today. We need a lawyer."

"Okay," she agreed robotically, keeping her eyes fixed on the whorls in the wooden counter so she wouldn't have to answer the questions she knew Sophie and Ray had about what she was hearing on the other end of the line.

"It's important, Esme. You need to find us a lawyer that can meet this afternoon. We need to get ahead of this. Just in case."

Even in her haze of grief, she felt her mind buck against his improper pronouns. It was only he who needed a lawyer. She hadn't done a thing. She pushed the thought aside.

"I'll handle it."

"They did tests, Esme. I agreed to them. The breath one and one where they draw blood."

"That shouldn't be a problem, though. You only had two glasses of wine."

Benedict's next words came out in a rush. "The wine. Who cares about the wine?"

"What are you talking about, Benedict?" Esme lifted her gaze and shook her head in confusion as Sophie and Ray stared at her questioningly. She could hear Benedict breathing.

"I took a pill. With Ranvir."

"What?" Her head pounded.

"It wasn't a big deal. A bunch of my clients were going out. We had a little champagne reception beforehand."

"Champagne and a pill?" Benedict's giddiness on the deck now made sense. "Like, MDMA?"

"Yes."

"Oh my God, Benedict. How could you start this all again?" Esme's head spun nauseatingly.

Benedict grew abrupt. "Look, I have to go. We can talk when I get home."

The line went dead, and Esme lowered the phone.

"Is he okay?" Sophie asked.

"No." She paused. "I don't know." Esme clenched the edge of the counter harder.

"Can he come home?"

"He says that he'll be back later, but it might not be for very long. Torn's dead." She said the last two words slowly. Numbness spread into her hands as Sophie clapped a hand over her mouth. Ray stepped back.

"It was an accident. I saw the whole thing, Esme." Ray rubbed his face. He looked even more exhausted than when he'd arrived.

"I should have told him not to drive," Esme said softly.

"Esme." Ray spoke as if he had not heard her. He laid his hands flat on the counter and squared his shoulders toward her. "I can testify for Benedict. I saw what happened. Whatever you need. We are here."

"Thank you, Ray. But you didn't see the whole thing. You couldn't have."

"What do you mean?" Sophie said.

"He was celebrating. One of his clients got into Paris Fashion Week."

"That's incredible." Sophie couldn't contain her enthusiasm for her former home, but she shook her head immediately at her own response.

"He only drank two glasses of wine with me, but he was acting strange. I should have known something wasn't right."

"What do you mean, Esme?" Ray asked.

"He was high. He took pills with his clients."

"At the agency?" Sophie's eyes were shocked. "What kind of pills?"

"MDMA." The acronym tasted bitter in her mouth. Ray's face twisted in anger and pain. After his brother had been killed by a drunk driver when Ray was nineteen years old, he had no tolerance for people being careless behind the wheel. Sophie noticed too and spoke to cover her husband's silence.

"Don't worry, Esme. We will figure it out. Whatever you need, always. Whatever happens. Okay? Anything." Sophie touched Esme's forearm, and Esme put her hand on top. Her eyes filled with tears at her friend's kindness.

"Thank you. It's such a mess. I just . . . I can't stop thinking that Torn would still be alive if it wasn't for Benedict's recklessness."

Ray's voice was sharp. "Benedict's definitely made his bed. Now we just have to figure out how much worse it's going to get."

Esme nodded miserably. Ray was right. This was only the beginning.

CHAPTER SIX

After her call with Benedict at Dix-Neuf, Esme walked back to Raven Lane with Sophie and Ray. On the way, the two had done their best to reassure her, but she knew they were just as shaken as she was. It had been a relief to say goodbye so that she could try to sort through her own thoughts. She couldn't believe that Torn was dead, that he had been riding without a helmet, that a car backing out of a driveway had been enough to kill him. There wasn't anything that her neighbors could say to make her feel better about the fact that Aaron was left without a husband, or that her own husband was to blame.

~

Benedict's unreliability had always been the thing she liked least about him, but at the beginning of their relationship, it had been easier to ignore. The first night they had met, he had been wearing a red knitted sweater that hugged his strong shoulders and chest. He looked more stylish in the unfashionable knit than anyone else in a bar filled with the hippest people in the city. Since the release of *Seeking Mercy* to huge box office numbers a month before, she had started to be ushered to the front of the lines of high-end nightclubs, the same places that used to make her freeze outside for hours. Despite her frequent visits to the clubs, she had never met a guy who looked like him before.

"I like your sweater," she said as she walked past him. He met her eyes, and she was disappointed to see his pupils were so large that she couldn't tell what color his irises were. *No thanks*, she thought as she kept walking. She remembered believing that the night was full of endless possibilities, with a seemingly infinite number of handsome men around her. The world was opening up to her. It had not seemed necessary to waste her time on someone too high to remember her properly.

Sometime later, he had appeared at her table, interrupting her mid-sentence by grabbing her wrist and tying a frayed piece of red yarn the same color as his sweater around it. She noticed that the bottom of his sweater was unraveling, as if it had been cut or ripped.

"You like it. You can keep it. So that you don't forget me."

His accent was so strong that she had to lean forward to understand him. He met her lips with his. The kiss lasted seconds; Esme had been surprised by how gentle he had been with her. She was expecting something rougher from the wild-eyed man who was still holding her wrist. A man had never been so careful with her. Had his touch been less delicate, she wouldn't have given him a second thought. But there was something so tender about the way he restrained himself as he held her, as if she was something precious. Someone who was easy to love.

~

Two hours later, Benedict called her from the police station for a ride. She parked carefully in front of the imposing building, wondering if any of the small windows that dotted the concrete facade like pockmarks opened into the holding cell where Benedict had spent the night. A few minutes passed before her tall husband emerged from the front doors, blinking as if the muted skies were still bright enough to hurt his bleary eyes. She smiled weakly as he opened the passenger-side door of the car and slid in. He smelled stale, like partially processed toxins and guilt. Once again, his pupils crowded his irises, making his eyes seem even more clouded than they had the night before. His face was as gray as the concrete slab of the station. She shuddered at the thought of what he would look like if he were forced to live within the confines of a cell for years on end.

"Esme. Thank God you are here. I thought I would go crazy in that place if I had to stay one more second." Benedict's rough whiskers scratched her cheek as he pulled her to him. She felt his hot breath on her neck.

"Shh, shh. It's okay," she said, though the words of comfort were a lie.

Benedict pulled away from her and wiped the tears from his face with the back of his hand. "Have you spoken to Kitty and Ray? They saw it all, right? They told the police that I didn't mean to do it. Esme, you know that I would never have—"

"Of course," she interrupted. "We all know it was an accident. That's what they told the police." She started the car, checked her mirrors twice, then twisted in her seat to make sure there was nothing behind her before pulling out.

"Did you call the lawyer?"

"Yes," she replied, thinking about her earlier conversation.

Besides her property lawyer, Jack MacDonald was the only attorney she had ever met. A quick online search for him after saying goodbye to Sophie and Ray had revealed that in the nearly two decades since they last spoke, he had begun a successful criminal defense firm in the city. Her hands were shaking as she thumbed the phone number from his website. She didn't expect him to remember her or to be available on a Saturday, but she crossed her fingers that she would be able to get a referral to someone who could take Benedict's case. Hope flared faintly when her call was picked up. After she explained herself, there was a brief pause; then his answering service had transferred her through to his cell phone. He insisted on taking the meeting himself after Esme explained the events of the prior evening. Nearly two decades ago, Jack had given her another chance after her life was turned upside down. She wondered if he could do the same for Benedict as she glanced at her husband's weary face beside her.

"How are you feeling?" she asked, trying not to let it sound like an accusation.

"Like a bag of shit," Benedict said. "But better now that I'm out of that place. It smells like death in there. I needed you, Esme." He placed his hand on her leg. It felt heavy, as if his grief and fear had increased the mass of his body.

"Let me make you something to eat," she said as she pulled into their driveway. She was relieved to see that none of their neighbors were in view.

"I'm not hungry. But thank you." Something in his words made her turn toward him, and she saw that he wasn't just thanking her for the offer of food. Her heart ached as she allowed him to pull her into another embrace.

"We've got an hour before Jack arrives. Is there anything I can do for you?" she said before she turned the handle to the front door. Their house was warm, and her headache lessened slightly as Benedict shut the door behind him.

Benedict said grimly, "I need a shower."

"Okay." He brushed her hand as he passed by. She watched his back all the way up the stairs.

While the water trickled through the pipes, Esme restlessly tidied the front room, gathering an armload of Zoe's science magazines, Benedict's sunglasses, an errant lip balm, and a pile of discarded business cards to bring upstairs. She heard the water stop as she stepped into the master suite. Benedict exited the bathroom with a towel wrapped around his waist. As Esme watched him stare helplessly at the closet, her headache pulsed again violently. She had never seen her husband look so lost.

"How about this one?" she asked, stepping to his side and pointing at a crisp button-down.

Benedict draped the shirt around his shoulders wordlessly. She handed him a pair of khaki pants, which he put on. Then he faced the full-length mirror on the wall, smoothing down the white linen shirt in an uncharacteristically self-conscious gesture. Esme wondered if he noticed the same resemblance to his father that she saw as she stood behind him, meeting his eyes in the mirror. Benedict rarely wore anything but casually luxurious clothes: light cashmere sweaters in the colder months and designer T-shirts in the summer. *Looking good is part of my business*, Benedict had told her. As a result, even though the agency still struggled some years to show a significant profit, his clothing budget had always been high. Esme suspected that Benedict did not want to be seen as older than the teenagers and young adults that the agency represented.

Benedict's father, on the other hand, had been the CEO of one of the largest banks in Germany, and his primary purpose in dressing had been to intimidate those around him. She had met him a handful of times before he died of a heart attack when Benedict was thirty. Each time, he had been meticulously attired in French cuffs, a starched shirt, and pressed slacks, even on the weekend, and had stayed reserved and quiet. She had never forgotten his look of disgust when three-year-old Zoe attempted to clamber onto his lap. He'd treated her as if she were a germ-ridden stranger rather than his own blood. Her mother's casual interest in Zoe had seemed like warm affection in comparison. Esme enjoyed their occasional trips to Benedict's home country much more now that his father was gone. Benedict's mother had changed so much since her husband had died, almost as if his passing had set her free.

Esme had never mentioned to Benedict how much happier his mother seemed to be now that she was all alone. She didn't know how to say it without revealing that it had made her understand how liberating loneliness must be.

"He should be here soon, yeah?" Benedict asked as he walked out of the bedroom. Esme followed, glancing at her watch. It was just after 1:00 p.m.

"Any minute. He said he was coming from downtown."

Benedict sat at the dining room table and riffled through the blank pages on a notepad she placed in front of him before standing up. "So, he's good?"

Esme thought back to the man who had won her the substantial settlement that had allowed her to secure the mortgage for their home and buy Dix-Neuf.

"He's very good," she said, resting her hands in her lap as her husband walked into the family room to stare out the large front window.

~

When Esme first met him, Jack had been right out of law school, the first lawyer she found in the yellow pages. She walked into his small office, thinking that he seemed young but just as good-looking as she had expected a trial lawyer to be: short blond hair, glowing complexion, and fit body. Later, he told her he had been a professional skier in his early twenties. He had watched her kindly as she choked out her story. He didn't say a word until she was finished.

"I am going to make Jed Matheson pay for what he did to you," he promised.

Unlike her, he could say the famous producer's name without flinching. He didn't try to take her hand. Instead, he laid his flat on the table, fingers spread, as if steeling himself for a fight. Then he had laid out the facts, being honest about what it would mean to go to court against Jed Matheson, one of the most powerful producers in the industry. Her name would be smeared through the mud, and even if she won, juries usually awarded less to victims than they could gain in an out-of-court settlement. *Taking Jed to court likely means that you will never work again*, Jack said. Esme had been horrified by the idea of losing her career almost before it could begin, so she had agreed to settle.

All she could remember of the settlement talk was Jed's smug face across the table from her as Jack detailed her case against him. His eyes were small and beady, like a pig's, and they mocked her the whole time their lawyers discussed the terms of the agreement. He wanted her to feel dirty for taking his money. She did, even as she told herself that agreeing to the terms would be enough to make her feel as if Jed had been punished. More than anything, she wanted to return to the career that was supposed to be her way out of an ordinary life. Nothing had made her feel the way she did when a camera was trained on her. Its glassy stare was intoxicating. For the first time in her life, everything she did was noticed. She couldn't bear to lose the ability to command attention so completely. Signing the paper seemed to be the only way to keep her childhood dreams intact.

It didn't take long to realize how foolish her decision had been. Technically, nothing had prevented her from finishing her second film, being produced by Jed Matheson. It was explicitly outlined in the settlement documents that she could return to the set. But the nausea began ten minutes after she had stepped onto the darkened soundstage, building until she was forced to sprint to the parking lot outside to throw up. She drove away, from Jed and from the life she had been building, ignoring the calls of the sympathetic director and the cast until they stopped. She knew Jed wouldn't dare sue her for breach of contract. The film had been recast quietly. He had more than enough pull to keep it out of the trade papers. Nobody heard from Esme Lee again, and she had no reason to reunite with Jack MacDonald. Until today.

~

"He's here," Benedict called from the living room.

Esme stood up to join her husband at the window. The car pulling up in front of the house was black, shiny, and expensive. An older version of the man she once knew emerged from the driver's side. He wore a lightly striped button-down and dark pants. He looked healthy and tanned. His shoes were a rich brown buttery leather.

She opened the door. "Hello, Mr. MacDonald."

"Esme. Please. Call me Jack." He reached out his hand, and Esme was relieved that he didn't attempt an embrace. She shook it, then stepped aside to allow him to enter. "You look wonderful."

"Thank you, Jack. And thank you for coming."

"It was no trouble at all. You must be Benedict." He greeted her husband. When the two shook hands, Esme felt a ripple of uncertainty as the reality of the situation hit her fully. Jack was here to discuss keeping Benedict out of prison. This time, she would be on the side of the accused, not the victim. The three of them walked down the hallway, into the kitchen, then turned into the dining room.

"Please." Esme motioned for Jack to sit at one side of the table as she and Benedict settled across from him. Jack pulled a yellow pad from his leather briefcase, uncapped a pen, and looked straight at Benedict.

"Before we begin, I need to tell you that my fee is normally a thousand dollars an hour. That will go up if I need associates and other experts to assist me, which is often the case. Today, I am here to discuss the case, and I will not be charging you. Esme and I go back, and I would like to try to help you if I can." He nodded at her. "But if I accept the case and you decide to hire me, each time we speak from now on, you will be billed. Okay?"

"Yes, that's fine," Benedict said impatiently. He had never cared about money. Meanwhile, numbers began to race through Esme's head. They had some savings, but those wouldn't last long at Jack's rate. She crossed her arms tightly across her chest.

"I'll be recording this. Is that okay with you both?"

They agreed, and Jack activated his phone, set it on the table between them, and tapped the recorder to begin. "Okay. Let's start with last night, the evening of September 7. What happened?"

"I hit someone with my car." Benedict's voice was tight, as if the lawyer was wasting his time. Esme glanced at Jack in embarrassment, but he seemed unfazed.

"Benedict, I'm here to help you. But I need all the information. Think of me like a doctor. We have an attorney-client privilege that began the moment I walked in the door. Let's start a few hours before the accident. Where were you?"

"I own a modeling agency. One of my best clients had a huge success, so we threw a little party. Nothing too crazy."

Jack motioned for Benedict to continue. "What time did you get home?"

"I have no idea," Benedict said, looking toward Esme.

"Seven fifteen p.m.," she supplied.

Jack turned back to Benedict. "Do you often work late?"

"Yeah, a lot of my clients are in school, so we have evening meetings. You have to start young in my industry."

Esme looked down at the table.

"Okay." Jack made a quick note. "Then?"

"Esme had a bottle of wine ready. She wanted to celebrate the news too. It's a big deal. Not every agent coaches his clients to such success." Benedict paused, as if Jack were about to congratulate him. Jack's face remained impassive. Esme chose not to mention that she had bought the wine long before she knew anything of Ranvir's accomplishment.

"How many glasses did you have?"

"We split the bottle."

Esme fought an urge to explain that her husband had consumed the lion's share as Benedict continued.

"Okay, so, we drank a bit and then I decided to get more wine. It was Friday night, you know?"

"So you were driving to . . . ?"

"Just up Main Street. There's a wine shop around Twenty-Fifth Street. I got in the car. Esme waved goodbye." Esme felt her cheeks warm at the memory of how she had said goodbye, but Benedict carried on smoothly. "She saw the whole thing. I was going slow; I was careful. The cyclist—Torn—came out of nowhere. It was an accident. The only reason it resulted in anything more than a bump was because Torn wasn't wearing his helmet."

Benedict ran his hand through his hair, and Esme was struck by the sadness of his unconscious gesture. She placed her hand on top of his.

She had also been tormenting herself with the idea that Torn could still be alive if only he'd taken more precaution.

"Other witnesses?"

Benedict looked at her, and Esme gave him Ray's and Kitty's full names, pulling out her phone to relay their numbers as well.

"They told me that they'll do anything to help," she said.

"Is there anything else you can tell me about your state of mind last night?" Jack said. He made no motion to switch off the tape recorder.

"No." Benedict sounded stubborn again.

Jack folded his hands together. "I can only help you if I know everything, Benedict."

"What do you mean?"

"The police suspected you were intoxicated even before you were detained. I called a friend at the station as I drove over here. There are notes on file saying you were overly emotional here on Raven Lane, and it progressed further as the night went on. At one point during questioning, you broke down sobbing, then immediately launched into a long and meandering story about the first time you met the victim. Your pupils were enlarged. You were sweating profusely. That's why the investigators requested a blood test. Before the results come back, I need to know what you were on."

Benedict shook his head hard. Esme touched his hand to calm him as he answered, "It was an accident. Torn is dead because he wasn't wearing a helmet and I was careless and we both were in the wrong place at the wrong moment. My actions caused a man to die, and I'll live with that forever, but the police can't really believe it was anything but terrible judgment on both our parts."

"It's going to be more complicated than that, Benedict. That's why I'm here. I made a second call to a friend at the DA's office." Jack's eyebrows knit together. "The police are working with the district attorney at this point—if anything illicit shows up in the blood test, it is going to be a real problem for you. You're lucky they released you this afternoon, Benedict, but they'll be coming back soon. You are only out right now because they didn't deem you a flight risk, and you've got no priors. But you need to tell me what they are going to find in that blood test. I have to be ready."

Benedict looked down, and Esme felt his body tense. For a second, she thought he was about to hit the lawyer. He hated being backed into a corner. Then his body slumped forward.

"It was Molly. MDMA. Pills were being passed around the party, and I took two there and pocketed another, which I took later, just after I got home."

Esme looked at Benedict in disbelief. "Three pills? You took a pill while you were with me?"

"I couldn't feel anything. It had been hours. It wasn't a big deal."

Esme's head pounded at his dismissal of her question, and she swallowed hard. Jack seemed to sense the tension and he looked down at his notes, then raised his head again to change the subject.

"Tell me more about Torn Grace. He was an author, right? Was he a friend?"

Esme felt sick at hearing Torn referred to in the past tense. She suddenly remembered a Monday night dinner in December. Torn had been sitting exactly where Jack was. He had eaten three servings of the meal she'd prepared. When Aaron had teased him about making it seem as if he'd been starving himself for days before the dinner, Torn had laughed and said he always fasted when he knew Esme was cooking. Now she'd never have the opportunity to cook for him again.

Benedict answered, "Yeah, good friends. Anyone on the street will tell you. Esme and I spent a lot of time with him and Aaron, his husband."

Esme took a shuddering breath, and Jack looked over. "I'm sorry for your loss. This must be so difficult, but it's good news for us. No motive is exactly what I was hoping to hear."

"I liked him a lot," Benedict said. His voice was rough, and he placed a wide, heavy hand on top of Esme's flat palm on his arm. "We both did."

"So, what's the next step? Are you willing to take Benedict as a client?" Esme asked.

Jack took a deep breath. "Yes. Even with the pills, I think we are looking at manslaughter, likely involuntary manslaughter, at worst. The DA will go for prison time, but I'll fight for that to be reduced. Your record is clean; you were friends with the victim. It was an accident. It should be fairly straightforward."

Esme's lungs felt tight, as if something were stopping them from enlarging completely.

Jack reached into his leather bag and pulled out a contract. "Before I begin, I need you to sign this."

Benedict passed it to Esme without glancing at it. Esme always handled all their paperwork since Benedict had signed a bad contract with an agent when he first arrived from Germany, which he still blamed for cutting his career short. Esme knew the truth was much more complicated, but she was usually happy to vet contracts and legal documents on behalf of both of them. Today, the words in front of her jiggled as if she were trying to read them while seated on a bike plunging down a bumpy hill.

"Ready?"

Jack was holding a pen out to her from across the table. She took it out of his hand and signed the last page. She hadn't read a word.

"Thank you, Jack," she said as she slid the papers back across the table.

"I want to let you know that it would be best to get your affairs in order. The arrest could happen at any time. You own this house outright?"

Her head pounded again as she nodded. Given the size of their down payment, it had taken only fifteen years for them to pay off the mortgage completely. After the shocking jump in real estate since then, their house was worth at least five times what she had paid for it. The equity was supposed to allow Zoe to attend the college of her choice, even without the scholarships she was sure to be awarded. Esme wasn't sure anymore if the plan would hold.

"Find the deed. You'll need it for bail."

"Okay."

"Once the arrest comes, we'll get Benedict out of jail as quickly as possible. Until then, it's better if he can carry on with life as normal. Keep working, and keep socializing with friends and family before the arraignment. It looks great to the jury, and it keeps everyone calm. Okay?"

"Yes," Benedict said.

"This trial is going to attract the attention of a lot of media. Have you received any calls or been contacted on social media yet?"

She and Benedict both shook their heads. What was the last thing she had posted? Had she made it private? She felt sick at the idea of a thirsty reporter reprinting a photo of Zoe in her bathing suit at the beach.

"Good. After I leave, restrict access to all your accounts and stop posting. If anyone calls, direct them to me. I don't want this case tried in the press, okay?"

"Okay." Esme tried to clear the lump in her throat as Benedict stood up.

"Yes. Is that all?"

"For now," Jack replied, standing as well. Benedict walked into the kitchen and out onto the deck without saying goodbye. His hands carved more pronounced paths in his thick hair as he paced. Esme followed Jack through the front room and out the door, pausing as he stepped onto their front step.

"Thank you for coming, Jack. We both appreciate it so much."

"This might not be as bad as we think. But there's one last thing," Jack said. "You need to prepare yourself to be called as a witness."

Esme had suspected that her account would be critical to Benedict's case, though the idea of testifying disquieted her. Jack patted her shoulder, then turned toward his car. She looked to the left, toward Sophie and Ray's house. The hedge seemed even more overgrown than it had the night before. Its gnarled branches were thick and tangled enough to block out the warm sunshine, casting a long, dark shadow on her as she watched Jack's car pull away.

CHAPTER SEVEN

After Jack departed and they both guarded their online presence against strangers, she encouraged Benedict to go for a run. It was what he did when he felt overwhelmed, and if the events of the day had been challenging for her, she knew her husband was barely holding on. Her headache had faded following Jack's visit, but as soon as the door closed behind Benedict, it returned. She was nauseated and in need of distraction, but everything she picked up—a long-abandoned knitting project, a new magazine—only blurred in her vision.

Until she saw Torn's book on Zoe's bookshelf. She had never finished it; Zoe had borrowed it when she was only a few pages in, and the book had sat on the shelves of her room for months. Esme had thought little of it. Her life had become too big for books in the months after she'd met Torn and Aaron. Now, suddenly, her world was small again, and she wanted to escape into a place of his invention. It felt like a tribute and a testament to her grief. She retreated to the bedroom, stopping only to take a painkiller before pulling the blinds. As she lay on the bed with the book in her hands, she couldn't stop craning her ears, waiting for the knock on the door that would take her husband away. She opened the pages to read Torn's words, trying not to think about the fact that his next book, which he had been fervently working to finish, would never be completed.

I saw a man on a street during the period media pundits would later call the Ides of March. At first, I thought he was just a typical panhandler who often loitered on the grand steps before the college I attended, seeking the leftover heat from the library that blew through the grates of the sidewalk. I had grown tired of being accosted for money or subjected to emotional battering by the unwell, unwashed individuals that called my school their home, so usually I hurried by their bodies without a thought. But he was different. I kept a safe distance as I watched him trace the lines of the sidewalk, painstakingly and intensely, his entire body held rigid as his extended finger scraped the flaws in the rough asphalt. He followed long lines, stopped and outlined collections of short cracks, and dug into the buckles between the paving stones as if the whole expanse were a map that he needed to understand to find his salvation. Then, as if he could feel my gaze, he lifted his face toward me, raising his finger to point at me. Even from a distance of ten feet, I could see that he had bloodied the tip to a meaty pulp with his scraping. A trick of light made his eyes flash white as he stared toward me, as if his madness had bleached the color. He began to rasp a word that I couldn't understand, the volume of his voice rising with each uttering until it became a tortured scream. I couldn't understand the gibberish. The word began with a hard *c* and ended with a long undulating *u*, but apart from those sounds and despite his ceaseless repetition, the rest remained unintelligible. When he saw my bewilderment, he stopped. Then he began again, in a language that I knew.

"Monster, monster, monster, monster," he cried, shaking his bleeding finger at me. A crowd began to gather, and I forced myself to break away from his terrifying, mesmerizing accusation. As I turned my back and continued up the stone steps, the call stopped. I dared a final look at the madman before I slipped into the imposing doors of the library. He had dropped to his knees and was tracing the broken pavement again, silently, as if his screams had never shattered the hum of the early-morning commute.

Esme closed the book, laid her pounding head on the pillow, and wondered what the madman would scream if he saw her on the street. In darkness, she woke up, disoriented and surprised that sleep had taken her so unaware. The pain in her head felt like two drills working inward from either side of her skull. She got up and unwrapped another migraine tablet, avoiding her face in the mirror as she dry-swallowed the pill. She returned to her bed, checking the time on her phone. It was 2:00 a.m. Benedict still wasn't home.

Esme woke again when Benedict stumbled in the door. Even before she heard him trip as he climbed the stairs, she could tell he had been drinking. She smelled his whiskey sweat as he climbed into the bed beside her, and she kept still to make him think she was asleep. Within minutes, she heard his alcohol-thickened snores, and her agitation grew with every wheeze of his nostrils. After years of marriage, nothing happened in isolation. Every moment between them was layered with the memories of those that had gone before. Esme's mind lurched as if a roller coaster had just pulled her around a sharp, speeding curve.

~

Eighteen years ago, during an August heat wave, José Padillo's call woke her from a deep sleep the night before her second film was about to begin shooting. She had just purchased the cell phone, and at first, its unfamiliar sound confused her. It took three rings before she realized it was coming from the pocket of her purse in her closet. A sinking feeling of dread filled her as she heard José's panicked voice on the line.

"Thank God I've reached you," José said hurriedly after she said hello. "It's Benedict. He's overdosed. I'm at the hospital now. I don't know what to do. He's not even awake. I found him on the bathroom floor at the club. There was blood everywhere; I think he must have hit his head."

Esme's first thought had been her call time the next morning. She had to be at the studio in less than six hours. Over the year and a half they'd been together, she had grown to nearly love Benedict, but his drug use had always stopped her from getting in too deep. She knew it was wrong to even consider telling José that she couldn't make it to the hospital that night, but she was tempted to do so. Then she remembered the previous Christmas, when he had given her a set of four chocolate letters spelling out her name, along with a lumpy pair of hand-knitted gloves. She couldn't leave him in the hospital alone. What if he died? She could never live with herself.

"Which hospital?"

Esme scrawled the name and address on a notepad beside her bed.

After she'd spent hours listening to ticking machines in the half light of the critical care ward at night, clutching his hand and watching José pace, Benedict had woken up. Despite his dulled eyes, he spoke with astonishing clarity as he assured José that he would never slip up like that again. After a half hour of assurances, José had left her and Benedict alone in the darkened private room. Benedict told her that he loved her and wanted to be with her, forever, and he knew the only way to do that was to quit drugs. She slipped into bed beside him, overcome with the emotions of the night. Esme had been surprised that Benedict was capable of sex after his body had been through so much, but the physical act had felt like even more of a promise than his vow to stop using.

Afterward, he made an international call to Germany to ask his parents for the money to enter a twenty-eight-day rehabilitation program.

Benedict's commitment to her and to getting clean thrilled her enough to carry her through her exhaustion on the first day of her second film, even if she wasn't completely sure she felt the same way. Her mother had so rarely expressed affection. Hearing Benedict say "I love you" felt like reason enough to stay with him long enough to find out if she loved him too. She was only twenty-two. If he failed, she could always leave. She had time to start over.

~

Somehow, the memory of Benedict's overdose lulled her into sleep. When she woke again, she was alone in the bed, and warm sunlight lit the room through the curtains. It wasn't as bright as usual, which confused her. Something felt wrong. It took a moment before she remembered Torn's death. Where was Benedict? She clumsily reached for her phone and gasped at the time. It was nearly noon. She couldn't remember the last time she had slept this late. There were several concerned texts from Sophie and Kitty. She replied to Sophie, told herself to remember to write back to Kitty later, then eased her way into a long, hot shower. The pulse of the water nearly erased the events of the last two days. It wasn't until she stepped out, toweled off, and got dressed that the details came flooding back.

On the kitchen table, she found a scrawled note from Benedict.

Esme:

I didn't want to wake you up, but I had to get out. I need to clear my head, so I'm hiking Grace Canyon today. I'll pick up sushi on the way home and we'll talk to Zoe together. Back around four.

xxx Benedict

Esme stood in the silent bedroom. Bright light still ringed the objects around her, and her eyes were sore from the pressure of her headache. Her mind kept skirting back to the image of Torn's body on the road, as if testing out her strength to accept that he was dead. Suddenly, she couldn't bear the thought of staying awake for another moment. With her hair damp from the shower, she crawled back into the bed that was still warm from her body. As her eyelids drooped, she set an alarm for 4:00 p.m. Zoe was due home at five. Benedict would be home by then, and they could all talk as a family.

Four hours later, she stirred in the dim room, opening her eyes gingerly. She was relieved to feel her headache had lifted, and she stretched her body out onto the sheets. In an instant, she realized Torn would never feel the whisper of fresh linen against his skin again. "Torn is dead," she whispered, feeling the words hit her like a dull mallet to her breastbone. She raised her body from the bed and slipped into her clothes. *Torn is dead.*

Benedict opened the front door just as she walked downstairs, pulling her fingers through her tangled hair.

"Hi," he said, looking exhausted. "How are you doing?"

Esme lifted one side of her mouth in a half smile. "I've been better."

She took the two bags out of his hands as he slipped off his hiking boots, making her way into the dining room to unpack the containers. Benedict followed her after grabbing plates and chopsticks. The routine felt as familiar as a choreographed dance. As they laid out the sushi, Esme noticed that Benedict hadn't included the house roll, which was usually part of their standing order. It had been Torn's favorite. The prick of tears made her blink hard. The fact that Torn would never sit at this table again seemed too enormous to comprehend. She stopped unloading the bags so she could look Benedict in the eye. She saw concern as he realized she was close to crying.

"Tough day."

"Any word from the police?" she asked.

Benedict sighed and shook his head. "Maybe no news is good news, yeah?"

Esme shrugged. Then the front door opened.

"Mom? Dad?" Esme heard a rustling of outerwear as Zoe placed her shoes on the rack and hung up her coat.

"In the dining room, honey."

Esme smiled as her daughter appeared before her, her backpack slung over her shoulder.

"Hello, dear Mother and Father. Did you miss me desperately?" Zoe affected Julia's vocal fry, and Esme couldn't help but smile as her daughter rushed toward her. Esme opened her arms, and Zoe tucked herself into the hug effortlessly. Esme savored her daughter's arms around her before Zoe pulled away and gave Benedict a similar embrace. He patted her back once, then pulled away.

"I wasn't sure you were here," Zoe said. "The SUV isn't in the driveway."

Zoe's dirty-blonde hair was pulled into a disheveled high bun more freed than contained, and her glasses were so smudged that Esme had to tell herself not to take them off her daughter's face and clean them herself. Zoe had started wearing glasses at the age of fourteen, and Esme teased her that she hadn't cleaned them since.

She looked back and forth between her parents. "What's wrong?"

"Nothing," Esme said, then kicked herself for the reflexive lie. "I mean, we need to talk to you about something, but it can wait until after we eat. How was the conference?" Zoe's AP physics class had been invited to a national meeting to discuss the possibility of establishing life on Mars.

"Awesome! Neil deGrasse Tyson was the keynote speaker!" Zoe's smile shone, and Esme felt her heart break at her daughter's exultation, knowing that the conversation they had to have would drag her away from her dreams of the vast universe and into a messy reality back on Earth. Zoe had seen Torn and Aaron at their home frequently over the last year, and Esme knew she cared about them both deeply, considering them slightly cooler versions of Sophie and Ray, but she had liked Torn best of all. At times, Esme had even worried that Zoe was beginning to harbor a crush on Torn, which made delivering this news even more difficult. Even worse than Zoe's imminent grief for their neighbor was that her first direct experience with death was going to be the worst kind imaginable: one that had resulted from her father's carelessness.

"That sounds great. Dinner is ready, honey. Let's sit down," Benedict said.

In one seamless motion, Zoe slid into her seat, unzipped her backpack, and pulled out a physics textbook and a pen, which she placed on the table before adding a selection of rolls to her plate. Zoe rarely read anything that she didn't underline ruthlessly, as if the words would escape her if she didn't imprison them with the inky lines of her pen.

"No books tonight. We need to talk."

"Okay," Zoe said slowly as she closed her book, looking worried at the change in etiquette. Years ago, Esme had given up on trying to get Zoe to stop reading at the table. Though she resented the physical reminder that someone else's thoughts were more important than her own, Zoe's coaxing had worn her down. Now their dinner table often looked like a college cafeteria during exam week, especially now that Zoe was preparing for her national exams. "What is going on, guys? You're both acting weird. Did Julia crash Kitty's car again?"

Her daughter's flippant joke made Esme's stomach turn. "No, it's not that. Zoe, we have to tell you something," Esme began, laying down the chopsticks she had just snapped apart. The sight of the beautifully made rolls did nothing to inspire her appetite.

"About what?"

Esme knew she couldn't mince words, which made it difficult to begin. Zoe liked facts. As a child, she had hated fairy tales. She was disgusted by the improbability of straw houses, century-long sleeps ended by a kiss, and hair long enough to be used as a ladder and had told her mother emphatically to "stop reading stories like that." She'd greeted the concept of Santa the same way. *What if he steals more than he gives us?* Zoe had asked, her eyes full of terror. *What if he comes into my room while I'm sleeping?* Esme had broken down three days before the holiday and admitted the truth in the face of Zoe's tears, though she had been heartbroken to replace wonder with logic. On Christmas morning, Zoe was overjoyed to open presents that had a clear, traceable supply chain, throwing her arms around Esme and Benedict after each gift was unwrapped. Zoe needed truth. She was like Esme's mother. Esme stared at her daughter, preparing herself to begin. But Benedict spoke first.

"There was an accident the night you went away," Benedict said. Esme released her breath, grateful that Zoe's puzzled eyes were focused on him and not her.

"What happened? Is anyone hurt?"

Esme looked at the table.

"Dad? Is everyone okay?" Zoe said, her voice a decibel louder than before.

"I backed out of the driveway and didn't notice that Torn was riding his bike until it was too late," Benedict said.

"What? Is Torn all right?"

"No. Torn is dead. Your dad hit Torn and he died shortly afterward." Esme spoke as plainly as possible, but her voice still broke on the last sentence.

"Torn is dead?" Zoe's eyes were enormous. "That's insane."

She turned back to her father.

"Wait, so you hit him with our SUV? Dad, are you okay?"

"I'm fine, Zoe. I mean, I'm struggling to comprehend all of this, and I feel terrible that I played any part in the accident, but it *was* an accident. The police are investigating. We met with a lawyer this afternoon. We need to stay strong, as a family," Benedict said, reaching across the trays of untouched sushi to pat her arm. Zoe looked surprised, then flushed, at the unusually emotional tone in his voice. "No matter what, we stick together. Okay?"

"Of course," Zoe said. Benedict withdrew his hand, and Zoe poked a California roll with the tip of her chopstick until it rolled onto its side. When she looked up, tears spilled from her eyes. Esme knew that Torn was the only adult she felt understood her passion for space and the universe beyond our imagining, because he so often dabbled in other worlds himself. During parties the two of them had often engaged in lively conversations about the possibility of time travel and where wormholes could really take someone. Even Kitty had remarked on it, wondering if Esme had noticed how close they were becoming. *I'm sure it's harmless*, their neighbor had said, but the wine made her face doubtful. At the time, Esme had dismissed the idea of anything untoward. Now she could see Zoe's grief was deep enough to suggest that Kitty had been right. The thought of her daughter harboring a secret crush on Torn made her heart ache.

"What happens next?" Zoe asked.

"Our lawyer says your dad could be charged at any time."

"So all we can do is wait?"

"Yeah."

"I can't believe this happened. I can't believe Torn is gone."

"I know. None of us have processed it quite yet. It was all so sudden and it's still so fresh. Just know that whatever happens next, I love you, Zoe," said Esme.

"We both love you so much," said Benedict.

"I know," she said, but Esme could see her cheeks pink up again at the words. She wondered suddenly if Benedict's often distracted parenting over the years had created the same need for affection in her daughter that she had felt growing up. The thought made her push her untouched plate of sushi away.

Zoe looked miserable as she glanced back and forth between Esme and Benedict.

"Will there be a funeral?"

"I'm not sure, Zoe. Aaron isn't back from Syria yet. We'll know more when he returns." Esme suddenly wondered if Aaron thought it was odd that she hadn't reached out to him. She had his phone number and his email address, but the idea of trying to construct a message made her head hurt again. She wasn't sure how to comfort a friend whose husband had been killed by the man she was married to.

"Will I have to go?"

"It's your decision, Zoe. We can talk about it once we know how Aaron wants to handle it."

Zoe looked down again. Esme watched her out of the corner of her eye. Again, Esme saw her mother in Zoe. Both appeared detached, almost unaffected, by the events around them, until something set them over the edge and they snapped. In first grade, Esme had been commanded to pick Zoe up from school after she had thrown a rock at a boy, which had cut his cheek and required a couple of stitches. The boy had been bullying Zoe for months, the teacher told her. No one had intervened because Zoe had seemed unbothered. Until she wasn't.

Zoe ate half her rolls, then asked to be excused. Esme nodded, picking up her own plate as she cleared Zoe's.

Benedict rubbed his jaw as he followed Esme with the uneaten food. "Let's save these for tomorrow."

The thought of day-old sushi made Esme wince, but she didn't have the energy to come up with a better plan. "Sure."

"Nightcap?" he said to Esme. She shook her head as he pulled out a bottle of scotch and poured himself a glass. She wondered how Benedict could even consider drinking alcohol after everything it had led to two nights ago, but she hid her judgment. The last thing her husband needed to see was her disgust.

"I'm exhausted, Benedict. I'm going to bed."

"I'll be up soon. I love you, Ez."

Esme smiled and made her way up the stairs, leaving her husband to stare out the front window alone.

CHAPTER EIGHT

Esme opened her eyes to sunlight flooding the room. The morning seemed bright and beautiful, like the world was still good. Just as she registered that her husband was beside her, he slid out of bed.

"Good morning," she said.

His eyes were bloodshot when they met hers. "Morning."

"What time did you come to bed?"

"Late," he replied slowly, sighing as he ran a hand through his unruly hair. His voice was thick with drinks from the night before. A whiff of his sour breath reached Esme. She squashed her irritation at his hangover.

"Are you okay?" she asked.

"No. Not at all. I feel like I'll never sleep again. I just keep hearing that sound."

Esme didn't need to ask what sound he meant.

"I know."

They looked at each other, and Esme felt her eyes fill with tears again.

"Are you going into work today?"

"Yes. Jack said it was best. Besides, I don't know what else to do with myself," Benedict said.

"I'll call Jack as soon as I can this morning for an update," Esme said.

"Good," he said before he slipped into the bathroom.

Zoe came downstairs as Esme was pouring her second cup of coffee. "There's granola and milk on the table."

"Thanks, Mom." Zoe's rumpled hair and ratty T-shirt made her seem fragile and young. Esme felt her heart pound at the idea of her teenage daughter having to deal with the things that awaited them all if the media took hold of the story as Jack had predicted. Torn had been an internationally known author, and both Esme and Benedict had achieved some celebrity in their early careers. It was bound to make the news. She couldn't bear to look at her phone, as if remaining in ignorance would protect her. Without proof, she could hold on to the hope that his death would be reported as just another cycling fatality, the kind that happened at least twice a year in Fraser City.

Esme wondered how Zoe would react to stories about her and Benedict's pasts. Their daughter knew that Benedict had modeled; when she was twelve, she had used one of his campaign shots as her desktop photo until a friend had asked her who the hot guy was in the picture. During that stage of early adolescence, Zoe had also screened *Seeking Mercy* dozens of times, remarking once that it was neat to see her mother back when she had been pretty. When she asked Esme why she had stopped acting after just one film, she had been satisfied with Esme's careful response that she had wanted to be a mother instead. It was oddly comforting to Esme how much easier it was for her daughter to accept a beautiful lie than the uglier truth.

"Zoe, you can stay home from school today, you know. Why don't we play hooky? Get manicures and watch terrible movies?"

Zoe met her mother's eyes and then looked down at the physics book she had left on the table the night before. "Can't, Mom. We have a prep test today in physics."

Esme swallowed her disappointment. "Well, how could I compete with that?"

Zoe laughed. Esme should have known her daughter wouldn't even consider the offer. Zoe never put school second. The creative aspirations of her parents and neighbors confused her. From the moment Zoe could express a thought, she had wanted to learn about the stars and the planets. At two years old, she used to bang on the bay window at the front of the house while staring at the sky, calling, "Moon, moon, moon," over and over, as if her words could capture its attention. Her knowledge of the universe had surpassed Esme's by the time she was six years old. Now she could name star systems that sounded like they came out of a fantasy novel as easily as listing breakfast cereal.

"Maybe you can convince Julia to stay home with you today. She's always up for missing a day of school," Zoe joked, before her expression darkened. "Actually, Dad would probably want to talk to her. She always knows what to say to him."

Esme smiled, though acid rose in her throat. "So do you, hon."

"Not like her," Zoe said, shoving her textbook into her backpack before turning to the door. "Gotta get dressed."

Ten minutes later, as Zoe strolled down the stairs in a pair of jeans and a flannel shirt, Esme casually met her at the front door.

"Are you heading out too?" Zoe looped her arm through one backpack strap, then the other.

"I'm walking you to school."

"Mom, I'm seventeen. My school is, like, six blocks away."

"I know, Zo. It's just . . . I thought it would be nice to spend a bit of time with you. To answer any questions that you might have after our talk last night."

"I asked all my questions last night."

Esme ignored the hint of sullenness in her voice and replied brightly, "Okay. I still want to take you to school, though."

Esme quick-stepped so she could stand in front of her daughter, stopping her in her tracks. Impatience flashed in Zoe's eyes, and Esme caught a glimpse of her father in her daughter's face. She pushed down the thought of Zoe turning out like him.

"Fine." Zoe shrugged as they stepped out the door together. Esme was relieved to see that no one else was out of their house yet this morning. They headed north to Wellstone High.

"So nothing else came to you? After we talked?"

"No, not really," Zoe said.

Esme changed tack.

"Tell me more about the conference."

Zoe smiled wistfully. "It's weird to think about it right now, but yeah, it was great. One of the teachers told me about a prep school that actually lets students apply for an internship on the International Space Station. It sounds incredible."

"Where is the school?" Esme asked.

"Its main campus is in New York."

"Oh, Zoe. Across the country?"

"I mean . . . it would be incredible to learn in a place like that. It would just be one semester. I know this is completely the wrong time to bring it up, but can we put a pin in it?"

"No way, Zo! You can't leave me all alone!" She had been trying for a joke, but her voice had a strange pitch. It sounded like panic. Zoe noticed.

"Mom. I wouldn't leave you alone. You would have Dad."

"Yes, of course. Sure."

"Are you all right, Mom?"

Esme trailed her hand along the petals of a dying dahlia, leaning out across the sidewalk from Kitty's house. "I'm fine."

"Okay, Mom. Don't worry about it right now. Let's just get through the day." Zoe gave her a smile. Esme remembered when her daughter's world had been composed of simple longings and transparent desires: milk, sleep, and the warmth of her mother. Now Zoe was no longer a little girl, and Esme often struggled to read her. Her thoughts were interrupted by a woman calling her name.

"Esme! Hi!" Kitty rushed down her driveway as quickly as her strappy sandals would allow. Julia trailed closely behind.

"I didn't think Zoe would be going to school today." Kitty swept Esme up in an embrace that smelled like lilacs and white musk: Chanel No. 5, her signature scent. She pulled back and smiled, though she looked as tender as Esme felt. Her carefully made-up eyes were threaded with fine lines of red.

"She insisted." Esme raised her eyebrows slightly, and Kitty nodded at the parental shorthand for *what can I do?* before turning to Esme's daughter.

"Of course. You are always so strong, Zoe."

"I have a test." Zoe looked at her mother. "Is it okay if I go on my own now? I really don't want to be late." She shot a glance to Julia, but Kitty's daughter looked away. She didn't seem to have the same concerns about punctuality.

"Sure. But call me if you change your mind and want to come home early."

"Okay. I love you, Mom." Zoe gave Esme a hug before turning to finish her walk to school.

Kitty didn't waste a second. "How is Benedict doing?" she asked, taking Esme's hand. "Did you get my texts? Have you heard from Aaron? Will there be a funeral service? Have the police found out why Torn left his house in such a rush?"

Kitty's voice was as raw as it had been fourteen years ago, when her husband had left her with five-year-old Julia for a wispy junior real estate agent from her own company. Esme had been devastated on her friend's behalf. She, more than anyone else, understood the deep blow that Kitty's husband had dealt to her. Not only had he betrayed the marriage, but he had left her alone to care for a child while Kitty was trying to get her realty practice off the ground. Juggling parenting and self-employment had connected Kitty and Esme even more than their shared pregnancies. *Whatever you need*, Esme had said to her shattered friend, *I am here.*

For the next few years, Julia had been a fixture at their home and Dix-Neuf, whenever Kitty needed a hand with childcare so she could do a showing. For years, Esme and Kitty had been the closest of friends. When Julia and Zoe started second grade, however, things changed. Sophie and Ray moved to Raven Lane. Kitty's realty practice began to boom, and she enrolled Julia in after-school care. As Esme and Sophie's friendship deepened, she and Kitty had grown further apart. But now looking into Kitty's eyes made Esme feel just as connected to her as she had the day they had shared too many margaritas and cursed every man alive. She knew if she spoke to Kitty for another second, she would break open like a pierced yolk in a soft-boiled egg.

Kitty's cell phone rang. Esme jumped at its volume. It sounded like a blast from a runaway train. Esme looked at her watch. "Listen. I've got to run, but I'll let you know as soon as I hear anything. If I hear anything."

"Of course. Please let me know, whatever you can. Julia, what are you waiting for? You're going to be late."

Julia locked eyes with Esme. She seemed about to speak, but Kitty burst in again. "Go."

Esme seized the moment to make her exit. She broke eye contact with Julia to look directly at Kitty. "We'll talk soon."

"Sure. But please, don't forget to tell me, whatever you hear."

Esme's smile died on her face as she hurried back in the direction she had come. Esme and Benedict used to be the first people that Aaron called when he got back into town. She was sure that wasn't going to be the case this time.

CHAPTER NINE

Esme hadn't been lying to Kitty, even if the truth had also provided her with a convenient escape from their conversation before it went too far. She did need to get to work. Since Anthony's promotion, she had been scheduling Monday morning tutorials to prep their most popular menu items and remind him of the nuances of each dish. Though Anthony had been running the restaurant alone for nearly six weeks, she felt anxious if she was out of the kitchen for too long, as if he were a nanny who spanked her children when she was away. Besides, she wasn't used to having days that were so empty. Until a permit was approved, she had little to do but rework her blueprints for the new space and test recipes, so she found herself slipping back into the regular service as Anthony's sous chef.

He didn't seem to mind her intrusions. Last week, he had told her that working alongside her was always more fun than running the kitchen alone. She needed to take him at his word today. After the chaos of the weekend, she was desperate to work with her hands, to quiet the fears in her mind. Her headache from last night was creeping back, sharpening when she realized that Benedict's impending legal fees might force her to abandon the plans for expansion altogether.

A light breeze lifted her curls from her forehead and rustled the leaves of a Japanese maple beside her, still desperately holding on to its green color despite the approaching autumn. She exhaled and focused on the tasks that lay before her. She couldn't solve Benedict's problems this morning, but she could keep her mind occupied until the way out came to her. She stopped at the house briefly to tidy up and send a few texts, then headed to Dix-Neuf.

Main Street was already jammed with parked cars. When Esme had first bought the space, Kitty had cheerfully described the neighborhood as "up and coming." It was real estate talk for "still not completely safe." In the early days, Dix-Neuf had been buttressed by a dingy laundromat on one side and a convenience store that had such erratic hours and limited products it seemed like a front for drug laundering. Now the rocketing prices of real estate in the city had brought an onslaught of new condo dwellers to her neighborhood, and her current neighbors were an upscale coffee shop and a craft shop for children. Instead of coaxing customers in, she had to turn them away. The risk she had taken in launching a restaurant with very little experience and a young baby had paid off. Besides raising Zoe, Dix-Neuf was her proudest accomplishment.

Esme knew every inch of this place like she had known the planes and curves of Zoe's body when she was a child, her small shoulder blades angling out of her back like the sprouting wings of a baby angel. She could still remember the crick in her neck from calls with suppliers while pinching the phone between her ear and shoulder and simultaneously cradling a crying Zoe in her arms. Zoe had taken her first steps in the kitchen, with Esme leaping in front of her wobbling daughter to get a pot of nearly boiling water out of the child's newly extended reach.

Once, when Zoe was two and a half, Esme had turned her back on her, leaving her to happily play with a stack of measuring cups, while she prepared an order. Esme had been busy enough to be careless with where she left her knife. She had wheeled around with a steaming poached egg dripping from her slotted spoon only to find Zoe pointing the knife toward her, inches from her soft stomach. Esme cried out in fear just as she stopped herself from walking into its point. The slimy egg spattered on the floor, and Zoe became hysterical at her mother's yell. It was up to Esme to comfort her. Zoe's tears ended quickly. As a woman and a mother, Esme was skilled at apologizing for her own terror.

The door chimed softly as she entered. She said hello to her cleaner, who was wiping down the baseboards. The young woman shot her a bright smile, her nose ring glinting in the sunshine that streamed through the windows. Esme slipped through the doors to the kitchen. It was strange to think that the biggest crisis in Esme's life was unfolding without any of her staff being aware of it, though she knew that wouldn't last long. When Benedict was arrested, she would be instantly connected to Torn's death, news of which was already taking over the social media feeds she had scanned earlier. The local blogs hadn't mentioned the suspicion of drug use, but Esme worried that the story was too salacious to be ignored by larger media outlets. If Jack discovered that the police had tested for drugs, surely a reporter with police contacts could just as well. She felt the same sense of dread as she had when her labor with Zoe had begun. Something was coming. The only question was when and how much it was going to hurt.

She needed to be prepared. *All the more reason to stock the fridge*, she thought as she pulled her custom-tailored chef whites from the hook beside the door. The last thing she wanted was the restaurant to suffer due to her husband's mired reputation. The financial repercussions of her restaurant going downhill would be only part of it. If Dix-Neuf failed, so too would Esme.

Anthony turned his dark head from the grill as she walked to her station. There were purple half circles under his eyes, and she wondered if the stress of his new job was beginning to get to him. She smiled, then ducked down to grab her knives. He stared at her without speaking until she turned to face him.

"Chef. I am so sorry. I wasn't sure if you would be able to work today." He bowed his head, and Esme was shocked to hear him choke back a sob. "Torn was a good man."

Esme was taken aback. How could she have forgotten that Anthony had also gotten to know Torn over the months he had been a regular at Dix-Neuf? Even here, there was no escape from the tragedy. Despite Torn's easy manner, the relationship between Anthony and Torn had never quite turned into a friendship due to Anthony's fanboy devotion to Torn's third novel. Though Anthony was often tongue-tied around his idol, he never failed to prepare Torn's food with great care, going far beyond the already high standards she had impressed upon him.

She walked over to embrace him, and his hold was fierce. "I'm so sorry," he repeated.

"I appreciate that so much. He was a good friend to us all," she said into his ear before pulling away. She smoothed her hands on her hips and gave Anthony a weak smile. "I came here because I needed to do something. Shall we begin?"

He cleared his throat. "Bouillabaisse?"

"A tribute," she said. It had been Torn's favorite dish on the menu.

"Perfect." Anthony straightened his shoulders. "The fish came in early. Halibut and snapper?"

She was relieved by his abrupt shift to the work at hand. Like Esme, Anthony rarely brought his personal life into the kitchen, and he always seemed to realize when he had crossed a line with her. In some ways, he knew her better than any of the other men in her life did, often giving her what she wanted before she realized her own desire.

"Yes. Let's stick it in the fridge out here. We'll need it shortly, but first, we need to prepare the rouille."

Anthony disappeared again, and Esme heard the rip of a box being opened. She began to sharpen her knives. Her head chef joined her after tucking several fish fillets on a shelf in the fridge, lined with butcher paper to prevent drips, just as she had taught him.

"Thank you," Esme said. She met Anthony's warm brown eyes and saw another unexpected rush of grief. She felt as if his sadness might break her apart. She broke eye contact and reverted to the teachings of her grandmother, even though Anthony had heard her say the same things many times before. She hoped it comforted him as much as it did her.

"This dish is a lot more than fish stew. Bouillabaisse is a staple, the heart of a meal and, really, of French cooking. It's a simple dish, but it can sing if chefs pay attention to two things: a good base and careful planning."

For Esme, the only difference between a good meal and a great meal was discipline, and she was happy to focus on the concrete tasks before her rather than the muddy waters that swirled in the rest of her life. Esme rattled off a list of ingredients from the top of her head. Anthony made a trip to the walk-in cooler, returning to deposit dark green leeks, aromatic fennel, and purple garlic to the workstation upon his return, as well as the fresh thyme that she had forgotten to ask for. Esme ducked into the pantry to find a jar of tomato paste. She and Anthony had spent several sweating days side by side, crushing and canning fifty jars in the heat of last year's summer.

"As you know, the rouille, the base, is our first step, and then everything else follows. If you know where you want to go, you don't need to rush yourself or your food. Every flavor, every piece of this dish, needs respect. So, separate an egg and mix the yolk with the garlic. Whisk them together and add a pinch of this."

Esme picked up a small bowl of paprika and rubbed the spice between her fingertips before sprinkling it into the liquid swirling around Anthony's whisk. Anthony smiled, and Esme pulled her hand away to wipe it on a towel. The red dust had ground into her fingerprints, like blood. *Out, out, damn spot*, she thought, surprising herself with a line from the first play she had ever been cast in, a high school production where she had played the female lead.

Her mother and grandmother had never understood that acting wasn't a passing fancy to her. As a teenager, she'd thought that never making it would be the worst thing that could happen to her. Being cast by Brian Smith had felt like the beginning of everything. She hadn't known then that it was better to dream about something beautiful than to succeed and learn how awful what you wanted really was.

As she and Anthony settled into their routine, the quiet kitchen offered her a chance to reflect. She breathed in the peppery scent of the spice, remembering a busy lunch service a year before.

~

She had been surprised to spot Torn alone at a corner table. It was the first time she had seen him since he and Aaron had come to Monday night dinner, three weeks before. She wiped her hands on her apron and walked toward him, a smile on her face to keep her nerves at bay.

"No food at home?" she joked.

Torn was so intent on the rich tomato broth in front of him that he jumped at the sound of her voice. "Esme! I didn't know you were working today."

"They keep me in the scullery most of the time."

He chuckled. "Well, it's a damn fine scullery. To answer your question, there's definitely no food like this at home. It was either cheese and crackers or a gourmet meal at the best place in town." Torn winked, and Esme's blood pulsed.

"I think you made the right choice."

"Can you sit down?"

Esme looked around the restaurant. The lunch rush had come to an end. There were only three other tables, and no one had a menu in front of them. "I'll have to get up if an order comes in, but I can stay for a minute."

Torn dipped a hunk of bread into his stew. "This stew, Esme, is incredible. I thought the food was good at your dinner party, but I've never had anything like this."

"I'm so glad you like it. What are you drinking?" Esme looked at his glass of water.

"Oh, I'm writing today. I don't need a drink."

"You must have the whole experience." She held up two fingers to her server. "Pernod, please."

Torn smiled. "You are a bad influence."

"You have no idea." Esme grinned back. Torn seemed different one-on-one. Friendlier and less arrogant. The server brought over two small glasses and a pitcher of iced water. Esme poured a few drops of water into each glass, and the yellowy-green liquid turned creamy.

"What kind of sorcery is that?" Torn was transfixed.

Esme laughed. It was simple chemistry: add the right ingredient, and each ordinary piece is transformed into something magical. Add the wrong ingredient and everything could be ruined.

"Try it. It's a great pairing with the bouillabaisse. Cheers." They touched glasses, and Torn took a small sip.

"Licorice?"

"Anise. Now try another bite."

Torn lifted his spoon and closed his eyes as the warm soup touched his lips. A small hum of pleasure escaped him. "Wow."

"Sweet and savory is my favorite combination."

Torn nodded without a reply. His mouth was full and his smile was wide. He reached across the table and laid his hand on top of hers. Later, she would think back to that gesture and wonder how she hadn't realized it was the catalyst to everything that followed. She had been wrong. Chemistry wasn't simple at all.

Anthony's voice brought her back to the kitchen. "Adding the tomato paste now."

She pulled out the fish and cut the heads off. As she deboned them and sliced the flesh into bite-size pieces, Anthony seasoned the broth with salt, pepper, and lemon juice, then pulled it off the burner to cool. He joined her to chop the fish. While his knife strokes hammered the counter, she took the heads and bones of the fish and put them in a large pot, covering them with water to make fish stock. Her grandmother wasted nothing. *Everything matters*, she used to say. *Save what you can and make the best out of what you have.* Esme had turned her grandmother's philosophy into her own mantra of "no wasted steps." Every movement and every word in the kitchen had a purpose.

Esme let the stock simmer and returned to the chopping block, where Anthony was scrubbing the scales and flesh from the wooden surface. Together, they sliced through the vegetables, garlic, fennel, and herbs. The kitchen began to smell salty and rich, silent besides the gentle bubbling of the pot. She hadn't always been able to make meals like this one that required precision and patience. Over time, she had learned to cook with care, being careful not to get ahead of herself, to rush into something for which she wasn't prepared. This dish had taken her years to master. It impressed her and made her proud that her protégé handled its complexities so easily.

Esme looked at her watch. "Okay, let's strain the fish. Reserve that liquid, then add oil to the pot to sauté the onions, fennel, and leeks."

As Anthony moved to the boiling pot, Esme felt her phone vibrate. "Give me a sec." She pulled the phone out of her pocket, then walked into the small hallway that led to their largest freezer. She recognized the number on her screen. She had to take this call in private.

"Hello, Aaron." Esme heard only silence and she pressed the phone to her ear, repeating her greeting. "Hello?"

"Esme."

Blood rushed to her feet, and spots of black appeared before her eyes at the sound of his voice. She took a deep breath. "Where are you?"

"I'm home. I got back this morning." His voice was dull.

"I am so sorry, Aaron. We both are." She couldn't bear to say Benedict's name out loud to Aaron. It seemed like an insult.

Silence again. She could picture Aaron adjusting his glasses and pinching the bridge of his nose, as he always did when struggling to speak.

"I don't . . . this might be inappropriate, Aaron. But if there's anything I can do."

"Thank you." He paused again. "Look, Esme. I'm calling because . . . the wake is tomorrow. You and Benedict should be there."

Esme bit her tongue. She knew he must have already spoken with the police, and she wondered if they had told him about Benedict's altered state of mind or what they planned to charge him with, but the questions seemed heartless. "We'll be there. Of course."

"It starts at six p.m. I'll see you." Aaron hung up abruptly, but not before Esme heard him choke on his tears. A sharp breath caught in her throat, turning into a sob as she dropped the phone back into her pocket. She didn't know if she was crying because of Aaron's loss of control or the smell of Pernod that Anthony was pouring into the steaming pot on the stove. Her tears could be for Torn, for Benedict, for Aaron, or for every single one of them. Most of all for herself.

CHAPTER TEN

Benedict was sitting on the couch in his running clothes when Esme returned from Dix-Neuf. His hair was damp with sweat, but his face was pale, not its usual after-exercise pink. When he turned to her, his eyes were full of fear. Esme's throat dried in panic. Had the moment they had both been waiting for finally arrived?

"What's wrong? Did Jack call?"

As Benedict shook his head, the brown spot in the corner of his eye caught the light. Esme knew she had to be imagining that the flaw had grown larger since Torn's death, but the mark seemed more jarring than usual.

"No," he said without affect. "Jack didn't call."

"God, I don't know if that's good or bad."

He shrugged. "Me neither."

Esme sat beside him, sliding close enough that their thighs nearly touched.

"Why are you home so early?"

"José told me to take the afternoon off."

"Why?"

"The police showed up at the agency."

"Oh."

"They wanted to ask me more questions. About you. And Torn."

"What kind of questions?" Esme could hear the alarm in her voice, though Benedict seemed not to register it.

"I don't know, Esme. It was so stupid. I was in the middle of a meeting when they interrupted. I got angry. They were trying to strong-arm me." Benedict paused, and Esme's stomach sank as his expression changed to guilt. "I lost my temper. I screwed up."

"How?"

"I told them to shove off." Benedict had learned English primarily through his British nanny, and normally his unusual turns of phrase made Esme smile, but not today.

"Oh, Benedict."

"It was stupid, I know. I just . . . don't understand what they're trying to get at. As if I don't feel bad enough already about what happened. About what I did."

Aaron's invitation needled into her still-aching head. There was no good time to tell Benedict. It might as well be now.

"Aaron is having a wake tomorrow for Torn."

"Oh."

"He invited us."

"No." Benedict looked out the large window that provided a clear view of the end of their driveway. A street cleaner had rumbled by earlier that morning. The sidewalk was no longer stained, though Esme guessed Benedict could still see the outline of Torn's blood in his mind's eye, just as she could. She doubted either of them would ever forget the discoloration at the end of their driveway. "I can't."

Esme fought to tame her panic at the idea of attending the event without him, though the alternative seemed just as fraught. She patted his hand.

"I understand. I'll go with Sophie and Ray."

She glanced at her watch, then stood up.

"I need to pick up Zoe."

Benedict nodded absently, not seeming to realize that Esme hadn't picked their daughter up from school since she was in fifth grade. He was too far away to see anyone but himself. Neither of them said goodbye as she slipped out the front door. She was grateful for the whisper of wind on her face to blow away the staleness of their house.

Thirty minutes later, when she and Zoe returned, the couch was empty and Benedict didn't answer when she called. She walked upstairs into their bedroom and found him sleeping on top of the blanket on their bed, still clad in his workout clothes. She fixed a light dinner for herself and Zoe, and they spent the evening watching a movie that Esme barely followed. Zoe seemed unusually quiet. Esme wondered what she had heard at school, but her daughter just smiled when she asked if she was okay. Before bed, Esme checked her email, scanning the articles that had come in through the search engine alert she had created for both Torn's and Benedict's names. She was relieved to see that there was nothing more than superficial reports of Torn's death and testimonials of how much his book had touched readers. She understood the feeling. Each section of *The Call* that she read drew her deeper and deeper into the world he had created, and it devastated her to know that there would be no more.

She adjusted the lamp to limit the glare on her sleeping husband, then picked up Torn's book once again.

I stopped at the grad student lounge for a coffee to calm my uneasy mind, still echoing with the voice of the man in the street. She was there, sipping on a coffee at a table scarred with the tips of long-forbidden cigarettes and still-permissible pints. My adviser elevated the atmosphere of the grubby bar into something like elegance. She said hello, and I asked her if she had received my latest grant application. It took her too long to answer, but she held my gaze the entire time as I waited for her response.

Finally, she said yes, stood, and walked out of the room. When she was close enough that I could smell the peculiar but appealing mix of cloves and jasmine on her skin, she said softly, "Not that it matters now."

Like the man's screams on the sidewalk, the words wouldn't leave my head as I picked up the coffee and dropped a dollar on the bar. The paper walls of the cup were not thick enough to contain its heat, and my fingers burned all the way to my office. The sensation grew so deep that I worried I would never stop feeling it, but I didn't drop the cup. When I finally set it down, and the radiant heat began to leave my body, I realized that a part of me registered its absence as a loss.

Esme tucked her bookmark into the pages, unwilling to damage a single one with a careless fold. The more the book puzzled her, the more important it seemed for her to read it, but exhaustion was clouding her ability to understand Torn's message.

In the morning, Esme woke to an empty bed. Benedict was sitting at the kitchen counter when she came downstairs.

"What time is the wake?"

"Aaron said to come around six p.m. I thought—"

Benedict cut her off. "I'll be there. I'm not letting you do this alone."

"Thank you."

Gratitude rushed over her. She couldn't remember the last time she had felt so fortunate to have him as a husband. She kissed him, and it felt as good as it had when she still believed his faults would change.

Eight hours later, they walked slowly to the house at the center of Raven Lane that used to be owned by two men but now belonged to only one. The chafing dish full of potato gratin was heavy enough to make her hands ache. As they climbed the stairs onto Aaron's cedar porch, she nodded her head at the door, indicating that Benedict should knock. He stared at her without a response, and Esme worried that his near paralysis from the day before had returned. The muted sounds of conversation coming from inside dampened her hands, and the metal handles threatened to slide from her grip. She tried to figure out a way to keep hold of the creamy potatoes and open the door herself.

Then her husband took a deep breath, twisted the doorknob, and flung it forward, as if expecting something horrible on the other side. She supposed a knock would have been unnecessary—no one would have heard it—but bursting in made her feel even more unwanted than they already were. Her stomach sank when she saw Aaron standing in the foyer, immediately in front of the door, as if he had heard their steps on the staircase and was about to greet them.

"Hello, Aaron," she said.

Her voice broke, and she felt shame at the evidence of her own grief. She leaned forward to kiss his cheek, but instead he extended his arms to take the dish out of her hands, keeping it between them like a shield as he stepped backward to place it on a side table. She tried not to let her sadness at the lack of kindness show. Of all people, she was not entitled to his compassion. Aaron looked tired. Like Anthony, he had black hollows under his eyes. Sorrow had beaten him like a fist.

"Thank you for coming, Esme."

Her hand fluttered at her side to touch him, but she stayed it almost immediately. She hoped her movement had been subtle enough to go unnoticed. Aaron seemed nearly unrecognizable without the warm gaze she was used to. He turned to Benedict. The look between them stopped Esme's breath. Then Benedict reached out his hand. Esme's chest tightened until she saw Aaron's response: a careful stretch of reciprocation. The two men touched, palm to palm. One shake, release. Aaron stiffened, then turned on his heel and walked upstairs. Benedict's and Esme's eyes followed, and she heard the click and turn of the lock when he reached the master bedroom. Only the slow plodding of

Professor coming down the hall toward them kept her from fleeing the house. She petted his thick brown, white, and black fur, nearly breaking into tears when he nosed her leg, as if gently trying to comfort her. She knew Professor drove Kitty crazy when he made his way into her backyard to do his business while Torn was distracted by his work, but she had always loved the big, friendly dog.

Through the door to the main room on their right, Esme could see a crowd of smartly dressed people. Though the Grace house was a mirror of their own, it was larger and felt very different, especially today, as the elegantly decorated main room buzzed with low conversation. The walls were covered in enlarged black-and-white photos. Some were scenic; others were portraits. All were somber, given that Aaron had taken them during his travels in the most violent parts of the world.

As usual, her eye was caught by a head-and-shoulders shot of a young girl, not more than five years old, staring out of a white frame mounted prominently on the main wall. Behind the little girl, a city street burned.

"Is that . . . Syria?" Esme had asked Torn the first time she had seen it, feeling hopelessly ill-equipped to even say the name of the country. Her throat had caught at her ignorance of what was happening so far away from Raven Lane.

"Yes," said Torn, quietly. "Aaron shot it during his last trip. He says telling the stories is what the people want. They think if someone could show the rest of the world what was really going on, they would help."

If only that were true, she thought.

"It's beautiful," she said feebly, vowing to ask Aaron what she could do to help as soon as he returned. She wanted to be different from other people, to be more like Aaron, to care about something besides herself.

"Yes. Haunting." Torn took her hand as she stared into the girl's huge dark eyes.

"Aaron really captured something in her."

"Maybe I'm not the only creative talent in our relationship."

Torn had laughed at how absurd he found his own joke. His strong sense of self had been so captivating at first. Something about the way he looked at her made it seem as if he could bring back the things she thought she had lost. She had been a fool.

As Benedict walked into the main room, Esme looked up the stairs where Aaron had retreated, feeling as if he had gone to collect his husband and both he and Torn were about to come down to meet them. Professor left her side and trod back to his pillow at the end of the hall. When Aaron failed to appear at the top of the stairs, Esme followed Benedict, regretting the fact that she had never asked Aaron about the little girl in Syria. Instead, her own life had consumed her. Now it was too late. She saw Benedict, Sophie, and Ray standing in a small group. Sophie noticed her entrance and turned to her immediately, pulling her into their ranks.

"Esme, how are you?"

Sophie laced her long, cool fingers into Esme's hand.

"It hasn't been easy," Esme murmured.

Benedict spoke in a low tone. "Things . . . well, Sophie. Things are shit."

"The bar is over there, Benedict."

He thanked her grimly, then walked toward it. Esme saw the quick glances of others as he passed them. Everyone here knew how Torn had died and who had been driving the car that hit him. Today the story had made national news, and social media had made sure it was shared widely. The articles and posts had been accompanied by side-by-side photographs of Torn and Benedict. Two handsome men, one dead, one responsible. It was an irresistible hook. Nervous anticipation began to hum through the voices around her. Esme's head thrummed with tension in response. She regretted coming. *Half an hour*, she told herself.

"Who are these people?" Esme asked.

"Editors and literary colleagues coming to pay their respects, mostly."

"Oh."

"Did you see Aaron?" Ray asked.

Esme looked at her friend, and her eyes filled with tears. "Yes."

Ray cleared his throat. "Esme, would you like a drink? I'm going to freshen mine up."

She shook her head as Sophie reached over to hold her hand.

"Oh, chérie. Just give him time. Benedict didn't mean to do anything wrong . . ." Sophie trailed off, sadly. "It was a stupid accident. We all have these moments, these lapses. For Benedict and Torn, the outcome was as terrible as it can possibly be."

"But the pills?" Esme said the words so quietly that Sophie had to lean forward to hear her. "People could consider that more than just an accident. It was reckless."

"Just like Torn's decision not to wear a helmet was reckless."

Esme stared at Sophie, trying to decide if she meant it or was trying to make her feel better. Sophie smiled at her reassuringly, before her face grew guarded as something over Esme's shoulder caught her eye. Esme forced herself not to look behind her.

"Here comes Kitty."

Esme spoke hurriedly to get the question in before Kitty joined them.

"Sophie, Torn's body? It's not here, is it?"

She knew that Torn had been raised half-Catholic and half-Jewish (and fully lapsed completely, he used to joke along with Benedict, who had also abandoned his upbringing in the Catholic Church). Some days, Torn had expressed relief not to have to conform to the restrictive religious practices of his parents, who had made him attend temple and church every weekend while he was growing up. On other days, he bemoaned the loss of spirituality in his life. When Aaron said this was a wake, her stomach had turned at the thought of seeing Torn's face filled with embalming fluid and manipulated into a neutral expression.

"No. Aaron said he couldn't bear it."

Esme relaxed slightly. Aaron was an atheist, just like her.

"Esme! I wasn't sure if you and Benedict would be invit—" Kitty cut herself off as if she realized how rude her observation was. She gathered Esme in a perfumed embrace to try to hide her lack of tact. Sophie let out a burst of air that exuded European disdain, while Kitty took her cue and tried to steer them back to friendly conversation.

"How are you doing, Esme? Have the police followed up with you too?"

Esme's heartbeat quickened. She hadn't heard a thing from the police since the night of Torn's death. If they had already spoken to Kitty and Benedict, she must be next on their list. Especially if they were digging deeper into her relationship with Torn.

"No. When did you speak with them?"

Kitty looked from side to side to assess whether anyone else was in earshot. Esme wasn't sure if she was hoping for more or fewer people to hear what she was about to say.

"They came to my house this afternoon. The cute one and Officer . . . Singh, I think? She asked all the questions, but I was hoping to hear more from her partner. If I'm being honest."

"Kitty. What did they want?" Esme hoped she didn't sound like she was speaking through gritted teeth.

"A few questions about what would make Torn leave his house so quickly. The cute one let it slip that there were no text messages or appointments on his calendar." Kitty raised her eyebrows reassuringly. "After that, they kept asking about you, Esme. They wanted to know if I suspected anything between you and Torn."

Sophie looked over at her with wide eyes, then took a sip of wine to recover. Esme suddenly wished she had a glass as well. She didn't drink often, but a prop would have been helpful in masking her reaction to Kitty's words.

"What did you tell them?" Sophie asked, looking over Kitty's shoulder disinterestedly, as if she were asking out of politeness.

"I—"

Kitty's sentence was interrupted by a sharp knock on the door. The room quieted. It was a knock of authority. It was a knock that made people shut up.

"Where is Aaron?" Kitty whispered.

As if his ears were ringing, Aaron came down the stairs. He didn't look over at anyone in the room. His eyes were focused on the front door. As he swung it open, it blocked Esme's view of who was on the other side, but it didn't matter. The voices were loud enough to carry through the entire first floor.

"We have an arrest warrant for Benedict Werner. We were told he is on the premises."

Esme's chest tightened. Zoe was home alone two doors down, having decided at the last minute that it would be too difficult for her to come. They must have gone to Benedict's listed address first. They must have told Zoe that her dad was going to jail before Esme could warn her, protect her, and keep her away from this.

Only one person moved. Her husband, the man who she used to joke was her tall Teutonic god, strode through the crowd like the room was empty.

"I love you, Esme," he said as he stopped in front of her, pressing a half-finished drink into her hand. "Call Jack."

She leaned into his kiss until he broke away, took a big swallow of the drink as he turned to the two officers, and then passed the glass to Sophie and followed Benedict to the door.

"Hello, Officers."

"Let's step outside, sir."

The officers flanked Benedict as they walked out the door. Once they were outside, Esme hurried to join them. She couldn't let them leave without getting some answers.

"What is the charge?"

"Second-degree murder."

Esme stepped backward and hit her heel on the bottom step. Jack had been so certain that it would be manslaughter.

Benedict paled. "Murder? What could possibly be my motive?"

Singh didn't respond, but her colleague snorted.

"Why don't you ask your wife?" he muttered. Apparently, he no longer felt the need to act as the good cop. Esme wondered if it had ever been more than a tactic, a mask he wore to lure the guilty.

Singh scowled at her partner. "That's enough."

Benedict's shoulders stiffened. He turned to Esme, and she saw him put together the questions the police had been asking earlier with the charge. She knew what he was thinking. The only reason that Esme would be able to answer the question of motive was if she was the motive. She steeled herself for Benedict's anger. Instead, she saw sorrow. She turned back to the party as she heard the front door open, only to see Aaron at the top of the stairs, his face etched with the rage that she had expected to see on Benedict's.

The murmur of secondhand thrills in the lighted house behind Aaron couldn't drown out the sound of the officer reciting the words to her husband that Esme had heard only on television. She turned back to her husband and kept her eyes locked on his until she heard the click of handcuffs on his wrists. When she looked back, Aaron was no longer on the stairs, and the front door had shut her out.

As the officers escorted Benedict to the waiting police car, Esme watched the red-and-blue lights flashing on Raven Lane, just as they had a few nights ago when Torn was killed. She stayed on the sidewalk as they ducked her husband's head into the back seat and began walking home to her daughter and what remained of her life only when the car revved its engine and pulled away. She wondered how many of her neighbors on Raven Lane realized what was really happening on their street. How many of them understood that they were all witnesses to this crime?

PART TWO

The request was simple. Embrace the things inside yourself that you have spent your life denying and you will be free, forever.

—*Torn Grace,* The Call

CHAPTER ELEVEN

At first, it had seemed like a joke.

"Don't be blue / Eat fondue? Is Kitty serious?" Esme held up the harvest-gold invitation to a '70s-themed party that Kitty had hand-delivered to their icy doorstep moments before. The freezing February rain was no match for Kitty in party-planning mode.

"Kitty is always serious about her parties. I, for one, am excited for a new addition to our annual party roster. This winter has been too dreary," Benedict said. "I think it sounds like fun. I'm going to wear that Armani fringed vest. *Easy Rider* with Peter Fonda, right?" Benedict shimmied his hips and then pointed straight up in the air with one arm while placing the other akimbo on his waist.

Esme held in a laugh. "Dennis Hopper was the one in the fringe."

"Okay, sure, whatever. So all I need is a motorcycle."

"I'm not sure I'm up for another get-together. Kitty's Christmas regifting party was only three weeks ago." Esme sighed in frustration. The endless winter rain was making her unnecessarily annoyed with Kitty's social calendar. "If I knew that part of home ownership on Raven Lane was mandatory monthly attendance at Kitty Dagostino's house, I might have reconsidered," she grumbled.

"What's so bad about being invited to a party?" Zoe asked, looking up from her book. Esme hadn't realized she was listening.

"I don't know," Esme said. "I guess I'm just feeling a bit antisocial these days." The daily routine of Dix-Neuf was making her feel dull and uninspired, and the fact that Esme never felt she could say no to Kitty's invitations was wearing on her. Declining the invite and then sitting in her living room across the street in her pajamas eating ice cream seemed rude, even if it was all she wanted to do in the dark days of winter.

"Come on, Ez. Zoe's right. It's just a party. Cheer up," Benedict said, revving an imaginary motorcycle and grinning.

"Maybe Dad will let you ride on his hog," Zoe said with a wide smile that nearly matched Benedict's.

Her daughter's joke released her laughter. "How can I say no to that?"

So, two nights later, she found herself tromping down a slippery street in six-inch platforms, a silver glitter blouse, and a miniskirt. She had blown out and teased her black curls into an enormous Diana Ross–size mop and ringed her eyes in thick black liner. Benedict had opted to wear one of her oversize printed blouses and the aforementioned fringed vest. Though the sleeves were several inches too short, he insisted three-quarter-length sleeves had been all the rage. His hair was styled into a feathered tousle. Despite her earlier reluctance, Esme had to admit that she felt surprisingly sexy in her costume. There was something about wearing fishnet stockings, even if she was freezing.

The electronic rhythm of Blondie pulsed through the door as Benedict and Esme reached the top of Kitty's steps.

"Should I knock?" Esme said, reaching out a fist. Her husband shook his head, swinging the door open before her hand could make contact.

"Happy Saturday, yeah!" Benedict jutted his hips one at a time as he half danced and half strutted into Kitty's main room. The partygoers were gathered in the large space. Esme was happy to see a few new faces in the mix; she recognized a couple of Kitty's staff (minus the wan blonde Kitty had fired immediately after learning of her husband's infidelity) and several other couples whom Esme guessed were her neighbor's former clients. There was a large velvet bag on the side table by the doorway. Esme found its placement in Kitty's usually immaculate house odd, but she thought little about it, having no idea what Kitty had in store. She thought that getting everyone into tight bell-bottoms and big hair was enough to satisfy Kitty's constant need for entertainment. She was wrong.

"Esme!" Sophie pressed a sweating smoked glass into her hand as she kissed her friend on the cheek. "Santé!"

She raised her glass. Both women paused to take a sip of their drinks. Esme tasted orange juice and gin. Lots of it. She nearly spat her mouthful back into the glass but managed to choke it down.

"What is this?"

"Kitty called it a Slow Screw," Sophie said, rolling her eyes gently. She thought their neighbor was hopelessly tacky.

"It's strong." After one sip, Esme already felt a warm wave rolling through her body.

"I know, chérie. Just look at Ray." Sophie's husband was speaking exuberantly to the quietest residents of their street, Miriam and Levi. They both looked dazed at his excitement. Esme guessed they would leave early, as usual. Their orchestra rehearsed most weekends, which they often used as their excuse.

"At least you know where your husband is. Mine seems to have disappeared."

Sophie cocked her head at Esme. "He was probably invited to sample Kitty's special party favors. It's not just the alcohol that's making Ray talk too much."

At first Esme was confused. Then her friend put one rose-colored nail to the side of her nose and mimed a sniffing gesture. *Oh God*, thought Esme, *it's going to be that kind of party?* She would have to find Benedict, and fast. Benedict had slipped into his old ways only a handful of times at Raven Lane parties since he had stopped taking drugs. *Abstinence is only one approach*, he said, and she had agreed, albeit grudgingly, after the first time, when his transgression hadn't resulted in anything worse than a staggering hangover the next day. It was always good, however, to keep an eye on him when he decided to overindulge.

"I'm going to track him down. I'll see you in a bit," she said.

Sophie kissed her on the cheek; then Esme walked into the kitchen, smiling at a woman she had met at Kitty's last party. Esme hoped she didn't have to interact beyond the warm facial expression. She couldn't remember anything about her besides a lingering impression of sadness. A lot of Kitty's friends were like that. She tended to attract people who were in need of fixing. Maybe it was because she presented herself as being so put together. More likely, it was because her parties always had lots of booze. And apparently tonight, drugs as well.

Torn and Aaron were leaning against the counter, and Esme walked toward them with relief. Since the fall, Torn and Aaron had become staples at Raven Lane events and at Benedict and Esme's home. They were the most frequent guests at Monday night dinners, and Torn had become Benedict's running partner. She and Aaron had whiled away many afternoons planning his garden for the spring. Torn was also one of her most loyal customers at the restaurant, often coming in for lunch and then staying throughout the slow hours of the afternoon, tapping rapidly at the keyboard of his laptop. Esme looked forward to the days when she could spare a break from dinner prep to join him for a Pernod or a glass of wine. He was good company, regaling her with stories from his encounters with excited fans.

"Hey. Have you guys seen Benedict?"

Aaron looked pointedly down the hall toward the stairs leading to the second floor. "He went that way, with Kitty."

Esme weighed her options. If the two of them had already established their position in Kitty's en-suite, it was probably too late to stop Benedict from taking anything, and her attempted babysitting would just make him angry. Besides, he was on vacation. He and José took a break every year after Christmas so José could go back to visit family in Mexico. This year, Benedict had tried to convince Esme to go on vacation as well, despite the fact that the month was one of the busiest of the year for her restaurant. He had never taken running his business as seriously as Esme, and her refusal to leave Dix-Neuf had resulted in a fight. Benedict accused her of being unable to have fun. She reminded him that the profits from her hard work were often what kept his agency afloat. As usual, the talk of money had been enough to silence him, though clearly it had not distracted him from his urge to let loose. She took another slug of her now dangerously smooth-tasting drink.

"I suppose there's no real point in me going up there now."

"That's probably for the best," Torn said. "I'm not sure you'd be interested in what they are doing up there."

He looked at her to see if he had guessed correctly. She realized that neither Aaron nor Torn had seen this side of their neighborhood parties yet. It was an infrequent occurrence for anything but alcohol to be served, but since Julia had grown old enough to make her own plans outside the house during her mother's adult gatherings, Kitty had started to dabble more often.

"You are absolutely right about that." She turned to Aaron, trying to take the bitterness out of her tone as she changed the topic away from her husband. "You must be heading back overseas again soon?"

"Yes. I leave the day after tomorrow."

"Such a hectic schedule," Esme said sympathetically.

"Yes, it has its drawbacks, but I'm sure owning a restaurant is no slouch either. How is Dix-Neuf doing this time of year?" Aaron asked.

"Great. Lots of cozy romantic dinners for two this month. And I'm looking forward to the reading. I've never had a literary event at the restaurant before." She smiled at Torn. "Should be fun!"

She realized suddenly how eager she sounded, getting excited about a party that was still six months away, but the event was fresh in her mind. It had been only last week when he had asked her if he could host a reading for *The Call* at her restaurant.

"I got so busy with the international tour that I forgot to schedule something close to home," he had said with his trademark mix of sheepishness and pride. "Any chance you could make room for me?"

"Of course," she'd said.

"For real?" Torn's eyes were almost as wide as his grin. "That would be awesome!"

"Fantastic. Give me the date. I'll book it right now." She'd grabbed the reservations book and written it in, grateful that the event was slated for an empty night. The last thing she wanted to do was rescind the invitation. "The restaurant is yours, my friend."

Torn's eyes had glittered. "Esme, I don't know what I would do without you. You just saved my life."

Esme had laughed and shrugged away his compliments, but all day, she had repeated the moment in her mind. It felt good to be appreciated. Tonight, his huge grin at her mention of the upcoming party inspired the same feeling in her. She smiled back, grateful that she had been able to shake her irritation at Kitty and her annoyance at Benedict's inability to say no to their neighbor. The night was turning out to be far more fun than she had expected.

"I'm just figuring out the appetizers. Any allergies I should know about?"

"No, no allergies."

"Except peanuts, of course." Aaron smiled, but his eyes looked hurt. "I'm allergic, as I'm sure Torn would have remembered to tell you. Eventually."

Esme smiled to cover the awkwardness between the two men. "Of course. I was also thinking of doing a braised short rib on—"

Her menu planning was cut off abruptly by Kitty's loud voice coming from the hallway. "Everyone in the front room, please! Come on!"

"What is happening?" Aaron asked under his breath. She shrugged in reply as the three of them obeyed Kitty's summons and walked down the hall. Esme caught a glimpse of Kitty's flushed cheeks before Benedict came flying down the stairs and grabbed Esme's hand with an overzealous grin.

"Benedict, you're hurting me," Esme said as her husband pulled her roughly into the room. He winked and mouthed an apology, then let go of her hand as he followed Kitty. Their neighbor caught the toe of her heels on the corner of the ivory throw rug and stumbled into Levi's lap. Miriam gasped audibly as Kitty cupped Levi's startled face between her hands.

"My hero," she said, planting a kiss on his lips before righting herself, grabbing Benedict's hand, and steering them both to the front of the room. She saw the shy man turn to his wife, his eyes wide with an expression that looked both horrified and excited.

Aaron and Torn came to stand on either side of her.

"Why do I get the feeling that something weird is about to happen?" Aaron asked.

"Come on, Aaron. It's a party. Lighten up," Torn said over his shoulder as he made his way to the place beside Kitty.

Esme whispered, "I'm with you. I think it will help if we both have another drink."

She grabbed two cocktails from the sideboard on their way to the main group, which had gathered on the jewel-colored furniture that Kitty had positioned in a circle. She was standing in the center, waving the purple velvet bag Esme had seen in the foyer. Esme realized it was the carrying bag that had come with bottles of whiskey when she was a kid, the same kind she used to stash her marbles in. She hadn't seen anything like it in years. Trust Kitty to find a period-appropriate pouch.

"Thanks, Esme," Aaron murmured as she handed him the drink. "My husband is pretty excited to get out of the house these days, but I would have rather spent the night in fuzzy socks in front of the TV."

Esme laughed. "You and me both." She raised her glass and they clinked, exchanging shy smiles at their lack of adventure. Esme lifted the glass, and the sweetly poisonous scent of the drink filled her nostrils.

"Aaron and Esme! Pay attention. This is important," Kitty admonished them before turning back to the others. "So, like I was saying, the 1970s were a time of risk. A time when people were willing and ready to throw off the rules of the so-called establishment."

Benedict hooted beside Kitty and raised both his arms to shoot peace symbols to the sky. Esme closed her eyes and issued a silent wish that Julia would stay out late and Zoe would be fast asleep by the time they got home. She tried not to let her concern for Benedict's mental state show. The last thing she wanted tonight was another argument, but she hated being with Benedict when he was high. It scared her to think that her husband could backslide into the person he used to be.

"Yes, Benedict! People were wild. It was a time to be free!" Kitty wiggled the bag again, and an odd jingle came from inside. "Soooo, in the spirit of the night, I invite you all to join Benedict and I in honoring a real 1970s tradition. The key party!"

Esme turned to stare wide-eyed at Sophie, who had come to stand beside her. She wasn't sure what irritated her more: Kitty's ridiculous game or the insinuation that Benedict was her partner in this venture. She watched as Kitty playfully pantomimed handing the bag to Benedict, only to snatch it away. *Definitely the latter*, Esme thought. She frowned and took another swig of her drink.

"What is a key party?" Torn called enthusiastically, suggesting he was up for anything. Kitty winked at him. Esme tried to ignore the sting of resentment that made her jaw tense.

"Sometimes, people called it wife swapping or swinging: a chance to dance with another partner, as it were."

Torn and Benedict laughed at Kitty's exuberant spin as she twirled into Benedict's arms. She pulled herself out of the embrace and shook the bag toward the surrounding group. "Let's live a little! There was a reason why I asked everyone to come with a date. Come on, people, put your keys in here with mine."

Sophie pointed to the couch as she laughed under her breath. "If anyone wants to swap husbands with me tonight, they are more than welcome."

Ray was lying facedown on Kitty's overstuffed love seat in the back corner of the room. Apparently, his brief explorations with 1970s abandon had been too much for him to handle. Thick snores underscored Sophie's amusement.

Sophie dropped her keys into the bag with a smile. "No hanky-panky, though, oui? Despite my husband's current state, I am a happily married woman."

Kitty looked disappointed. "Well, that's not really the point."

"Come on, Kitty. You don't really expect us to . . . ," said Esme, her cheeks flushing with color before she could finish her sentence. She took another drink to cover up her embarrassment, even though it was beginning to taste like the headache she knew she would have in the morning. Kitty's gaze rested a fraction too long on Benedict, who was waving his keys above his head, before she turned to Esme.

"Of course not. I mean . . . it's up to you. One partner will draw the keys and choose their partner from the matching couple. And remember"—Kitty had a gleam in her eyes—"I know this is a 1970s tradition, but there's no reason to be heteronormative. Why not try something different?"

"Yeah! Girl on girl." Benedict's louder-than-necessary voice made the words even more lurid as he dropped his keys into the bag.

"Benedict, come on. I don't want to do this," Esme said. Kitty's eyes narrowed at Esme's impatient tone.

Sophie stepped to Esme's side and whispered, "Don't worry, I will pull out your keys. We can go back to your house and watch *Real Housewives* and stick Ray and Benedict together."

Esme softened at Sophie's suggestion. Going back home was all she wanted to do. The fever of the party was too heated, the drinks were too strong, and her growing annoyance at her husband's antics was too real. She could sense the mood in the room begin to shift as the expressions of the people she hadn't met yet turned both hostile and eager. Neither sentiment felt like something she was willing to engage in, and she shuddered to think of what it would feel like to be paired off with a stranger.

"Okay."

"Yes!"

Benedict cheered. Kitty smiled. Neither of them seemed to see the negative reactions their actions were generating. Esme watched as Miriam elbowed Levi in the side, prompting him to stand up at the same time as her. Miriam's face was frozen into an expression of disgusted disbelief, while her husband seemed paralyzed by fear, as if hiding from a large predator.

"Actually, um, we have to get going. Er, rehearsals. Tomorrow. Thanks for the party," he stuttered.

They both walked toward the door, coats in hand. They were in such a hurry that they didn't even bother to put them on before they walked into the frigid night. One other couple that Esme didn't recognize wore the same confused and contemptuous expressions as they followed them out the door. They didn't bother to say goodbye.

"No surprise there. I shouldn't even have invited them," Kitty said breezily, turning back to the group. "Okay, everyone else, throw in."

Esme could see Torn looking excitedly at his partner, while Aaron shook his head no. Sophie noticed as well.

"Aaron, mon cher. It's all in the name of fun. No one is expecting anything."

"It's not a good idea," he said. "Men can get . . . weird in situations like this."

"Look, I'll make sure to pull your keys," Esme said quietly as she realized that Kitty's suggestion was even more awkward for Aaron than it was for her. She glanced toward Sophie, who agreed with the change of plans. "Then you and I can go watch *Real Housewives*."

"Make it *Project Runway* and you've got a deal," Aaron said, smiling gratefully at Esme.

"Is that okay, Sophie?" Esme asked.

"Of course, of course. I suppose I can always try for that guy." Sophie looked toward a tall man who was staring at her. "We can tell Ray all about it when he wakes up."

"I think that's Kitty's date."

"All the better," Sophie said, and Aaron laughed before nodding to Torn, who threw his keys into the mix.

"Let's get started! Torn, last one in, first one out. You draw first!" Torn reached into the bag Kitty was waving before him before any of the three of them could stop him.

"Wait, I want to draw," Aaron cried, trying to jostle through the crowd to get to the front. But it was too late. Torn reached in before Aaron had a chance. Esme sighed with relief when she saw Benedict's leather key chain dangling from Torn's fingers.

"It's okay," she whispered. "That's us."

The look of relief on Aaron's face was almost as palpable as the disappointment on Kitty's. Esme swallowed her anger at the fact that Kitty had clearly been trying to go home with her husband with another gulp of her stiff drink. The alcohol dissolved her annoyance slightly. Thank God that fate had derailed Kitty's ill-advised plans for Benedict. Esme knew they would all be grateful in the morning that the party hadn't turned into something that they couldn't control. She made a mental note to ask Kitty not to include historically accurate drugs at her next costume party. It was not beyond the realm of possibility that her neighbor would get a kick out of MDMA at a rave-themed party.

"Torn! Who do you choose: Esme or Benedict?" Kitty recovered fast, still seemingly intent on throwing herself into the spirit of the night.

"Esme." The group burst into cheers as Esme looked helplessly at Aaron. Benedict rushed toward Aaron, gathering him in a bear hug.

"Aaron!" her husband cried. "I can't promise you anything but more drinks. Though you never know." He winked lasciviously, and Aaron forced a laugh before turning to his partner, who was now standing in front of Esme.

"You owe me a binge day of *Project Runway* with Esme, Torn."

"You got it!" Torn turned to her, his blue eyes shining. "Your place or mine?"

Benedict interrupted. "Aaron and I are heading to our place. I've got more liquor. You like schnapps?"

Aaron smiled gamely. "Sure."

The two men walked out of the room. Right before they reached the front door, Benedict grabbed Aaron's hand, swinging it dramatically. Kitty's date let out a loud whistle, and Sophie grinned.

"Wish me luck in the next draw," she said as Esme kissed her friend's cheek. Torn grabbed her hand as well as they walked out the door. His skin was warm and softer than she expected, though his grip was firm.

"Well, Kitty is never dull," Esme said as the noise of the party faded behind them. "I'm glad to be done with that party."

"So am I. It's nice to be alone." Torn's voice was surprisingly intense.

"Yeah," she said lightly.

The night had taken a strange turn, and she realized suddenly how much she enjoyed Torn touching her. He made her feel like she had in the days before she quit acting, when she had enjoyed the slow dance of desire with so many men. She and Benedict hadn't been serious at first, and she remembered the sweet power her smile used to have over the fans seeking her autograph and the agents seeking to sign her. For a moment, the world had been hers to enjoy. Torn's unpredictability reminded her of how she used to give and take in those interactions, always careful not to go too far and damage the relationship she had with Benedict while still leaving the men something to think about.

Torn seemed to understand the wax and wane of desire better than most. His mood was like the tide. Some days, storms would cloud his eyes and close his world off. Other days, his swell of joy carried her along. During his afternoon visits to Dix-Neuf, there had been moments when she'd felt a shimmer of what she could describe only as attraction. It was foolish, of course. But tonight, it felt less so. The air was cold enough to hurt as she breathed in the darkness, lifting her head to see that the clouds had parted and the stars were painting points of light across the black sky.

They reached Torn and Aaron's house and walked up the wide stairs to the front door. Though it had the same design, the house was nearly twice the size of the others in the neighborhood. *The jewel of Raven Lane*, Kitty had described it in the listing. The thought of Kitty triggered a latent flash of annoyance. She turned, about to ask Torn what he thought of their neighbor's antics, when she felt him step close. Closer than he'd ever been before.

"I didn't pull your key out by accident," he said. His breath warmed her lips.

"What do you mean?" She knew she should step away. One slight move from either of them would be enough to irrevocably change their relationship.

"I've been waiting for this for so long. Please tell me you felt it too, Esme Lee."

His words blew away the things she was supposed to say. Then Torn's lips were on hers, and her life began to fall apart.

CHAPTER TWELVE

In the early morning the day after Benedict's arrest, Esme made her way from the courthouse back to the largest police station in Fraser City after the bail hearing Jack had managed to schedule before regular court hours. "The judge had a tee time he didn't want to miss," Jack had joked as the bailiffs took Benedict away to wait until she posted. Esme hadn't laughed. During the hearing, Benedict's face in profile had looked as bleak as the cold streets. She hadn't been able to see his eyes as he wouldn't turn to meet her.

Their SUV was still being held by the police, so Esme was driving their second vehicle, a fifteen-year-old car they had debated selling last year. The streets were as dull as the sky, empty save for scavenging crows and the occasional still lump of a person huddled in a tattered sleeping bag. As she entered the station to follow Jack's instructions on how to post bail, the mottled stone walls pressed in on her, and she wondered how her husband had fared overnight in a cell. Benedict had told her that last time he was detained, the police had kept him in an interview room with no place to lie down. She hoped he had been given a bed this time—alone. It made her stomach clench to think of him surrounded by other inmates, as if he were already one of them.

She assumed her place at the end of a long line of people queuing in front of a reception desk, avoiding eye contact with the others. She tried to distract herself from her bounding thoughts and the unpleasantly strong body odor of the man in front of her by reading the faded posters about bike safety and neighborhood watch that were taped limply on the walls around her.

Normally, her phone would be her companion, as it was for most of the other people in line, who were swiping at their screens. This morning, however, she dreaded looking at her social media feed, knowing that the worst events of her life would be the main subject of interest. She had foolishly opened her page before leaving the house, only to see that several blogs were speculating wildly on the "love triangle of Raven Lane." One link to a gossip site read: Actress. Model. Author. Murder. She couldn't bear to click through. Just reading the headline had been enough to make her drop her phone as if it were an unexpectedly scalding frying pan. She had known that a skilled reporter would unearth her and Benedict's past professions, but it made her nervous that the information could also have come from a source closer to them, maybe even one of their neighbors. The phone felt heavy in her purse, like a suitcase she wasn't strong enough to carry.

Esme dropped the irony of fixating on a poster instructing her how to properly fit a bike helmet and let her thoughts drift to Zoe. The last thing she wanted was for her daughter to hear about her infidelity through a prurient online story. Last night, after a long phone call with Jack, it had been late by the time she had tucked her daughter into bed, nipping in her quilt around her body as if she were still a child. Esme had been sadly grateful for Zoe's state of shock. She was so focused on how they were going to get Benedict out of jail, it hadn't occurred to her to ask why he had been put there in the first place. Esme hoped with every fiber of her being that her daughter was still sleeping. For once, Zoe had agreed to miss a day of school so she would be home when Esme and Benedict arrived.

Esme envied the unequivocal desire her daughter had to see Benedict freed. As much as she wanted to bail Benedict out, she knew he wouldn't forget to ask her about what she had done to their marriage.

Each slow step she took to the front of the line moved her closer to his impending demand for explanations that she wasn't sure how to give.

And he wasn't the only one looking for answers. It wasn't just news stories that Esme was avoiding by keeping her phone cloistered in her purse. Sophie, Ray, and Kitty had been sending her texts since Benedict disappeared in a squad car, but she hadn't answered a single one. At first, she had been too busy comforting Zoe and calling Jack. Then, as she found herself alone in the dark hours of the night, all she could do was stare at the messages on her phone screen, unsure of what to say to the people she considered her closest friends. Her problems had become too large to describe with a tiny keyboard. She ignored the insistent tremors until they had stopped, but she knew in her heart that, like Benedict's, their questions would have to be answered soon.

The man ahead of her walked to the desk, leaving her exposed at the front of the line until she was also motioned forward. She stated her reason for being there to the disinterested clerk and received a pile of forms that seemed to require every detail of her financial history since birth. Benedict's bail had been set at $100,000. She had to come up with 10 percent. She painstakingly transcribed the details from the deed of their house on Raven Lane, cringing at the way it was described on the form. Who knew her dream home would end up as collateral? When she finished the paperwork, she clutched the pile in her hands until a tall man with a deep voice called to her from the end of the counter.

"Esme Werner?" He pronounced her name incorrectly: Ez-Mee instead of Ez-May. It was the same way Jed Matheson had said it, and her head pounded with tension as she moved forward to the bail clerk. Her shoes squeaked on the soft linoleum. The clerk began to review the papers. In the bureaucratic pause, Esme couldn't stop herself from remembering the first man who had destroyed her life.

~

Jed Matheson was a star maker. Landing a role in a film produced by his company, MirrorMirror, had felt like a fairy tale, though the daily shoots had been difficult. Esme was confused by the director's harshly shouted commands between takes and embarrassed by his frustration at her inability to understand. His aggressive style was so different from the quiet suggestions of Brian Smith. Each night when she returned home, she felt exhausted and terrified that she was about to be fired. She wished she could call Benedict, but the rehab center that his parents had paid for didn't allow any outside communication for the first twenty-eight days.

Two weeks into shooting, she found a dozen red roses in her trailer and an invitation to go to Jed's house for a meeting. She hadn't questioned for a moment whether she should accept. If she could establish herself as someone marketable, Jed's clout would make a success of the film and bring myriad new offers for her, regardless of how much her current director seemed to despise her. Her dreams were finally coming true.

She had arrived at his house in Fraser City's wealthiest neighborhood the next afternoon, marveling at the enormous glass and rawwood structure perched on the edge of a cliff like a castle. The ocean crashed below. A maid wordlessly took her coat and led her into an office that was twice the size of her apartment. Jed Matheson appeared through a side door after she was shown in. He was a big man, more than six feet tall, and loose pounds hung on his body like bloat on a beached whale. The mint green of his golf shirt cast an unflattering light on his acne-scarred face.

"Esme Lee. A pleasure." He held out a meaty hand. Esme shook it with a smile, careful not to register her distaste for its dampness or the singsong pronunciation that made her name rhyme, like a goofy character in a children's television show.

"It's nice to meet you, sir."

"Sir," he guffawed, causing a slight sheen of spittle to coat his lips. "Please. Call me Jed."

"Thank you." She smiled. He looked at her expectantly. "Jed."

He kept staring at her, making sure their eyes met before sweeping his gaze pointedly up and down her body. She had chosen a fitted black dress—professional but appealing, but she wondered now if the neckline was too low as his gaze lingered on her chest. She didn't want to seem too desperate or inexperienced. With only one film under her belt, she knew she had to present herself as someone who was skilled beyond her résumé. She reminded herself that she was lucky; most actors had to work for years to get breaks this big, and she wanted to make the most of her opportunities. Jed was acting aggressive because that's how he acted with everyone. It was what had made him a success. It wasn't anything to be nervous about.

He likes actresses who make an effort to please him, her agent had told her when she called him about the meeting. *Wear something nice.* Once more, she felt Benedict's absence keenly as she tried on and discarded several possible outfits, wishing he were there to guide her with his strong knowledge of fashion. She hoped that when they were finally allowed to speak again, she would be able to tell him that MirrorMirror had offered her another role.

The only thing she had felt confident putting on was an expensive bra and underwear set she had splurged on. With Benedict gone, no one else would see them, but the feeling of the luxurious silk against her skin made her feel confident. Esme used the thought of her secret armor to hide her discomfort at being so blatantly appraised. She broke eye contact and crossed the room to look at the dozens of photos on the wall of Jed with the biggest celebrities of the last ten years.

"You could be up there someday, you know," Jed said.

"Oh, wow. If only," she said. Her voice was higher than normal, like a serf paying homage to a king.

Jed waved at a linen love seat positioned near a floor-to-ceiling window in the corner of the room. "Please, sit down."

Esme dutifully took a seat on the edge of the love seat, smoothing her dress carefully. The small salary she had made from *Seeking Mercy* was nearly gone, and she couldn't afford regular dry cleaning, especially after spending so much on lingerie.

"Would you like a drink?"

"I would love a Coke."

"I was thinking something a little more fun. How about a gin fizz?"

Esme was only twenty-two. Her distaste for alcohol hadn't diminished after a year of being legally permitted to indulge, and she didn't drink much, especially before dinner. She didn't want Jed to think she was unsophisticated, however, so she said yes.

Jed walked to the dark oak bar against the far wall and began mixing cocktails, crossing the room with two glasses when he was finished.

"Here you go."

"Thank you."

He sat on the love seat and patted the spot beside him, indicating she should come closer. She moved toward him despite the unease pooling in her stomach. She left six inches between them, smiling and following suit as he lifted his drink. She shifted her knee subtly to give herself a little more room, fighting the adrenaline that was making her hands shake. Something felt off, but she told herself it was just her nerves. This was the biggest chance she had ever received. She had to make sure not to blow it. She took a long sip and forced herself to swallow. It tasted like gas. She set the drink down on a side table.

"Too strong?" Jed chuckled as he spoke. His light-brown eyes sparkled with mockery. She felt embarrassed.

"It's delicious."

He smirked. "Glad you like it. I've been watching the dailies. You have a real talent."

"Thank you so much. That means a lot."

Esme flushed with relief. Jed must have been aware of how hard it was to work with the director. It wasn't her fault that things had been so tense on the set. The combination of the strong drink and Jed's reassurance made the muscles in her body relax. He seemed to notice, shifting a few inches nearer. Up close, the pockmarks on his face were more pronounced, and his color was uneven, as if his internal organs were having a hard time keeping up with his lifestyle. Jed was renowned for having wild tastes.

Matheson parties were legendary among the young professionals in the city. In their first month of dating, Benedict had broken a date with her to go to one. She hadn't seen him for three days, and when he returned, he had been a shell, haggard and lethargic for a week as his brain struggled to rebalance its chemical equilibrium.

Jed finished his drink and set it down. In one smooth gesture, his hand was on her thigh, just inches away from the hem.

"You have what it takes to go far in this business, Esme. I know people. I can introduce you."

Esme's skin crawled as she felt his hand slip up and under the cotton of her dress.

"Please stop." Her face burned, and she stood up. Jed anticipated her movement and rose with her.

"Stop what?" he asked slyly, grabbing her wrist and pulling her close. His belt dug into her stomach. "Helping launch the career of the world's most sought-after starlet?"

"What are you doing? You're hurting me."

"No, sweetheart," he whispered hoarsely in her ear. His breath smelled rotten, like a hard-boiled egg left in the sun. "I'm giving you an opportunity you can't refuse."

"No. Stop." Her voice was loud enough to be heard outside the room, but she wasn't surprised that no one came to help as he raised his hand and backhanded her across the face. This was not a place where women were rescued. She had never been hit before. She hadn't realized

how much it would hurt. The pounding of bone on bone made her brain thud inside her skull as her head roiled back. Blood crawled down her cheek like an insect. Absurdly, she wondered if the makeup artist would be skilled enough to cover the bruises tomorrow on set. Had Jed required them to learn how to do so on past actresses who foolishly had agreed to meet with him? Or maybe none of the others had resisted.

He pushed her back onto the love seat, kneeling between her legs, then turned her over as he positioned himself behind her. As he finished, he ground her head into the upholstery. It smelled like cigarettes, and Esme wondered if Jed smoked or if the scent had lingered from other guests whose own careers were shaped by the same crooked hand. As soon as he pulled away, she stood and ran to the heavy wooden door of the office. His voice was calm as she jerked it open.

"I'll be in touch."

It was ten minutes later, her hands shaking almost too hard to keep the steering wheel straight, when she realized she had left her expensive underwear there. She kept driving, sickened by the knowledge that they were with the man who had already taken so much.

When she got home, she stripped robotically before stepping into a steaming hot shower. She felt disgusted by the deceptive property of the water beading on her skin, as if her body had the ability to protect her from harm. She knew that she might be washing away evidence, but she couldn't bear another second of feeling him on her body or risk triggering a criminal case by allowing the police to perform an exam. The thought of being caught up in a public trial that would ruin her career made her retch.

When she had regained control of herself, she turned off the water and wrapped herself in a robe that used to feel comforting. She examined the clothing crumpled on the floor, relieved and disgusted to find the inside of her dress was now stained with the remnants of what he had done. Her logical mind took over. She had washed herself, but maybe what remained unclean would be enough. She took a photo of herself, naked except for her bruises, in her full-length mirror, holding up a copy of the note Jed had left for her and a newspaper with the date, thankful she had recently acquired a digital camera. The idea of having an image developed in a lab was more than she could bear, even in her current detached state. She walked to her bedroom and burrowed under her covers.

Two hours later, her phone rang in the dark apartment, waking her from a deep but troubled sleep. She let the answering machine in the hallway pick it up. The sound of her agent's excited voice made Esme shiver under her quilt. Three scripts had arrived at her agent's office from MirrorMirror, each offering plum female roles opposite huge, bankable stars. Her agent signed off with three words: *You impressed him.*

Esme curled into herself, cringing as her bruised parts rubbed against the blankets. Prior to meeting Jed, it had felt as if she lived in a glass house that conformed to her body, protecting her from evil. She had taken its protection for granted until Jed Matheson fired a bullet. Now the walls were cracked and fragmented. She needed strength to rebuild them. She spent the rest of the weekend in bed, getting up only to relieve herself and eat a handful of pieces of buttered toast.

On Monday, she returned to the set, but the first mention of Jed made her flee. Unsurprisingly, her agent had severed their relationship after she told him she would never accept another role on a film financed by MirrorMirror. *If you want to commit career suicide, I can't represent you,* he'd said. His tone had been sad enough to make Esme wonder if he knew what really happened at Jed Matheson's mansion on the cliff. She hadn't even bothered to say goodbye as she hung up, then opened the phone book. Both Esme and the lawyer she found, Jack MacDonald, had been surprised at how quickly Jed had offered to settle. She had never reported the assault to the police, but the photo and dress seemed to be damning enough. For someone like Jed, even the hint of a scandal was too much to risk.

During the negotiation period, she had never felt so alone, and her thoughts kept circling back to Benedict, who was also all by himself in the treatment center. Her heart ached for him, and, in his absence, she realized that his words and actions after his overdose had made her fall in love with him. She needed him more than she had ever needed someone before.

He returned to her, with clear eyes and glowing skin, days before the settlement finalized. She told him there had been an accident on set while he was away and that she had suffered a severe concussion. She was okay, but she needed to rest, and she'd been forced to quit the movie. The money was compensation for her injury, and she was meeting with a lawyer regularly to negotiate the terms. Benedict had been nearly overcome with concern. He insisted on staying with her and cared for her night and day. She could still remember how soft his hands had been on her back as he stroked her into sleep every night. It felt like she was Benedict's new addiction.

~

It took close to an hour for the police administrators to process Benedict's bail and lead him into the waiting room to meet her. Once again, she had to work hard not to recoil at his scent of panic and unwashed clothes as she stepped forward to embrace him. He refused to raise his arms, so she dropped hers in turn. They stared at each other in the dirty room.

"I'm so sorry. I can explain, but not here."

He didn't meet her eyes, so she turned toward the door that led outside. They walked to their car in the parking lot in silence. Esme ran through her apology in her head, beginning to speak the moment Benedict slammed the passenger-side door.

"Torn and I did sleep together," she said.

Benedict looked at her with accusing, self-righteous eyes, and she steeled herself against the unfamiliar, unfair realization that she was the one who needed to apologize. Benedict's eye had wandered too many times to count. He had flirted with Kitty blatantly in front of her for years. But, in his mind, she had crossed a line he had never dared to step over: an affair made public, a betrayal that endangered every part of their life. *Underneath the anger is pain*, she thought. It made her next words come more easily. "I'm sorry."

"How many times?" he asked, turning his head to stare at the pitted concrete building instead of her.

Esme gripped the steering wheel, then released. "More than once."

"How many times, Esme? Just answer the question."

Esme shrugged helplessly. "I'm not sure. It went on for a few months."

Benedict's face sharpened with anger.

"How many men before him?"

Esme bristled. Benedict was lashing out. He couldn't possibly believe she had ever done this before. "None. None, I swear. Torn was the only one."

"When did it start?"

"The night of Kitty's key party," she said, scanning his face closely for a reaction. His mouth dropped open slightly before he buried his face in his hands.

"That stupid party."

"We all behaved badly that night," she said. He glared at her, as if his behavior were suddenly beyond reproach. "It didn't mean anything,"

Benedict snorted. "The police certainly think so. So does everyone else in the world." He pulled a plastic bag from his pocket. Inside were his wallet, keys, and phone, all the trappings of a modern life that had been sealed away from him upon his temporary imprisonment. His finger scrolled across the screen before he stopped to read something.

"They've found out who we used to be," he said, shaking his head dolefully, but Esme knew him too well not to see that the corners of his mouth turned up slightly at the sight of himself as a young man. She remembered how much Benedict had loved to be on her arm when the cameras were flashing.

He let the phone drop, then rubbed his hand against the short blond hairs that had grown on his face overnight. In the bleak light, Esme could see some had faded to gray. Another betrayal for a man who still considered himself young.

"I'm so tired, Esme. I can't think straight. How could you do this to us? To me? My darling wife." His tone was so bitter it made Esme want to spit.

"I'm sorry," she repeated.

"That's not enough," he said.

The silence in the car grew thick, and she forced herself to respond. "I know."

"If this goes wrong, I will never be able to forgive you." His voice was robotic.

Tears clouded her eyes and she blinked hard enough to make them spill.

"We need to get back," he said. "Zoe is waiting."

As she pulled onto their street, she couldn't shake her dread. She backed into the driveway and turned off the ignition, then braced herself to face Zoe. For the first time in seventeen years, stepping into the white stuccoed house with its bright-red door didn't fill her with a sense of safety.

"Zoe?" Benedict called as he slipped off his shoes.

A muffled reply came from her bedroom.

"Can you come downstairs, honey? Dad's back. We need to talk."

Esme heard the door open and Zoe walked downstairs, her eyes soft with sleep and her hands mercifully free of her phone. She embraced Esme, then Benedict. This time, he was not the first to let go. When his arms finally relaxed enough for her to step back, Zoe's face shone with pride at being able to comfort her father.

"Is there coffee?" she murmured.

"I'll make a fresh pot," Esme said. "Why don't I meet you in the family room? Benedict, please wait until I get back."

She took his silence as consent. As she boiled water for the French press, she could hear Zoe asking how he was. The compassion in her daughter's voice made her ache with fear. Would Zoe ever feel sympathy for her again after she learned the truth about what she had done with Torn? Was it possible for a seventeen-year-old to understand that mistakes like this did not happen in a single moment but were crafted and shaped by every single thing that had happened in a life? In a marriage? When the kettle screamed, Esme poured its contents into the coffeepot, hoping this was not the last time her daughter would accept the acts of love she had to offer.

Esme walked into the white-walled room where she and Benedict had hung the bright paintings and prints made by friends and beloved artists they had met over the years. The energetic art didn't lift her spirits today. Instead, they fed the frenetic panic rising in her as she poured her daughter and husband steaming cups of coffee. Zoe doctored hers with milk and sugar as Esme settled on the chair opposite them on the couch, cradling her warm mug. Her daughter's face was stained with tears. Esme didn't know how to begin, but she spoke anyway.

"Zoe, the police have charged your father with second-degree murder. They believe he had a motive to hit Torn."

"What? Why would Dad want to hurt Torn?"

"Jealousy. They believe he acted out of rage." She paused to take a breath. "I haven't been honest with you. With either of you. I had an affair with Torn."

Zoe visibly paled. "Torn? You and Torn?" The pain in her voice confirmed Esme's suspicions about the depths of feeling she had for their neighbor. She shuddered at how deeply she had betrayed both of them the moment she had convinced herself that what happened between her and Torn could exist separately from the rest of her life.

"I'm sorry. I have no idea how the police learned of it, but it's given them reason to believe your dad did this on purpose."

Zoe looked to Benedict for confirmation. "But it's not true."

"It's definitely not true, Zo. I didn't even realize your mother had been . . . unfaithful," he said, furious grief pulling down his mouth. Esme rubbed her pounding forehead.

"Mom! You have to tell them that Dad didn't know. How could you do this to him?" Zoe gripped her father's hand, and it nearly made Esme break down in tears. Even though her chair was less than three feet from the rest of her family, she felt as if she were miles away.

"I will. I've already spoken with Jack, and we'll go over it again tomorrow morning in more detail. I'm so sorry. I regret it. I can never apologize enough for how I've hurt you both. Please, please understand that I know I will not go unpunished," she said. *None of us will,* she thought, but she couldn't say the words out loud.

Zoe stared at her as if she were a stranger.

"I'm sorry," Esme said, to them both. Benedict wouldn't even make eye contact.

"I just . . . I need some time, Mom. I need to be alone right now," she said.

Zoe walked out of the room with Benedict's arm around her shoulders. Esme gathered the cooling cups of coffee and returned to the kitchen, alone.

CHAPTER THIRTEEN

An hour after her confession, Esme heard a knock on the front door. Her stomach flipped with fear as she grasped the doorknob, wondering if she would find the police on the other side returning to take Benedict back to jail. Instead, it was Kitty and her daughter. Julia was poised halfway up the short staircase that led to the front deck, her body tense. Kitty began speaking before Esme could say a word.

"We need to talk. The barbecue party is a disaster."

Julia rolled her eyes behind her mother's back. Esme opened her mouth and then closed it, trying to control her frustration at her neighbor's selfishness. This year, Kitty's annual back-to-school barbecue had been slated for last Saturday, the day after Torn died, but she had sent a late-night group text to Raven Lane residents after Officer Singh had finished her questioning, telling them that the party would be postponed for a week. Seconds after scanning the text, Esme had forgotten all about the invitation.

Now, the day after Torn's wake and Benedict's night in custody, Kitty had come to discuss salvaging the party. As always, Esme was in awe of her neighbor's nerve. It wasn't only that Benedict had just been arrested or that Torn had just been buried. Kitty seemed to have forgotten that last year's barbecue was the event when Torn and Aaron had debuted on the scene at Raven Lane. But that was Kitty. She always acted this way. Why would she change now?

"Why don't you come inside, Kitty." Kitty nodded gratefully and stepped past Esme. Julia hesitated on the doorstep. "You too. We need to sort this out."

Julia nodded without meeting Esme's eyes. Her entrance into the house was slow and careful, like she was reluctant to enter the dwelling of a man accused of murder. Kitty was already sitting on the couch in the main room, tapping at the screen of her phone, when Esme and Julia joined her. Kitty turned the screen toward them, and Esme caught a glimpse of the party-planning app that Kitty used to coordinate events.

"Look! Miriam and Levi are a no, and no one else has even responded. How can I throw my barbecue without any people? Esme, if you and Benedict commit to being there, everyone else will think it's okay. We need to do this. For Benedict. For Torn. For the neighborhood." Esme wanted to say that bowls of salad and grilled meat hardly seemed like an appropriate memorial, but Kitty's expertly contoured face crumpled into tears. She cast a quick glance toward her daughter, who was pulling at a thread on her shirt. "Esme, I don't know how to do this."

Esme took the seat beside Kitty and pulled the crying woman into her arms. *This isn't about the party*, Esme realized as Kitty sobbed.

"Kitty, I'm here for you. Please. We have to be strong."

It was odd for her to be the one offering comfort, but Kitty was on the verge of breaking. The last week had been devastating for everyone on Raven Lane, and Esme knew that Kitty had been through more than most of them. She had seen the crash. She had watched Torn die.

"The prosecutor has been calling me. I think they want me to testify for them instead of the defense. Oh God, Esme. I can't. It's too much!"

Esme took a deep breath. "Listen, it doesn't matter if you are listed as a witness for the prosecution, Kitty. Just tell the truth. That's all that is important. You know what you need to do."

Julia leaned against the doorframe, glaring at her mother. Kitty seemed to sense her daughter's disdain. Her tears ended abruptly and she sat up straight, dabbing at the corner of her eyes with a tissue Esme handed her from a box on the side table.

"You are right. Oh, Esme, I'm sorry. How is Benedict? How are you?"

Esme struggled to reply to Kitty's question. Both she and Julia stared as Esme opened, then closed her mouth without an answer.

"You know what? We are all overwhelmed. I'm just going to cancel it. It will be the first time in twelve years, but there's just too much going on." Kitty reached for Esme's hand. "I should be thinking about you and Benedict right now. Have you been able to . . ." She paused before using the unfamiliar language of legal dramas that had become the reality of Esme's life. "Bail him out?"

Esme was grateful to find a quick response. "Yes. We got home about an hour ago."

"So Benedict is upstairs right now?" Julia's voice raised an octave.

Esme nodded silently.

"Oh my God," Kitty said. Her eyes shone with renewed tears. Esme was so distracted that she didn't hear her daughter's footsteps coming down the stairs.

"What are you doing here?" Zoe's inability to keep her emotions in check affected Esme more than Kitty's tears. Her daughter rarely treated others with disrespect.

"They just stopped by to see how we were doing, Zoe. They're here to help."

"Have you spoken with Jack?"

"Not yet."

"What?" Tears began to spill down Zoe's rosy cheeks. "Mom! We have to focus on Dad right now. He needs us!"

Kitty met Esme's eyes, then returned her gaze to Zoe.

"Zoe, this is so hard on everyone. We know exactly what you are going through, honey," Kitty said.

"Really, Kitty? You think you understand because your husband cheated on you?" Zoe emphasized her name with the same ferocity usually reserved for curse words.

"Zoe!" Esme's shock at her daughter's outburst turned to anger when Zoe gave a cold shrug.

Esme turned to Kitty. "Kitty, I'm sorry about this. Clearly, I need some time to talk to Zoe. I'll call you later."

"Please do. Anything you need," Kitty said, and she stood. Julia darted from the room so quickly that Esme heard her open the front door before Kitty had reached the front hall.

Esme turned to her daughter as the door swung shut. Zoe glared at her.

"Zoe, how could you say that?"

"I want to come to court with you." Zoe's words were tough, but the tears clogging her voice made her sound like a little girl. Her angry expression melted into gut-wrenching grief. Esme's stomach dropped as she gathered her daughter in her arms. She was relieved that Zoe allowed her to do so. For the second time that afternoon, she let another woman's tears fall while she stayed dry eyed.

"Oh, honey. I don't even know if I'm going to be allowed in," Esme murmured into the top of Zoe's head.

Zoe pulled out of her embrace with eyes widened by panic. "I mean it. I want to be there to make sure everything is going to be okay."

"It will. I promise."

"When?" Zoe said.

"I don't know."

Zoe was out of the room before Esme's last word was finished. She heard her daughter's fast steps race up the stairs as she sank into the couch, trying to figure out how to explain what she meant. Suddenly, she stood up and crossed the room to open the window. The day was cool, but the lingering scent of Kitty's perfume on the air felt thick enough to choke her.

CHAPTER FOURTEEN

After Kitty left, Esme tried for a sense of normalcy by preparing a meal for the three of them. As she set the roasted chicken on the table in front of Zoe, hunched over a book, Benedict banged the front door shut. Esme's stomach seized. She and Zoe stared at the steaming pot. It looked cheerful on the table, as if waiting for a happy family to come to dinner.

"I'm not hungry either," Zoe said, her face twisted with anger.

Esme felt overcome with misery at her failure as a wife and a mother, but she did her best to hide it with a warm smile. "Can we talk?"

"How many times did you sleep with him?" Zoe asked. "He was married! So are you."

"Oh, Zoe."

"Sorry, Mom. What did you want to talk about? The weather?"

Esme swallowed hard. "More than once."

"He was so much younger than you! Did you love him? Were you planning to leave us?" Zoe looked disgusted.

Esme shook her head, trying to contain her tears. "No. Never you, Zoe. I would never leave you."

"But you were planning to leave Dad?"

"I don't know what I wanted, Zoe. I wasn't thinking straight. It seemed to happen far away from what we have as a family, almost as if it weren't really happening at all."

Zoe shook her head. "Well, it did happen." She closed her eyes and took a deep breath. "And Dad might go to prison. Because of you!"

Her heavy footsteps out of the room, down the hall, and up the stairs made Esme want to weep. Instead, she placed the lid back on the untouched chicken and unset the table. She left the roasting pot where it was and walked up the stairs. When she saw the closed door of the guest room, she realized her husband would not be sharing her bed that night, or possibly ever again. Benedict was not a man who forgave easily, especially when it wasn't in his best interest to do so. Once he had run into his former agent at a talent scouting event and had refused to shake his hand, leaving Esme to fumble through a quick hello.

She picked up Torn's book. At first, the words blurred in front of her eyes, but she kept going until the pages calmed her jumpy thoughts.

After the ides, those who had experienced the madness without killing themselves came to their senses and began trying to explain what had happened to them. The accounts were eerily similar. Each dream began the same way. A distant bell, gong, chime, or alarm sounded as the horrors of an unnatural world were unleashed. It was a notification of a new age.

When the call came, those who could hear it were changed forever. For some, it was a scream of unbearable agony. For others, it was the song of a siren: an invitation that they could not resist. In fact, they had been waiting for it all their lives. The request was simple. Embrace the things inside yourself that you have spent your life denying and you will be free, forever. For some, the price was too high, but others would have paid more than what was asked. There was nothing they wouldn't give for the chance to be released from the burden of their feigned morality.

In the dreams, as soon as the call's last toll ended, the monsters arrived. Tentacled, oozing leviathans that only the darkest oceans could breed sucked ships and water-front cities into churning depths. Impossibly jointed, thousand-legged creatures from the deepest depths of earth writhed higher than the tallest skyscrapers, blocking out the sun. Mesmerizingly huge and shockingly fierce flying swarms with knifelike stingers descended from the sky to carve their way through countries. Then, after they finished their blood feast, the monsters went quiet. The dreams ended in the disquieting calm of a monstrous world hiding, waiting to be revealed once again.

She closed the book, feeling disturbed. Instead of laying it on her bedside table, she placed it carefully in the top drawer and slid it shut, as if the wooden drawer could stop it from infiltrating her thoughts. It took her hours to fall asleep. Benedict returned around midnight. Esme fell asleep listening to him pace in the room beside her. Over and over, his footsteps jerked her out of a light sleep, convinced that something was coming for her.

When she woke up, the skin around her eyes was tight and tender, as if she had been crying. Zoe had already left the house and didn't respond to Esme's texted question about whether she was going to school that day. The pot of chicken was still on the table when she came downstairs. She took it directly outside to the trash bin and upended it before placing the empty pot in the sink.

Benedict was in the front room, dressed in a suit jacket and jeans, waiting for her. They were both scheduled to meet Jack to go over the information he had received from the prosecution. *We need to prepare for the preliminary hearing,* Jack had said, noting that hard proof of her infidelity had surfaced. Esme felt queasy at the thought of it. As they left the house, she wondered if her husband would ask her to drive, but he grabbed his keys without hesitation. She could never have operated a car with confidence so shortly after killing a person with one, but she knew it would be just as much a mistake to question his decision as it would have been to look sideways at the number of drinks he was consuming each night. At this point, she was in no position to judge him.

Her phone rang when they were halfway across town. It was Anthony.

"Hi. Is everything okay?" Esme half hoped that there was an emergency at the restaurant so dire that it would require her to skip the meeting with Jack.

Anthony sounded uncharacteristically agitated. "The restaurant is packed with reporters. They want to know where they can find you, where you live."

"Have you told them anything?"

"Of course not. The staff know not to say a thing as well. But I'm worried about you. Do you want me to come over?"

Esme sighed with relief. "Thank God. Tell them if they want to stay, they have to order. Maybe we'll get a good lunch rush out of it." Her attempt at a joke fell flat.

"You got it, Chef. I'm sorry he did this to you, Esme," he said forcefully.

"Thank you," she said, too distracted to do anything but respond automatically. "I won't be able to get to the restaurant until this evening."

"I can hold down the fort, Chef. You don't need to come in at all. Just take care of yourself and Zoe."

"I will. Thank you." She hung up, knowing that the omission of Benedict's name was no accident. Anthony had disliked Benedict since Esme had hosted a thirty-fifth birthday party for him at the restaurant. After preparing an incredible meal, Anthony had left the kitchen pristine for the next day's service. Ray and Benedict, made bold by too many whiskeys, had crept into the space and instigated a food fight without Esme's knowledge. The next morning, Anthony had walked into a kitchen so filthy, he had been forced to close Dix-Neuf for lunch.

"There are reporters at the restaurant," she said numbly.

"This is a nightmare," Benedict said as they circled the underground parking lot for a space, going lower and lower until her lungs felt tight.

"I know. But Jack is very good. If anyone can get you out of this, it's him," she said.

"He won you a workplace settlement, Esme. That doesn't exactly make him equipped for a criminal case. I should have hired someone else." The sunless space made it too dark to see Benedict's expression, but she could hear the frustration in his voice. Even after all these years, it was strange to hear her lie repeated as truth. Immediately after his release from rehab, Benedict had been so focused on his sobriety that he never asked for details about the incident on set after their initial discussion. Then the check was issued, and it felt like their lives were beginning again, with the search for a new home and the start of their new jobs. There had been no time to dwell on the past. Esme wondered if her lack of honesty was the reason she had come full circle, back to Jack and the hurtful chaos of legal wrangling.

Benedict finally pulled into a tight spot on the sixth level, the tires squeaking painfully as he maneuvered into it. Esme had to edge sideways between the vehicles to join Benedict as he strode across the echoing concrete, but she didn't dare complain. As soon as they exited the elevator, Jack's assistant led them to a boardroom. Esme willed herself to focus on the sophisticated muted blue walls and blond wood furniture instead of her growing dread at seeing Jack. He had been curt, but professional, at the bail hearing, but she could tell that he would no longer be treating her with the sympathy he had in the past. She was now just another client, stained by her own mistakes.

The office was located on the twentieth floor of a large corporate building on the edge of downtown where a scarcity of land in the city had led to massive redevelopments over the last two decades.

The boardroom was bright with unexpected late September sunshine. Floor-to-ceiling windows ran the length of the room, showcasing the city and the sparkling ocean beyond its shores. Cranes spun on the tops of surrounding buildings like spiders weaving iron webs.

Esme and Benedict chose chairs that faced the view, leaving an empty seat between them. Esme rested her arms on the whitened wood of the huge table, wishing suddenly that her family could stow away on one of the barnacle-covered freighters lurking in the bay and sail away from this shining city forever. A lump of guilt sat in the back of her throat. Zoe, Jack, and Benedict all blamed her for the current situation. They weren't wrong to do so, but it still made her feel sick that they believed the story had only one side.

The assistant hovered at the head of the table. "Would you like coffee?"

She waited to make sure Benedict said yes before she did the same. She felt cautious about her every move, hoping that if she stayed on her best behavior, he might forgive her. Even in profile, Esme could see the damage that fatigue and worry had carved on his face. He had shaved, so the gray hairs she had noticed before were invisible now, but he looked aged. His green eyes were sunk back into his face, surrounded by fine lines. She had seen similar evidence of the stress they were both under this morning in the mirror. Neither of them had been sleeping well.

Jack and his assistant entered the room together, and the lawyer waited until Esme and Benedict received their coffee before he began to speak.

"Benedict. Esme. Thank you for coming."

Esme took a drink as Jack opened a folder. The coffee was too hot, and the skin on the tip of her tongue blistered painfully, but she didn't make a sound. Jack looked up at them once his papers were arranged, laying his hands flat on the table, just as he had after she told him what Jed had done, so many years ago.

"I'll get right to the point. As you know, the judge will decide tomorrow if there is enough information to uphold the prosecutor's charge of second-degree murder. I'll be honest. Tomorrow's hearing is just shy of a formality. I'll do my best, but it's very likely that this case will go to trial. As a result, I want to give you a sense of what to expect in the next few months. I met with the prosecutor yesterday afternoon, and we went through the information."

Benedict placed his coffee cup on the table hard enough to send a sharp crack ringing through the room. A brown tongue of liquid lurched over the side.

"This is such bullshit. All they have on me is my wife's affair, which I didn't even realize was going on."

Esme looked down at the ring of coffee pooling at the base of her husband's cup. The rage in Benedict's voice made the hair on her arms stand up with fear. Benedict was acting like a person she no longer knew, and she was the reason he had changed.

Jack continued to speak.

"I know how difficult this is. For a lot of my clients, this is the hardest part. Obviously, it's no picnic to spend a night in jail, but the period between the initial charge and the trial can be excruciating. How did you sleep last night?"

"Fine," Benedict said before taking a large gulp of coffee.

"Eating?"

"Fine. Please, let's get to the point."

Jack paused, then picked up his papers. "Good. We have work to do. I have a copy of the arrest report and a few witnesses the prosecution plans to call. From what I can determine, the focus will be on your motive. Opportunity is weak, so the prosecution is going to need to prove that you learned of the affair shortly before Torn Grace was hit. I can only assume that they are going to frame this as a crime of passion. That you found out about Esme, then saw Torn on the street and acted on impulse."

"I didn't know a thing about Esme and Torn. I had no motive, so I wasn't looking for an opportunity. It was an accident. You have to prove that," Benedict said.

"Of course. Our defense will focus on showing without a doubt that you had no reason to kill Torn. If we can do that, there isn't much of a case. I want to call as many character witnesses as possible to show your good standing in the community."

"I had no motive," Benedict repeated as he shifted in his seat. "I had no idea what Esme was doing behind my back."

Esme met Jack's eyes as her stomach dropped in panic. She hoped her guilt didn't show on her face. She had to learn how to take responsibility for what she had done if she had any hope of getting through this. There would be so many more people to defend herself against as the trial continued.

"Do you know how the police found out?" Esme's voice was quiet. It was the first time she had spoken.

Benedict looked away, but Esme saw his jaw clench.

"Yes. It was detailed in the arrest report." Jack pulled a series of fuzzy images from a folder beside him. "The police found these in your SUV during their search. Under the driver's seat. They dusted them for prints but there were none to be found."

He slid the photos toward her husband, who glanced at them so fast that Esme would have assumed he hadn't seen them at all were it not for his disgusted expression as he spoke.

"I've never seen these before in my life."

He shoved them toward her, acting as if the papers were hot enough to burn his fingers, then pushed his chair back and walked to the window, his back toward them. Esme looked at the photo on top. It was a close-up of her and Torn. Neither of them faced the camera, but their side profiles were clear. Her hand was woven through his hair like she was pulling him toward her, even though his lips were already pressed against hers so tightly that both of their mouths were obscured. She turned it facedown and looked at Jack. The images were much grainier than they had been on her phone.

"Esme, have you ever seen these before?"

"Yes, we took them . . . together. It was stupid, just a game. We used my phone. I'm sorry," she said miserably, not sure if she was apologizing to her husband, her lawyer, or the world at large. She could see Benedict's hard eyes on her in her peripheral vision, but she didn't turn her head.

Jack's eyes showed no sign of the contempt Esme had been expecting. "Did you print them? Tuck them under the seat to keep them hidden?"

"No, of course not." She would never have tried to hide something in such an obvious location, as if begging for them to be found.

"Did you send them to Torn?"

"No, no. I was the only one who had a copy. They were on my phone." Benedict exhaled loudly as Jack continued.

"Do you leave your vehicle unlocked?"

"Sometimes," Esme admitted, surprised that her guilt could be compounded even further.

"How careful are you with your phone?" Jack said. "Could someone have stolen it? Found those images and put them there for Benedict to discover?"

Esme tried to still her racing thoughts. "I don't know—"

Benedict cut her off. "The artists' showcase. Last spring. You left your phone somewhere and couldn't find it. The next morning, it was on our doorstep, but no one ever told us they dropped it off."

"Oh my God," Esme murmured.

"It had to be someone on the street," Benedict said. The airy, bright room suddenly felt suffocating. Jack cleared his throat.

"Look, I'm going to be blunt. These pictures are damaging but not insurmountable if we can present them in the right way. We can't deny the affair, but I have a plan and I need you both to get on board with it. We know the affair is going to be the meat of this trial. It's really the difference between accidental death—manslaughter, which I thought was the direction we were heading in until I learned of the extenuating circumstances—and second-degree murder. As you both probably realize, the key element that differentiates those two things is intent. Without the affair, it was a simple accident. With it, the situation is a lot more complicated."

"I didn't know," Benedict said. His voice was louder than necessary. Esme stared at his back. A cramp of guilt folded her stomach unpleasantly.

Jack cleared his throat. "Denying knowledge of the affair is not our best strategy, even though it's the truth."

Benedict shook his head.

"The jury might think you're lying or, worse, that you didn't know until you discovered those pictures the night Torn was killed and the discovery made you react in rage. My job is to convince the jury that the information in these photos is inconsequential. That it didn't matter to either of you the night that Torn was killed, and it still doesn't matter."

Esme looked at her hands. It seemed impossible. "How will you do that?"

"I won't." Jack paused. "You will."

"What?" Esme said.

"I want you to testify that you and Benedict have an open marriage and that you left the pictures in the car. It was careless on your part, just a handful of shots you had taken in fun with Torn that slipped out of your purse. You can convince the jury that the affair wasn't something worth killing over because, in your eyes, it wasn't an affair at all but a mutually agreed-upon relationship outside the marriage. I want you to tell the court that your marriage was based on complete honesty and allowed both of you to sleep with other people. In other words, the affair wasn't a betrayal. It was a way of life."

"But it's not true."

"Sometimes, plausibility matters more than truth," Jack said, and Esme's head pounded as the full ramifications of what he was suggesting came to mind.

"Would it be more . . . plausible if Torn wasn't the only person we had done this with?"

Jack looked at her gravely. "Probably."

Esme began to ask if Jack expected her to make up false lovers when Benedict spoke, his lips curled in disgust. "So I have to lie about people I've slept with, because otherwise the jury will think I'm lying?"

"Actually, I don't want you to say anything, Benedict. I think it's better if you don't take the stand at all."

"What? No. I want to testify on my own behalf."

Jack took a deep breath. "Benedict, that is not advisable. Juries don't respond well to emotion, and it's difficult to testify on your own behalf without it. The majority of defendants who get their charges dropped never take the stand. I have a better way to get the job done, to tell your side of the story. We need to let Esme tell this part of the story."

"Won't the jury consider me just as unreliable?" Esme asked. "I was sleeping with the man Benedict killed."

Her words were sharper than she intended, and, out of the corner of her eye, she saw Benedict flinch. Jack responded smoothly.

"Actually, your presence on the stand will show how strong your marriage is. Not every couple could get through what you have and still stand by each other's sides. When the prosecution brings up Benedict's history of drug use and the blood test from the night of his arrest, it will be much less damning if you can show that you've supported him all along. You got married right after he was released from rehab, right? That will play well for us too."

Benedict shifted his body to stare at her, and she saw his doubt that their marriage was strong enough to sustain these blows. She had to prove to him that she was still in his corner, despite everything she had done. She shifted her gaze to Jack.

"What do you want me to say?"

"That the two of you agreed, early in your marriage, to total honesty. That if either of you felt attracted to another person, you would discuss it with your partner and decide whether it was acceptable to act on the attraction. That nothing was off the table, so long as the decision was reached by both of you, together."

"So we had an understanding?"

"Yes." Jack held up a sheet of paper and pointed at a typed name too small for Esme to read. "Levi Stein, your neighbor from across the street, will be testifying in the preliminary hearing. Presumably he saw Torn and you together. I'm not ruling him out as the source of the photographs. If you can think of any reason he might have a grudge against you, I'm all ears. In any case, I'm guessing that they will be calling him and Officer Singh tomorrow."

"I've barely said two words to Levi Stein in my life. What could he possibly have against me?" said Benedict. Esme remembered the hateful expression on Miriam's face at Kitty's key party. Not everyone on Raven Lane was as accepting of Benedict's wild behavior as he thought.

"Just keep it in mind. If we can track down who got those photos into your SUV, it could make our case even stronger. Sophie Bernard is also on their list, though not for the preliminary hearing. I'm assuming she was aware of what was going on between you and Torn?"

"Yes, she was," Esme said in a voice so low it was barely audible.

Benedict snorted in disgust. "God, you have made such a fool of me, Esme."

Jack spoke again before Esme could respond to her husband's anger.

"I think the prosecution is doing us a favor with her. She's a good friend, right? She won't speak poorly of either of you on the stand, especially if we can defuse her knowledge of the affair with Esme's testimony about the open marriage."

"Sophie knows our marriage is not like that," Esme said.

"Nobody really knows what goes on in a marriage, Esme."

Sometimes not even the people that are in it, thought Esme as Jack continued.

"Keep this strategy between us. No matter how close you are to Sophie, witnesses can't share information. Besides, it will look good if Sophie is just as surprised by your testimony as everyone else."

She swallowed hard. It seemed the punishment for her dishonesty was being forced to lie again.

Benedict sighed heavily. He ran his hands through his hair. "Who else is on the list for the prosecution?"

"So far, they just have Levi and Sophie, but it's early days. They can add whomever they like as their case builds. I will let you know as soon as I hear about any changes."

"So, who will speak for me?"

"Our witnesses need to show who you really are. I want to call Kitty Dagostino and Ray Peters. Two people that saw the event and remain on your side. In the arrest report, they were both extremely sympathetic to you, and they swore repeatedly that it was an accident. They've been your neighbors for years; they'll do a good job of establishing your character."

Jack turned to Esme.

"The secondary witnesses are important, but your testimony will prove the open marriage. It will show your loyalty to your husband. It will give the jury a real man and a real woman in a trusting, open marriage. Remember, this was a very private agreement between only you and Benedict. You did not share this with friends, no matter how close. And it wasn't something you wanted your daughter to be aware of. No one else knew."

"Except Torn," Benedict said bitterly.

"You can get that kind of anger out here, Benedict, but I want you to present a united front whenever you are in public, okay? This is a happy, open marriage, and Esme's testimony is the key."

"What if I can't convince them?" she blurted before she could stop herself. Benedict blinked hard.

Jack sighed. "Esme, this is a critical part of the defense. It's the only strategy I can come up with that feels solid. You used to be an actress. A good one."

Esme swallowed hard at Jack's pointed words, worried suddenly that he might assume Benedict knew everything about the settlement. She was losing control of the details.

"I can help you, Esme. That's my job. I need you to let me do it to the best of my ability." Jack's mouth was set in a firm line.

Esme took a deep breath. "Is this Benedict's strongest chance for acquittal?"

"I believe so."

Benedict looked at her across the table, and Esme was struck by the force of his need. "Esme. Jesus. You're the reason I'm here in the first place. You have to agree."

Esme took a deep breath to rid herself of her disbelief that despite everything he had done, her husband now felt comfortable putting the entirety of the blame on her, but she knew she had to agree.

"Yes," Esme agreed, her mind spinning.

"Thank you." He sat down again, across the table. Esme carefully slid his almost full cup of coffee across the table and he picked it up. The tension in the room eased as Jack spoke again.

"This is good. Really good. I truly believe this is our best defense. Your lives are unconventional by most standards: your past in the entertainment industry, the neighborhood parties. We don't need to fight those aspects of you. Instead, we can embrace them and use them to our advantage. The police have based a lot of their evidence on assumptions, and we need to turn those on their head."

Benedict nodded and Esme did her best to follow suit, though her trepidation made the gesture almost imperceptible.

"Great. Excellent. I know this seems overwhelming, but we are in good shape. There are several big weaknesses in the state's case." Jack began ticking items off on his hand. "Number one, Torn's schedule was erratic and his husband was away. No one even knows where he was going that night. The police checked his cell phone, and there were no messages to arrange a meeting, nothing set up in his calendar. The police are assuming that he either got a knock on his door or that he remembered something that he needed to attend to immediately. Number two, he wasn't wearing a helmet. Both points will make it extremely difficult to prove that Benedict had any intent to kill. The state has to argue that this was a crime of opportunity, but Esme, you will state that the hedge blocked the view, that Benedict couldn't see anyone biking down the path. Police forensics back that up. There was no way for Benedict to know that Torn was going to be behind him, precisely at that time. It will be hard, hopefully impossible, to show that Benedict planned any of this. You have witnesses stressing it was an accident. If we can take away the blight of the affair, the state has very little."

Benedict's shoulders dropped as Jack kept going. Esme could tell Jack's words were reassuring him. She wished she felt the same.

"I think they're reaching, Benedict. I think they got pissed off once they learned you were high, and they are trying to throw the book at you. They might have had a case for manslaughter, but with this charge, I think we are looking at an acquittal. Maybe even a dismissal."

Benedict said solemnly, "I hope you are right."

Jack stood up. "I am. I've got a lot of work to do. I'll see you both tomorrow morning for the preliminary hearing. Esme, it's necessary that you attend each session of the court, though you won't be permitted in the courtroom until you testify. I want to show the judge that you are a loyal wife, despite the prosecution's accusations of the contrary."

"Okay," Esme said, grateful for the first time that she had made herself superfluous at her own restaurant.

"The days will be long, so make sure to bring what you need to stay calm and focused."

She and Benedict stood. It wasn't lost on either of them that Jack was billing by the hour. When he said they were done, they listened. Esme excused herself to visit the restroom as Jack walked them to the elevators. She needed a moment to catch her breath. It was an enormous amount of pressure to be the only thing standing between her husband and a prison sentence. She owed it to him to make sure the jury reached the right decision.

CHAPTER FIFTEEN

The night of Kitty's key party, Esme pulled away from Torn after a single breathless kiss, slipping down the icy sidewalk still feeling the press of his lips. She felt grateful—and frustrated—to have ended it before it went too far. The house had been quiet when she returned, which surprised her. She had expected Benedict and Aaron—especially Benedict—to be drunk at the dining room table. Part of her had been prepared to laughingly confess what had happened between her and Torn, blaming Kitty's cocktails and the surreal nature of the night. Instead, she was left alone as both the alcohol and honesty dissolved in her system.

She looked in on Zoe, snoring softly in the soft light Esme let in from the hallway, then took a shower. The warm water made her feel clean enough to fall into a sleep that was so deep she failed to wake when Benedict crawled into bed beside her. The next morning, through half-lidded eyes, Benedict told her that he had taken Aaron to a nearby bar to watch a soccer match, but Aaron had left shortly after they arrived, due to fatigue. Benedict hadn't come home until much later, staying with other sports fans to see the end of the game. Before Esme could prompt Benedict for more details, her phone had rung with a question from her pastry chef about oven settings, and she lost her chance to confess as Benedict drifted back into sleep. Normally she would have questioned him about the cocaine and the way he had behaved with Kitty the night before, but it hardly seemed appropriate after what she had done.

Benedict stayed in bed to nurse his hangover, and Esme found herself at loose ends as she fought through her thirsty headache to try to make something of the morning before her shift. Zoe was barricaded in her room with a bag of cheese puffs, a carton of pineapple juice, and several textbooks to study for her physics exam, so Esme was alone. She began testing dessert recipes. By midmorning, however, neither member of her family had come downstairs, and Esme felt like she was about to drown in profiteroles. In her increasingly restless state, she even considered calling her mother before she remembered that her breeding program had just begun at an East Coast zoo. She thought about going for a walk, but the cold rain and a lack of desire to chat with her neighbors on Raven Lane kept her housebound. She wasn't ready to debrief with Sophie about Kitty actively trying to seduce her husband, and what had happened with Torn felt too precious and bewildering to put into words yet. She couldn't stop feeling his lips on hers, wondering if it would happen again and feeling horribly guilty that it might.

She saw her laptop on the side table and found herself typing "Torn Grace sexuality" into a search engine, looking over her shoulder as if she were about to view pornography as she clicked the first video link that came up. It had been posted less than a year ago and seemed designed to appear less like a formal interview and more like a conversation between friends that happened to be recorded. This time, the interview setting was decidedly edgier than the black stage of the previous video. Torn, clad in a soft-blue denim shirt, sat at a glass-topped table beside two people in their twenties. One wore thick black glasses and had a knit cap perched precariously on top of his head. The other had a nose piercing between her nostrils that glinted oddly in the warm lights, making it seem as if she were in need of a tissue. Her catlike eyeliner was expertly applied, and her deep-purple lips parted expectantly as she stared at

Torn. Behind them, floor-to-ceiling bookshelves were crammed with paperbacks in every color of the rainbow.

Eyeliner leaned toward Torn, revealing a glimpse of a pleasantly curved breast peeking out the top of her ripped tank. She began speaking with no preamble.

"So, what got you so interested in Lovecraft? Isn't he the guy who said that no human could pronounce the name of his monster?"

"No human until now," Torn laughed. "I think I do a pretty good job."

Eyeliner toasted him with her cocktail before changing the subject. "So, you're getting married?"

Esme wondered if the interviewer began every sentence with the same word as Torn wiped a thumb on his cocktail glass before lifting it to his lips and taking a drink. The gesture made Esme blush. "I am indeed. To the man of my dreams."

"Have you always identified as gay?" the young man in glasses asked. Eyeliner shot him a look.

"I don't remember ever saying that I *identified* that way." Torn smirked. His emphasis made Glasses slump against the red leather seat before asking his next question.

"Do you use any word at all to describe your sexuality?"

Esme sucked in her breath, furtively glancing toward the door that led to the hallway to make sure that neither Benedict nor Zoe had sneaked downstairs without her realizing it.

"Desire shouldn't have a label. I love who I love. I'm not attracted to men or women. I'm attracted to strength. To courage. To extraordinariness."

"And your fiancé is all those things?" Eyeliner asked.

"And more," Torn replied. "Being with him makes me a better man."

"But why marriage?" Eyeliner pressed. "What's the point?"

"Why not?" Torn said. "I'll try anything once."

He finished his drink and lifted a finger to signal for another one. The video stopped on a freeze-frame of his face, one eyebrow lifted. Esme clicked a tiny X in the corner to make it disappear from her screen, snapping the laptop shut. She glanced at her watch. Finally, it was time to go to work. She left a note for Benedict and Zoe on the off chance that either of them noticed she was gone.

When she arrived, she found Anthony plating ramekins for French onion soup, which they were featuring that day.

"Is Benedict coming in later?" he asked.

She had asked Benedict to reorganize the shelves in their walk-in cooler that afternoon, since they were too high for her to reach, but she doubted that he would remember. After all, she had forgotten to remind him. "He's a bit . . . under the weather. Maybe I can stand on a ladder. We need to get it done today, before the sides of beef come in."

Anthony looked at her for a beat too long before agreeing. "Sure, we can try and make that work. That new server, George, is pretty tall. Maybe he can help."

"Great," she said as she heard a chit come in. "Order up."

It settled Esme's mind to meet the demands of the busy shift, working in a steady, comforting rhythm with Anthony by her side. She was making far too big a deal out of a simple kiss. After all, Benedict had been snorting coke and had practically made out with Kitty the night before. Sophie had been flirting shamelessly with Kitty's date. *We all got carried away*, she thought as she walked toward the door between the kitchen and the dining room. If anyone was to blame, it was Kitty for creating such a wild atmosphere. Her justifications vanished the second she saw Torn hunched over his laptop at his usual table. His presence warmed her from her head to her toes.

Torn raised his eyes nearly as soon as she'd spotted him, as if he could sense her gaze. Without asking, she set down her water glass and poured them both Pernod. His eyes didn't leave her for a moment as she crossed the room.

"Hi."

"Hi."

She offered him the small glass, and he smiled.

"Can I tell you something?"

"Sure."

She leaned in, half hoping he would say something she didn't want her staff to overhear. Like why he had kissed her. Or what he wanted to do to her next. Instead, Torn set his glass down on the table with a half smile.

"I really hate this stuff."

Together, they both looked down at the cloudy liquid swirling in the tiny glass. Then she laughed, and Torn joined her.

"Why have you been drinking it?"

"I was trying to impress you." His tone was sheepish.

"How many glasses of this have you choked down?" *He is trying to impress me?* she thought.

"Quite a few," he said. She suddenly remembered the gassy taste of the drink Jed had forced on her and shook her head to dispel the thought.

"How about a beer?"

Torn agreed with a smile. Esme hurried to grab a cold bottle for him, as if he would disappear from her life if she took too long. When they both had drinks and she'd finished doctoring hers, he spoke.

"Are you okay? After . . . ?" He trailed off, and Esme was struck by how different the man in front of her seemed from the one she had seen at Kitty's party.

"I feel wonderful." Her words were as rushed as her movements had been. She paused, worried suddenly that he was asking her only so that he could apologize for having gotten out of line and remind her that they were both married. "You?"

"Are you kidding? I got to kiss Esme Lee. I'm the luckiest guy in the world."

She smiled at his enthusiasm but felt a little sad. "Esme Lee was a long time ago. Now I'm Esme Werner, wife, mother, and restaurant owner. Pleased to meet you."

Torn returned her smile briefly. He was so young, the wrinkles that it caused around his eyes disappeared when his expression changed to something more intense.

"Come on. The woman you've always been is right in front of me."

"Sure," Esme said. "But Esme Lee was before Zoe. Before Dix-Neuf. I'm more than that now." *And less too*, she thought.

Torn's eyes were shining, as if she hadn't spoken. "When I was a teenager, I used to watch *Seeking Mercy* over and over. I thought I was going to fry that DVD. There was something about you that I couldn't resist. I could never tell if I wanted you or I wanted to be you." He paused. "I guess I finally figured it out."

He winked, and she laughed again, this time loud enough to turn her server's head. Esme waited until he went back to folding napkins before she spoke. Torn's flirtation made her bold enough to ask the question that had been stuck in her mind since his lips had touched hers.

"But . . . didn't you know back then that you didn't want women at all?"

Torn's face turned serious. "Not really. I'm still not sure. Adolescence was . . . a confusing time. I felt drawn to a lot of people, both men and women. But with men . . . it seemed easier somehow. So that's the path I stuck with. But I was always open to more."

Esme took a deep breath. "So, you've never . . ." She trailed off.

"You are the first woman I've ever kissed."

Torn's eyes were soft. He seemed uncharacteristically vulnerable. Esme had never been the first for anyone. Benedict had been so experienced when they met that she didn't want to seem unworldly. She never told him that she had been with only one other man before him, a summer fling with a lifeguard who never called her after he left town to return to college. Neither man she'd been with had treated her as if she had something special to give them in that regard. She had learned early that sex was nothing precious, and what happened with Jed had only reinforced that in the ugliest possible way. But Torn was acting differently. The air between them was charged as she took another sip of her drink without breaking eye contact.

"There have been other women that have captivated me, but it's never gone very far. Physically, I mean."

Esme felt Torn's leg brush hers under the table.

"What about Aaron?" Her voice was so husky that she sounded as if she were pitching it deeper on purpose.

"What about Benedict?"

They locked eyes. Then Torn raised his glass and she followed suit. All her senses felt heightened, like his presence made her better than she was. The light chime of the glasses touching seemed like the first note of a beautiful song. Esme could smell the malt of his beer. She could see a dark shadow on the bottom half of his freshly shaved face.

"Why did you stop?"

"Acting?"

Torn nodded. Esme took a deep breath.

"It's a long story, Torn." His eyes didn't leave hers. "Acting isn't like people think it is. There's a lot that goes on behind the scenes."

Esme expected Torn to change the subject, as Benedict always did when her past career came up. Instead, his dark eyebrows drew together and he pressed his leg against hers more firmly, like he wanted to give her support as he asked his next question.

"Did something happen behind the scenes that you didn't like?"

Esme paused. His leg was warm against hers, and it felt both comforting and tempting. She had never spoken about Jed's actions to anyone, not Benedict, not Sophie, and certainly not her mother. But Torn seemed to really want to know. He looked so kind. She took a long sip of the sweet anise-flavored drink, startled by a memory of sneaking a piece of licorice from her grandmother's candy bowl and hurriedly putting it into her mouth before realizing that it was covered in ants. Sweetness coated her tongue. She surprised herself as she said, "Yes."

"What happened?" Torn sounded concerned, but there was a note of curiosity that raised Esme's guard again.

"It's not something I can talk about, legally and, well, psychologically, I guess. I signed a nondisclosure agreement. It's a sealed record."

"Whoa. That sounds bad."

"Yes, it was," Esme said as she finished her liqueur. The restaurant was now empty. Torn's beer was almost drained. She shrugged, gave him a wry smile, and stood, wanting to change the mood without ending the conversation. "Want another?"

"Why not? I'm not driving." Torn laughed and gestured to his bike outside. She walked behind the bar to refresh his drink, grateful for a moment to flush the memory of Jed from her mind. As she sat back down, she smiled.

"Okay, my turn. Is Torn your real name? Or is it just a sexy author thing?"

Torn laughed again. "You think I'm a sexy author?" His eyes seemed to turn bluer, and Esme realized that the afternoon sun was getting low. Zoe and Benedict would be expecting dinner soon. She didn't have much time.

"I think we've established that," she replied with a smile.

"Okay. Torn isn't my real name. My parents called me Todd. I know. I had much grander aspirations for myself. I was an adopted teenager who liked boys and was obsessed with monsters from the deep. My parents told me that my birth mother came from the north, and I got it into my head that she was Inuit."

"Is that true?"

Torn looked wistful. "I'm still not sure. Adoption records are only unsealed by the permission of the biological parents. My mother didn't want to be found. She asked that they be kept private. At the time, those online DNA tests didn't exist, but I would have taken one in a heartbeat. It felt like I would only know who I really was if I knew what I had come from."

"I'm sorry, Torn. That must have been devastating."

"It was at the time, but looking back, I think that it was a gift. The mystery gave me a chance to invent my own story. Sometimes, I think it's the reason I can write. By the time it became possible for me to figure out my genealogy, I had lost the desire to do so. Anyway, I found the term 'Torngarsuk' in the earliest draft of Lovecraft's work. It stuck out at me like it was jumping off the page, so I read more about it. The Torngarsuk was one of the most powerful gods in Inuit mythology. Kind of a demon, actually, but that was part of the appeal when I was sixteen."

"So you changed your name to Torn?"

"Well, I was a teenager, remember. My parents were incredibly supportive of my search for who I was. Maybe too supportive, actually. They told me to wait until I was eighteen and then make my decision. It was only two years. My mind didn't change. So now my full legal name is Torngarsuk Grace."

"You named yourself after a demon?"

Torn grinned. "Still think I'm sexy?"

The sunlight hit his face full force, and Esme was struck by the wave of lust that rolled over her.

"Surprisingly, yes." She tried to keep her tone light, but her voice contained something too powerful to be masked.

Torn cleared his throat. "Hold that thought."

He rose and walked to the hallway between the kitchen and the dining room. Esme watched him, fighting the urge to follow. She looked around again. Her server was on the other side of the restaurant now, sweeping the wooden floor before the dinner crowd arrived. There was no one else around. Five minutes passed. She got up. The restrooms at Dix-Neuf were unisex, large spaces with a toilet and space for a wheelchair. She turned the handle on the one door of the three that was closed. Torn hadn't locked it. Her heart raced as she stepped inside the small room. Torn was standing at the sink. She met his eyes in the mirror. He didn't look surprised to see her. Instead, he spoke as if he was expecting her.

"Come here, Esme Lee."

She stepped forward as he turned toward her. He touched the back of her neck, pulling her gently toward him as she stood on tiptoe to meet his mouth. He tasted like beer and salt, and his touch sent fire from her lips all the way through her body. She reached for him, and his body was hard all over, and the groan that came from his lips vibrated through her.

"Please, Esme," he whispered. "Like this."

She felt a flicker of panic at the positioning, but his hands were warm on her hips, and she allowed him to turn her body toward the mirror. His lips brushed her ear and her neck as his hand reached down to pull off her loose chef pants and lacy underwear. She closed her eyes at his touch. It had been weeks, maybe even a month, since she and Benedict had been together. After years of marriage, nothing he did to her ever made her feel like this. She wondered how Torn knew what to do as his finger traveled to the small spot between her legs that mattered so much. She drew her breath in sharply as he made small, gentle circles. It was almost too fast.

"Look at yourself," he whispered. "Look at me."

He stopped rubbing her, and she heard his belt buckle jingle. The sound sent a frisson of fear and pleasure through her body, knowing she was about to cross a line. Despite his urging, she kept herself in darkness. His voice whispered in her ear again.

"Open your eyes."

Then his light fingertip was back, and he touched her slowly as she lifted her eyelids and locked on his gaze in the mirror. She could feel his breath on her neck and his finger on her as he slid into her.

"Look at yourself. You are amazing."

The last word came out in a moan as part of him became part of her. He didn't stop looking right at her eyes, and in that moment, she saw herself as beautiful again.

"Esme Lee, Esme Lee, Esme Lee," he said softly as they moved together. His finger circled more rapidly and her breath quickened at the same rate.

"Torn." The word sounded like surrender, and his eyes seemed to contain worlds beyond worlds as the moment overcame them both. He shuddered into her and she leaned back. The air around them seemed to wobble. They both gasped for breath. When he pulled away, she felt cold, as if she had lost something, like she always did after sex was finished.

"Was that okay?" he asked without meeting her eyes. He fumbled with his belt clumsily.

She waited until he was done, turned her body, then raised her lips to his again. She kissed him, gently. "Torn, that was incredible."

"I was worried that I would hurt you."

Esme traced a line from his jaw to his cheekbone, realizing Torn was the first man she had been with who cared about whether his actions caused her pain.

CHAPTER SIXTEEN

On Friday morning, Esme and Benedict followed Jack up the steps of the Fraser City courthouse, through the crowd of reporters shouting their names. Esme ignored the shouts of "Esme Lee," as if turning toward the cries would change her to a pillar of salt. Benedict had barely said a word to her since their meeting with Jack. When she tried to speak to him and Zoe after the meeting, both seemed completely detached. His withdrawal reminded Esme of how he had been in the month of his heaviest drug use, when he had retreated so far into himself that she had been forced to rely on friends for updates about how he was doing. That period had been extremely difficult, but it was nothing compared to now.

Esme's nerves jangled as their footsteps echoed on the thick marble floor. Jack walked purposefully toward the room Benedict had been assigned for his preliminary hearing, pausing to point to a seat across from the door leading to the courtroom, where Esme would be sitting throughout the trial. Benedict gave her a quick, tight smile that didn't change his eyes, then looked away.

"Right there. Just like we talked about," Jack said. The bench was already occupied by Levi and Miriam Stein. The couple faced forward, averting their gazes as she settled a few feet away from them. She focused on the wood grain, noticing it was the same shade as the boardroom table had been during the settlement negotiations with Jed.

She wondered if every decorator in the legal system got a discount on the dark stain.

She tried to blink moisture into her tired eyes. She knew she was wearing her lack of sleep like the wrong shade of foundation. Her insomnia had been caused by worry about the arraignment hearing and the hollow space beside her in the bed.

Anthony had done nothing to relieve her anxiety. He seemed distraught at what she was going through, sending her a flurry of messages each day asking her to call. When she did, panicking that the restaurant was in peril, he asked her over and over how she was holding up, what he could do to help her, whether she thought Benedict would be sent to prison. She was able to distract him only by going through the minutiae of that evening's restaurant service, and the calls were draining. After the trial, Esme knew she would have to have a serious discussion with Anthony about boundaries and convince him to find a grief counselor to help him overcome the sadness Torn's death had caused him. But in the meantime, there was nothing she could do for him besides listen. It took everything she had to survive the long days. Each evening, Esme crawled into bed too exhausted to sleep, then lay awake until the darkest hours of the night with only Torn's book to comfort her. She knew her husband was sleepless as well. The soft murmur of videos on his phone in the room next door sounded like whispers of people speaking ill of her.

The door to the courtroom was opened by a stunning woman in an expensive suit. Esme recognized her from the news as Selena Wong, the prosecutor who would be trying Benedict's case. In the interviews she had given to the media about the trial, her voice had been clear, strong, and full of contempt for Benedict. As Ms. Wong entered the courtroom, Esme glimpsed a line of defeated-looking people in garish orange prison jumpsuits through the open door. Esme's breath caught in her throat. Benedict would be among them, if it weren't for Esme's willingness to trade the security of their home on Raven Lane for his freedom.

Esme rubbed her forehead, trying to ward off another headache.

The defendants were called in alphabetical order, which meant Benedict would be close to the last summoned. She had searched this morning for her copy of Torn's book, growing frustrated at its absence from her nightstand but unwilling to risk the fragile peace of her household by asking Zoe if she had borrowed it again. It had been on her nightstand, but now it was gone. In its absence, she was left with nothing but her own thoughts for company.

She knew that she should have forced herself to come clean the night after Kitty's party when it had been just one kiss to confess and not months of lies and sex. If she had told Benedict the next day, after Torn came to Dix-Neuf, she could have asked him about his own secret. Now, as she thought about the judge reading the allegations against Benedict, she wondered what he would have said if she had asked him. What happened between her and Torn had grown so fast that it became a part of her before she realized what was happening. She was so used to keeping parts of herself from her husband that the deception came naturally.

Besides, the months after Kitty's party had been busy. Zoe had begun a twice-weekly study group that met at their house. Benedict and José had thrown themselves into expanding their international recruitment, which meant many late nights for Benedict at the agency. Her affair with Torn had become just another element of her life, separate from her family. Benedict was good at not asking too many questions. When she married him, she thought his ability to accept her without digging too deep was a lifeline. Now she realized it had been the worst part about them.

~

Though Benedict had convinced himself in later years that his modeling career had been sabotaged by a bad contract, Esme remembered the message on his answering machine the day he arrived home from the treatment center during the final days of her settlement talks with Jed. His agent had been apologetic, even supportive of Benedict's newfound sobriety, but he had told him that it was too late to salvage his career. Benedict had blown off too many gigs in the months before when all he had cared about was pills, cocaine, and champagne. Esme had been terrified that the agent's dismissal would lead Benedict to relapse. Luckily, Jed cut the check three days after the call came in, and Benedict's idle days were filled with the hunt for a house.

They both knew the money meant that, even though both their careers were in tatters, they still had choices. Benedict was picky as they looked at house after house, telling Esme that it was worth waiting for the right one to come along. She didn't mind the exhaustive search. It distracted her from what she knew was happening. She waited eight weeks after her first meeting with Jed before she took the pregnancy test to confirm the suspicion that had grown stronger with each bloodless day that passed. When it turned out positive, she told herself it was just as likely Benedict's as Jed's. She couldn't bear for Benedict to know the truth and worry about the paternity of the child for the rest of their lives. She was young enough to think that the end of one path was just the beginning of another, so she told him about the baby and then she proposed.

She wasn't sure what stunned Benedict more, but he had hesitated for only a brief, sickening moment before gathering her in his arms and sweeping her off her feet. Even as she swung in the air with Benedict saying over and over that he loved her, she could still feel Jed's hands crawling all over her. The money and the marriage had to erase the past as quickly as possible. They entered city hall that afternoon in jeans and raincoats. She left forty-five minutes later as Esme Werner, the person she thought she wanted to be.

It was exactly what she needed to make her feel like the future contained more for her than just Jed's awful stare. Two months later, when they found the house on Raven Lane, it had seemed like the perfect next step. She made sure that both of their names were on the deed. As soon as she stepped into their new home, she knew she had made the right decision even though she had been wrong about what the settlement could do. The money didn't get rid of the feeling of Jed's coarse fingers cutting and bruising her flesh or the lingering smell of his sour sweat-drenched body. It didn't get rid of the memory of his thick tongue lapping at her like a monstrous dog. But it did make her feel safe again and allowed her to rebuild her walls thicker and strong enough to withstand everything.

In the early days and long nights of their marriage, alone with only a small crying baby who screamed so loud she seemed to hate her mother, Esme scared herself wondering if the settlement would disappear up Benedict's nose. Instead, the opposite had occurred. Two weeks after they moved in, José approached Benedict with the idea of cofounding a modeling agency. The agency had consumed Benedict so much that he stopped asking if she would consider returning to acting. Years later, when he had experimented with drugs again, she had held her breath and waited for it all to fall apart. But it hadn't. Not until they met Torn Grace.

~

The large doors to the courtroom opened and Benedict and Jack exited. Benedict met Esme's eyes. He shook his head slightly, his mouth turned down. Esme knew exactly what he was telling her. The judge had not dismissed his charges. Her husband was now on trial for murder.

CHAPTER SEVENTEEN

Benedict spoke as soon as he pulled the car away from the curb.

"Levi saw you," he said quietly.

She paused as she tried to figure out what Benedict meant. The signal indicator ticked as loudly as a timer.

"Torn and I?"

"Yes. The night of Kitty's party. It was late, he said. He couldn't sleep. That guy is such a creep," Benedict muttered. "He probably skulks around the neighborhood all the time trying to spy in our windows."

Esme had never considered Levi to be anything more than a timid musician, perhaps slightly too beholden to his wife, but she murmured her agreement before seeking the more important information.

"Did he mention the photographs?"

"No," Benedict said. "But Jack is planning to ask him about it during cross."

Esme sensed her husband withdrawing again, and she spoke quickly.

"What about the officer?"

"She just stated what Jack told us. The photos were found in our SUV, tucked under the seat. No fingerprints. It looks horrible for me. The judge didn't ask for much more detail. Just the fact that they were there was bad enough. It felt like the decision was made to go to trial before anyone got on the stand." Benedict rubbed his jaw roughly. "I just hope the jury hasn't made its mind up about me in the same way. Listen, Esme, I know it's been hard between us, but Jack is right. Your testimony is what's going to change their mind, yeah? You know what happened that night. Why I was . . . distracted. It had nothing to do with Torn. I didn't even look in my rearview mirror."

Esme didn't know how to respond, so she stayed silent. For the rest of the drive, she mulled over how to tell a jury about her bold action on the front steps. She could sense Benedict's frustration growing with each quiet mile. He turned into the driveway and stopped the car's engine before he looked at her. Esme saw something worse than anger in his eyes. She couldn't remember her husband ever appearing so desperate. In spite of herself, she cupped his cheek with her hand and he leaned into it, like a puppy searching for affection.

"I know what I did. I'll do my best to talk about it on the stand," Esme said.

Relief relaxed his features. "Thank you."

"Did the judge set the date?"

"November 15," he said. "We've got six weeks to prepare."

"Okay," she said. "I need to tell Sophie. Will you be okay if I leave for a few minutes?"

Benedict's expression changed as abruptly as a slammed door.

"Of course," he said. "I'm fine. Remember what Jack said, though. The plan remains between us."

Esme walked around the hedge and up Sophie and Ray's front path. As she swung open the door to their house, she breathed in the strangely comforting scent of perfume, mint tea, and hot glue.

"Hello?"

"In here," Sophie called from the front room to Esme's right.

Unlike the other residents of Raven Lane, Sophie and Ray did not use the largest room in their house for entertaining. Ten years ago, when they'd first moved to the neighborhood, Sophie had been certain that Ray would finish his novel and be able to leave his position as a sportswriter, so creating a central space as a home office was paramount. They had divided the room in two. The front half, which enjoyed most of the natural light from the street-facing window, was Sophie's studio. A large white table took up most of the space. Today, it was covered in clay, paint, ribbons, and glue. The walls were a collage of images that inspired Sophie. The back half of the room was Ray's, who had furnished it like a Raymond Chandler detective's office with a rolltop desk, green banker's desk lamp, and gray metal filing cabinet. In between the two spaces was a sliding barn door. Today, Sophie had left it open, and Esme could see that Ray's desk was covered in a thin film of dust.

Though Sophie earned the bulk of her income as a freelance photographer, mostly for catalogs and Instagram feeds, her personal art was far more important to her. She had a small but loyal following for her collections of miniature scenes, and the tiny figures sold well to both private collectors and museums. The problem, Sophie admitted to Esme, was that the work was too laborious and time consuming to provide them with the income that they needed, especially since Ray's salary hadn't increased in ten years and his novel remained unpublished.

It was Sophie's personal art that had brought the two women together. Ten years ago, during a slow day at Dix-Neuf, Esme had left the kitchen early to take a walk, excited to pop into a small gallery that had just opened a few blocks away on Main Street. The opening exhibit was called *Small Curious World*, and Esme had been mesmerized by the painstaking detail the artist had captured in each scene, despite the fact that the figures were less than an inch tall. The show was a series of six tableaus, each depicting the same room in a house in different historical eras, including a stuffy turn-of-the-century parlor, a tiny 1930s speakeasy, and a modern family glued to a television. After two hours, Esme had reluctantly relinquished the provided magnifying glass. She was so captivated by the precise brushstrokes that rendered emotions on the figures' faces that she kept picturing the almost painfully exquisite art when she went to sleep that night.

The next day, Esme returned to see more and was thrilled to be introduced to Sophie, the young artist behind the work. The two women began a conversation that ended six hours later at Dix-Neuf, with a bottle and a half of red wine and two bowls of French onion soup. Sophie spoke about her husband's new job as an in-house sports-writer, expressing enthusiasm that his stable employment had created an opportunity for them to finally purchase a house of their own. Esme learned of her neighbor's decision to sell his home weeks later, and, after a quick word to Kitty, Sophie and Ray had become residents of Raven Lane.

Today, Sophie greeted Esme with a kiss and waved toward the seating arrangement in the middle of the room. "Do you want some tea? I just made a fresh pot."

"I would love some."

To further demarcate the two spaces (and provide seating on the very rare occasions that they entertained), Sophie had arranged a group of vintage chairs around a small art deco table in front of the barn door. The effect was haphazardly beautiful, like Sophie herself. Esme set her purse down on one of the chairs before walking back to look at Sophie's current project.

"What are you working on?" Esme asked.

"I'm not completely certain." Sophie laughed as she clicked the off button on her glue gun. "I had an idea last night about the carnival in Venice, but it's turning into something closer to the Day of the Dead."

Esme leaned down to look closely at a grouping of women clothed in black. Their faces were painted like skulls, and they all carried beautiful red roses.

"It's beautiful. A bit macabre, but I suppose that's appropriate, given recent events."

"Merci." Sophie seemed nervous as she carefully placed the small figures to the side. "Let's sit down, Esme. We need to talk."

Esme followed her instruction and returned to the center of the room, settling into the comfortable curves of an Eames chair as Sophie poured her a cup of tea.

"This smells delicious."

"I dried it last month."

Esme took a sip of the spearmint tea, savoring its round, sweet flavor before turning to her friend. Sophie started to say something at the same moment that Esme began to speak. She waved for Esme to continue.

"I just came from a meeting with Jack," Esme began.

"I think I know why you are here." Sophie leaned toward her, her hand shaking a little as she placed her small cup on the table between them. "The prosecutor called me this morning. She told me that I shouldn't even be talking to you."

"Yes, Jack warned me as well."

"But who are they to tell us what we can say?" Sophie pinched the bridge of her nose before looking directly into Esme's eyes. "Oh, Esme, I'm so sorry. I cannot lie for you."

"Lie for me?" Esme felt her eyebrows draw together in confusion. Her mind began racing with possibilities. How could Sophie know about Jack's strategy already? She took a sip of tea to calm herself.

"I will be sworn in, non? I have to tell them. About you and Torn."

Esme released her breath.

"Oh, Sophie. Of course you have to tell the truth about Torn and me. I would never ask you to lie. About the affair or anything else that comes up during the trial."

Sophie's warm brown eyes grew even bigger as tears magnified their appearance. Esme had not been able to keep the affair from her best friend. Sophie had been the only person she confided in about Torn. She knew Sophie would understand, at least in part, her astonishment at being seduced by someone so unexpected and so alluring. She also knew that Sophie had felt that what they were doing was wrong and that she hated being caught up in their dishonesty, so Esme hadn't told her any details after their first encounter at Dix-Neuf. Knowledge of her affair had been a heavy burden for her closest friend to carry, however, and she guessed Sophie was relieved that it had finally come out in the open. Sophie's tears welled over and spilled onto her slightly flushed cheeks. She jumped from her chair and wrapped Esme in an embrace.

"Esme. Thank God. I was so worried you were going to ask me to deny it. You know I am a terrible liar. Tell me, how did the police find out about you and Torn? Why do we even have to talk about it?"

Esme pressed her lips together and shrugged. "There was an envelope of photos under the seat of our SUV. Benedict swears he didn't know they were there."

"Photos?"

"Of Torn and I."

"Oh my God." Sophie wiped away a tear. A small streak of eyeliner blackened a spot below her eyelashes. On anyone else, the effect would have been sloppy. On Sophie, it appeared avant-garde, as if smearing makeup in strange places were the next big trend. Her expression became suddenly defiant, as though her words were at odds with her thoughts.

"I'm going to find out who put them there, Esme. It had to have been one of our neighbors. Who else could have done it?"

Esme shook her head. "Sophie, no. I don't want you to get mixed up in this any more than you have to."

"It's the least I can do for you and Benedict," she said, her mouth set in a firm line.

Esme took another sip, miscalculating the angle of her cup and filling her throat with more hot liquid than she intended. The scalding of the back of her mouth made the burn on the tip of her tongue from earlier throb in sympathy.

"Diminishing the importance of the photos was mostly what the meeting was about today. Jack, Benedict, and I just agreed on strategy to try to . . . I guess, nullify the effects of the affair. Jack thinks we have to acknowledge the affair with my testimony. He says it's the only way to assure the jury that Benedict didn't have a motive."

Suddenly, Esme felt very tired, but Sophie leaned forward encouragingly, keen to hear more.

"How so?"

"I don't want to drag you into that part of it. Forget this conversation after I leave, if you can. I just needed someone to talk to." Esme felt conflicted about once again burdening Sophie with the truth.

"Esme, please. I want to help."

She should have predicted that Sophie wouldn't want to remain in the dark. She sighed, then admitted what they had discussed. "Jack thinks we should tell the court that our marriage was open, that we often slept with other people."

"But that's not true!" Sophie gasped.

"I know. You might be asked about it too."

"Okay."

Sophie stretched out her hand to hold on to Esme. Esme could feel her friend's tension in the touch.

"This is so difficult," Sophie said after a moment of silence.

"It's awful."

"How is Zoe doing?"

"She's terrified," she said.

"Poor thing. I can't even imagine how hard this must be for her. It's making everyone fall apart, even the adults. Kitty came over to talk earlier. She is on edge, just like me. She left right before you got here."

Esme finally placed the top note of the scent she had noticed when she first arrived. Kitty's perfume.

"What did she say?"

Sophie bit her lip. "She told me the prosecutor had been asking a lot of questions about her and Benedict, and it was hard to be honest."

Esme laced her hands together, practicing a meditation technique she had learned, where the instructor had asked them to place their less-dominant hand on top to calm themselves with an unfamiliar touch.

"I'm not surprised about that, given the way she acts toward him. But the prosecutor isn't going to care about their flirtation. I can't call her. Jack would kill me. But if she asks again, just tell her to keep it simple and stick to the story. She knows what to do."

"I will."

"Thank you for everything, Sophie."

"You are welcome. And don't worry. I'll find out who planted those photos."

Esme kissed her friend on the cheeks, murmuring thanks. As she crossed the room to the door, she cast another look back at Sophie's new pieces. The tiny skulls winked at her as the sunlight flashed through the window.

CHAPTER EIGHTEEN

On the first official day of Benedict's trial, Esme pulled her wide-brimmed hat low over her eyes so she wouldn't be recognized as they climbed the steps to the courthouse. It was a feeble attempt, and the calls of "Esme, Esme" made a small muscle in her eyelid pulse unpleasantly. Esme felt chilled by the incessant voices and shivered under Benedict's arm, which lay heavily across her shoulders in a coached sign of solidarity. In the months between Benedict's arraignment to today, Torn's death and Benedict's trial had generated so much coverage that the entrance steps were clogged with not just bloggers and media but also the general public, rabid fans, and curiosity seekers. Some were there to grieve the loss of their favorite author, others to condemn Benedict. Both camps cursed her existence.

Esme's last turn in the spotlight as an up-and-coming actress had been nothing like this. It was one thing to be followed due to admiration. It was another to be known and despised. The second time she worked up the courage to log in to her social media profile since Benedict's arrest, she had been sent a message alert about a forum created to house the comments of hatred that her social media restrictions wouldn't allow on her own page. Despite herself, she opened the group and found herself awash in evil words. She couldn't close the window fast enough to avoid seeing messages like Die Esme Lee and Whore. For a full day, she couldn't bear to pick up her phone, imagining it teeming with millions of tiny, relentless monstrosities that would infest her skin if she touched it again.

She now entered Dix-Neuf through the back door to ensure no one knew she was there. They had never been so busy, and she knew Anthony appreciated her help. Two weeks ago, the attacks on their house had begun, and only the presence of a marked police car on Raven Lane had managed to deter the spray painters and egg throwers who had sought to vandalize their house late at night. Even with the police outside, every noise in the night jerked Esme from restless sleep to fearful insomnia. The rampant media coverage had led to the judge and the prosecutor consenting to Jack's request for a closed courtroom, meaning only Torn's family and close friends could watch the proceedings.

As she stared through the windows at the back of the building, which looked into an empty courtyard that was inaccessible to the public, she saw a skeletal tree shaking in the cold November wind. She felt an unfair longing for her daughter. *Zoe wants to be here*, she reminded herself, *but it's too much for a seventeen-year-old to be her mother's sole companion at her father's murder trial*. Her daughter had been heartbroken to be sent to school rather than accompany her parents to the courthouse for the first day of the trial. Esme's worst fear was the scars this ordeal could carve on Zoe. She knew it couldn't be easy on her daughter to have to walk into rooms that quieted as soon as she entered or see the furtive looks trying to discern telling details from her when others thought she wasn't watching. Esme hated it herself, and she was a fully grown adult. Luckily, Julia and Zoe seemed to have rekindled their friendship through the hardship. Zoe had let it slip to Benedict that Julia was patrolling Zoe's social media and shutting down people who tried to post anything about the trial.

Alone on her side of the bench, with Miriam and Levi pointedly looking away, she felt like she was attending a wedding for a well-liked bride and a despised groom. She wasn't supposed to be by herself as the lawyers presented their opening statements, but yesterday Sophie had been called away on a last-minute work assignment. A tension headache began to build inside Esme's skull. She knew Benedict must be feeling the same way as he faced scrutiny all alone in the courtroom. Raven Lane seemed to have turned against them. No one besides Sophie and Ray had knocked on their door or visited them since the arraignment. Esme had heard from them that Aaron had asked for a long assignment overseas and planned to be away until shortly before the trial. Esme knew that, technically, Kitty, Levi, and Miriam were respecting the rules of the court by refraining from speaking with her before the trial, but the silence felt strained.

Her house was just as quiet. Zoe spent nearly every available moment in her room, and Benedict had been out often, alternating between running and drinking. As the winter rain began to fall and the days shortened, Esme had found herself living in a full home that felt emptier than one that had been abandoned. As a result, she had doubled her usual hours at Dix-Neuf, helping Anthony with the crowds. He was the only person who treated her exactly the same as before, as if he realized that sometimes compassion took the shape of familiarity.

The entrance doors in front of the courthouse opened, and the hum of the crowd rose like a kicked wasps' nest. She dared a quick look and saw Aaron walking in with an older couple. Esme recognized them as Torn's parents from the wedding photos she had seen on their walls. She wondered if Aaron stared at those pictures now, remembering the way Torn's eyes had sparkled when he was proud of something he had done but knew it would be boastful to admit it. His parents looked kind, though grief slumped their shoulders. His mother had a wild head of curly gray hair, and his father's head was a close-cropped mix of salt and pepper. Torn's mother had Aaron's hand sandwiched between both of hers. Esme wished suddenly that she could have met them before this moment so that they would know she was more than a woman who slept with married men. More than the wife of their son's accused killer.

It was a stupid thought. After all, they probably thought she was the cause of his death, like so many others. Esme saw Torn's mother swipe at her face and felt a catch in her own throat, but she swallowed hard before it could dissolve into tears. She didn't deserve to mourn. Not here. She kept her face as neutral as possible. The last thing that Aaron or Torn's parents needed to see was her crying over the death of her lover at the hands of her husband. Fortunately, the three of them entered the courtroom without a glance in her direction.

Esme wished she had a coffee, though she had already consumed too many cups that morning. She reached into her purse and pulled out the copy of *The Call* she had found in Zoe's room. It broke her heart to know that her daughter had borrowed it without permission for the second time, as if wanting to read Torn's words both before and after his death were something shameful. She had taken the book back into her own possession without a word, realizing that she too felt guilty that Torn's book still existed in the world even though he did not. She wondered if Zoe had noticed it was gone.

As she opened the pages, Esme could hear the sharp rap of the judge's gavel through the closed doors. Benedict's murder trial had begun. She narrowed her vision to the typed words on the page before her.

I wasn't part of the teams of learned scholars trying to delve into the damaged human psyches. Psychology wasn't my field. After my professor's death, I immersed myself in my thesis so deeply that I barely registered the current news stories and personal accounts of what had befallen so many people. I was a student of iconography. I didn't dream at night, unlike many others around me, who had begun to be prescribed heavy sleeping pills to obliterate their minds enough to rest.

Despite my professor's death, the world of monsters felt far away from me. I was surprised when I got the letter from the law firm executing his will. He had left me a statue, quite an unusual piece, according to its description in the letter. I was to go and collect it at my earliest convenience at their office downtown. My former teacher had been extremely explicit that the item was not to be sent by courier or post. It had to be placed in my hands by the head of the firm. I was to come alone and tell no one of the statue's existence.

Though he died tragically by his own hand, my professor had been a practical joker, and I attributed the strange bequest to an elaborate ruse, half expecting a small statue with a comically enormous phallus to be my gift. I agreed and arranged to come in to the office in a week's time. I went about my studies and research as usual, without thinking much about the meeting to come. The day of my appointment, I entered the law firm office and was confused by the presence of police in the lobby. When I gave the receptionist my name, she looked at me with wide eyes and wordlessly passed me a shoebox from an expensive men's shoe store over her marble desk. I asked to speak with the lawyer who had called, but before I could finish my request, tears ran down her cheeks.

"You can't speak to him," she choked out, barely containing her fear.

"Why not?" I felt horror coming off her in waves at my question.

"He left this box for you. He told me to make sure that no one but you touched what was inside. Then he went up to his office and shot himself."

I swallowed hard. "Did he say anything else to you?"

"He told me that the monsters aren't coming. He told me that they are already here." She burst into tears again and I stepped back, cradling the box in my hands as I tried to make sense of her words and what I had been given.

Esme jerked at the creak of the courtroom door opening. She shut the book and shoved it into her purse. She didn't want to be caught reading Torn's work in public, especially not here. Aaron was the first to leave, and she steeled herself for his disgust as their eyes met. Instead, she saw heavyhearted sorrow. She realized he was searching her to determine if what Jack had stated about their open marriage was true, if she, Torn, and Benedict had all been a part of breaking his heart. She looked away, terrified he would be able to detect that it was a lie. They were all relying on Aaron being away enough to doubt his own knowledge about the relationship between Benedict, Esme, and Torn. She had not anticipated how much it would hurt him to have to second-guess the bond they had all shared. There were already too many betrayals to keep track of, and the trial had only just begun.

Benedict and Jack came out next and she stood to join them, slipping her hand into her husband's as they walked out the door to face the crowd. His hand felt like it belonged to a stranger.

CHAPTER NINETEEN

Esme never dreamed she was a person who would cheat on her husband. In the week after her first encounter with Torn in the washroom of Dix-Neuf, she had been racked with guilt. Her remorse prompted her to work long shifts at the restaurant, ignoring chores at home so Benedict wouldn't see the shame she suspected was written all over her face. Neither Benedict nor Zoe picked up the slack of the household duties, so a week after Kitty's party, despite the sixty hours she had worked, she was still the one forced to deal with all of their overflowing laundry hampers. As she sorted through the lights and darks, she smelled perfume. It was faint but unmistakable. Neither she nor Zoe wore any, which would have made her grandmother roll in her grave, but fragrances made Zoe sneeze. When Esme held Benedict's boxer shorts to her nose, she found the source. Someone had been close enough to Benedict's underwear to leave a scent. She was not the only one who had been unfaithful.

Esme's stomach turned. Her guilt about cheating dissolved in an acid wash of anger as she realized why Benedict had been so cagey about the end of his evening. He didn't stay at the pub. He must have circled back to Raven Lane. To Kitty's party. His obfuscation about that night hadn't been a result of his blurry drunkenness. He had been hiding his adultery the same way she had. She was furious at her husband and at herself for allowing what she thought was a harmless flirtation between him and Kitty to continue for years. She never would have guessed that it had blossomed into something real that night, but she should have. Kitty had plied him with cocaine. She had flirted with him all night. She had even designed a party game to tempt him into her bed, right under Esme's nose. For the entirety of their marriage, it had been Benedict's drug use that frightened her the most, the thought of him slipping back into his old ways. His flirtation with other women had always seemed so over the top, too ostentatious to be real. It was both infuriating and liberating to realize that she had been wrong to trust her husband, just as he had been wrong to trust her.

Through her anger, Esme realized that Benedict's betrayal had cleared a path for her. She didn't have to feel guilty. His affair had set her free to explore what could happen with Torn, so long as she could control her temper and keep it a secret that she knew of his infidelity. If Benedict was hiding something from her, he would be too distracted to realize she was also hiding something from him.

Two days after her discovery, Esme walked toward the large house at the top of Raven Lane. She had heard a car coming to collect Aaron late the night before; the sound of the engine at midnight had roused her out of bed from a sleepless state beside Benedict. She stood at the bedroom window, hidden in the darkness behind the glass. Her heart had started beating faster as the airport taxi pulled away from his house with Aaron in the back. He left late at night only when he was taking the red-eye flight to Syria. It was then that she had decided to surprise Torn the following day.

In the bright March sunshine, she felt less confident as she closed the distance between her house and his. *It isn't strange to come to his house when Benedict is at work and Zo is at school*, she told herself, aware that Kitty could pop out of her house if she saw Esme walking up the street. Everyone knew that Torn relied on takeout and orders from Dix-Neuf when Aaron was out of town, so she was bringing him a basket of beignets and a six-pack of beer. *It isn't suspicious to stop in on a friend.*

She stepped onto the cedar deck. The front window was open, and Esme could hear the music playing on the stereo. Torn was an unashamed fan of the early Rolling Stones. Once, she had teased him for listening to "old man music" and Torn had grinned, saying he hoped he could grow up to be as much of a badass as Mick Jagger one day.

As Esme knocked, a surge of nerves prickled her hands. There was a long pause, and she began to doubt that Torn was home. Maybe he'd left his stereo playing while he went for a walk. She looked for a place to lay down the basket in front of his door, telling herself that it was probably better that he wasn't there. Crisis averted; the whole thing could end before it even got started. Then the door swung open. Torn looked quizzical as he peered out, blinking hard as if he hadn't seen sunlight all day. Judging by his faded T-shirt and sweatpants, he probably hadn't. Esme knew that his agent was pushing him to get his fourth book finished as soon as possible. He was writing. She shouldn't have interrupted. But when their eyes met, his face changed into a smile with another expression lingering underneath it. An expression that made Esme's toes curl in her black flats.

"Hello, Ms. Lee."

"Hi." She tried to feel flattered that Torn seemed unable to see her as she was now, not as she once had been. He cast his eyes up and down her body, then stepped backward, and she followed him.

"I brought you some food." She lifted up the basket, and he smiled. The melancholy melody of "Ruby Tuesday" flowed around them.

"Know this one?" He pointed up as if the song were in the air, then leaned forward and finished singing the stanza in her ear, whispering the lyrics as he unbuttoned her blouse and kissed her collarbone, her breasts, and her stomach. His voice was off-key and broke on the last word, but she loved it anyway.

As the chorus soared, he pushed her against the wall, gently pressing on her hip bones with the flat of his palms. In one motion, he knelt down and pulled up her skirt. Her breath caught in her throat. This was the moment when she always stopped Benedict. She started to speak as Torn slid off her underwear, but then the song filled her ears as he filled her body. It wasn't the way it had been with Jed, an assault of her dignity, or with Benedict, a routine so familiar that she could almost choreograph it. Torn was gently hungry for her. She closed her eyes to a deep shade of black as his warm mouth flooded her. She moaned. She cried his name and he kept going. Everything between them seemed connected. In less than a minute, her body clenched as if trying to pull him inside her. She gripped his hair and shuddered against the wall. His hands were around her shaking thighs as she said his name weakly, like a prayer.

She looked down at him kneeling before her. He took her offered hand as he stood up and kissed her. Her legs felt weak.

"Thank you." She couldn't manage more than a whisper.

"I think I should thank you."

Every man she had ever been with would expect something in return for that, but he just smiled at her. His eyes weren't expectant. He looked content.

"Want to come in?"

They both laughed sheepishly, and she followed him back to the dining room, which he had turned into his office. Professor was lying on a big cushion, and he raised his head sleepily as she patted him. Torn's desk took up nearly the entirety of one wall. Above it hung several framed copies of different covers of *The Call*: the German, Spanish, and French translations; a shiny embossed version announcing the sale of one hundred thousand books; and a piece of art signed by a well-known artist who had been captivated enough by the story to produce a line drawing after reading it. The desk itself was covered in disastrous piles of leaning papers, half-full cups of coffee, and a plate with a curling crust.

The other corner of the room contained two black leather chairs, positioned to look out into the naturally landscaped backyard. Aaron had worked hard on their garden since his lessons with Esme, but she felt a flash of irrational guilt as she saw that the weeds were beginning to take over the beds. She should come over when he returned and help him clean them up. Esme shook her head to clear her mind of what she and Torn were really doing to their husbands. She placed the basket of pastries on an ottoman before offering Torn a beer, which he accepted with a laugh.

"You are the best visitor I've ever had. Please come anytime."

Esme blushed at his words, and Torn heard the double meaning at the same time. He laughed softly.

"That's not what I meant . . . but that too, I guess."

"I suppose I would be a fool to say no to either invitation." She smiled.

"You would definitely be a fool to say no to me," he said.

He raised his bottle, and she clinked hers against it, drawn to his bravado. She had been raised in a world of women; her father had died when she was still a baby, and her mother hadn't dated anyone since, to Esme's knowledge. Who knew what happened when she was away, which was the majority of the time? Her grandmother had also been widowed young. Torn's world was almost purely masculine, and he moved in it with the strength and certainty of a shark. Benedict's confidence, which had attracted her to him, seemed to pale in comparison to Torn's unwavering belief that he belonged, that he was owed everything he could possibly desire. She pushed the thought of her husband from her mind nearly as quickly as it had arrived.

"Maybe. Most men don't do it like that."

Torn raised an eyebrow.

"Sometimes, it can be unpleasant, like it's just another way for a man to control you." Esme felt her anger rising. At Jed. At Benedict. At all the men who had considered her something that could be easily manipulated, then discarded when she was no longer useful.

"That sounds awful."

The record ended, and the silence in the room seemed louder than the music had been.

"It is. It was." Esme's voice caught on the last word.

"Is that what it felt like today?"

"No. Today was different."

Torn looked relieved. "I don't want to hurt you."

"I can tell."

He paused before he spoke again. "What happened with the person who did hurt you, Esme? Did you report it?"

"It wasn't like that, Torn. I couldn't go public. At least I didn't feel like it at the time. Now I wonder how many other people he's done it to. I think I handled it all wrong. I wish I could have been stronger. I wish I hadn't let myself be bought."

"What do you mean?"

"I went to a lawyer. I had evidence, but I was afraid of being humiliated, so I took a settlement and signed a nondisclosure agreement. I quit acting. I sold myself out. I never told anyone else about it, not even Benedict."

"That's why you only made one movie?"

Esme was surprised to feel tears spring to her eyes. "Yes."

"Just because you took his money doesn't mean you sold out."

"I think that's the definition of the term," Esme said sadly.

"Who was he?"

Esme paused. Even now she felt frightened to say his name. "He was a producer."

"Jesus."

"Yeah."

"So he exchanged sex with actresses for better roles?"

"Something like that," Esme said. Torn nodded as if he understood that she didn't want to call it what it was. Rape. Sexual assault. The words were too ugly to say out loud.

"When did it happen?"

Esme responded to his question unthinkingly. His words seemed to come from far away as she remembered the faint scent of cigarettes in the rough upholstery. "About nine months before Zoe was born."

In the silence, he reached over for her hand, and his grip was tight. "That must have been so hard," he said softly.

"At first, it was unbearable. Then I learned how to not think about it, I mean her, like that. Nothing else matters because she became mine."

It had taken her over two years of Zoe's life to fully shed the dread of her child that had clung to her like the extra pounds around her midsection, but she had done it. The cold sunlight from the window lit Torn's eyes. She could almost see herself reflected in them. She cleared her throat and pulled her hand away, suddenly shocked at how much she had told the man in front of her. Esme looked around the room and saw an adoption brochure lying haphazardly on the side of Torn's desk.

"What's this? Are you considering adoption?" She was veering dangerously close to speaking about Aaron, but she felt desperate for a change in the subject.

Torn sighed. "I am. I think of it all the time. But, for Aaron, it's different." Esme watched him carefully as he said his husband's name, but she couldn't detect any change in his voice or face. She was surprised Aaron was the one resisting children. Of the two, he seemed far more equipped to handle a dependent.

"Different how?"

"He sees kids that are hurt or worse, all the time. He says that he can't bear the thought of seeing his own child like that. He thinks it would destroy him."

Esme thought of the black-and-white photo of the lost girl in their front room. "I understand that. I mean, part of it. Zoe fell down the stairs when she was two years old. Her forehead was gushing blood. It was awful. She needed six stitches and she screamed the whole time, and all I could think was that she came so close to not existing and it was all my fault." She felt cold at the memory of the doctors turning her baby's neck to check for spinal injuries. From that moment forward, Esme had never considered Zoe to be anything but hers, as if her doubts had been obliterated by her daughter's pain. "I know that's nothing compared to what Aaron has seen. I can only imagine watching a child die in front of you and being powerless to stop it. It's not a love that anyone can take lightly."

"I don't take it lightly." Esme was surprised at the irritation in Torn's voice, as if her general statement had been accusing him of something.

"I didn't mean that."

"Aaron always tells me that I'm too hedonistic to have a child. And now you. Why does everyone think of me as such a frivolous person?"

Something in Torn's frowning face reminded her of Benedict, and she took a drink before answering, hoping to tamp down her annoyance at his ability to pivot the conversation to his own ego. It was good that Torn didn't seem to have realized the enormity of what she had said. It meant her secret was still safe. Torn looked at her impatiently.

"I didn't mean—"

"I'm going to change the record." Torn walked out of the room.

She drank the last of her beer and debated whether to follow him. She hadn't come here for an argument. He was setting the needle when she walked into the room. He spoke before she could tell him she was leaving.

"I want children and not because I think they would be fun. I believe in adoption. I was adopted into a good home. I was just a baby; I never knew what it meant to be abandoned like the children Aaron has seen. I have a mother and father that I love with everything I have. I want to give a child that. Just like my parents, we have the means to make a kid's life amazing." Torn flashed a proud smile. His mood had changed as rapidly as a sun escaping from behind a cloud.

"I understand that," Esme said.

"Esme, I see what kind of mother you are. I want to be that kind of father. I know Aaron could be too, if he could find a way to not be so bitter all the time."

Esme was surprised at the harshness to Torn's voice. Disagreeing on children was poison to a partnership. Five years ago, Esme had watched Sophie and Ray come close to disintegration over the same conversation. For Sophie, being a mother was never an option. She loved her life and her freedom. Besides, she had laughed, no child would survive in her studio. Ray had taken a long time to come to terms with the fact that being with Sophie meant not being a father. It had been hard. But he stayed. Esme wondered if Torn would too, if Aaron never changed his mind. A treacherous part of her wished Aaron wouldn't. Maybe neither she nor Torn were meant to be with the ones they had married.

Otis Redding's voice brought the room to life again and Torn turned, his hand out.

"A dance, a drink, and a walking tour of the house? I'd love to show you the bedroom." He winked. She looked at her watch, then slipped her hand in his. She still had an hour before Zoe would be back from school. She was lucky to be so close by. It made what she and Torn were doing feel like home.

CHAPTER TWENTY

The second day of Benedict's trial was rainy. Esme's back felt damp and cold where her jacket seams had leaked during her run to Sophie's car. They pulled into the underground garage. The abrupt end to the patter of rain on the windshield and roof of the car surrounded her and Sophie in silence. Jack had asked Benedict to come to the courthouse early to go over the details of the cross-examination he had prepared for Levi and Miriam Stein. Luckily, Jack had secured passes for two cars to the private parking garage so they didn't have to weave through the thickening crowd at the front of the building.

Sophie parked in a spot close to Benedict's car, and the two of them walked across the chilled concrete floor to the drafty stairwell. Once they reached the main floor, they crossed the polished marble floor to the bench outside the room assigned to Benedict, and she spotted Miriam and Levi exiting the elevator about twenty feet away from them. She arranged a small smile on her face on the off chance that either Levi or Miriam would look at her in greeting. Neither did. They walked to the opposite end of the bench, as far away from her and Sophie as possible, without making eye contact. Esme felt her cheeks burn as her smile faded.

"This is ridiculous," Sophie whispered loudly. "We have known them for five years."

"They've treated me like that for months," Esme said, meeting her friend's red-rimmed eyes with a grimace. She knew Sophie must have been exhausted. Her flight had arrived at midnight the night before. Esme had never been so grateful to her. Sophie winced, then patted Esme's forearm as she tried for a note of levity.

"He is acting like he just got invited to another of Kitty's parties," she joked, and Esme tried to smile at the memory of Kitty's aggressive affection.

As if on cue, the courtroom doors opened and the bailiff summoned Levi inside. Esme watched out of the corner of her eye as the thin man stood up. Levi fidgeted with his tie as he walked. Esme was glad to see that he looked nervous. She wondered if the jury would feel sorry for him or find his nerves distracting.

"I hope he doesn't vomit on the stand," Sophie said.

"I kind of hope he does," Esme said.

Sophie shifted closer to Esme, as if she needed to be reassured by her friend's warmth. Esme wondered if she was feeling nervous about giving her own testimony tomorrow. She too felt in need of comfort. Her headache hadn't left her, and her mouth was dry with lack of sleep. Esme had heard Benedict turn on a soccer game at 4:00 a.m., and she'd listened to the faint cheers for hours, until the sun came up halfheartedly behind the clouds and forced her to drag her body out of bed.

Officer Singh walked past them to the doors of the court with quick, sure strides. She was dressed in a fitted black suit and white shirt. Her lipstick was deep red, and her gold earrings flashed as she moved. She looked beautiful, wise, and authoritative. Esme's head pulsed.

A sharply suited young man followed her in. He had a mounted poster lodged under his arm, image side out. Sophie gasped. It was a blown-up photograph of Esme, blindfolded with a man's tie around her eyes. Torn's head was in view lower in the frame, turned slightly toward the camera, inches away from Esme's lower stomach. They were both smiling.

Sophie swore under her breath. "Merde. Esme, this is outrageous."

Esme shook her head and looked in Miriam's direction. The woman had placed earbuds in and was reading sheet music. Esme could hear the faint, low whine of an oboe, Miriam's instrument, bleeding out. Her lips felt numb as she lowered her voice to whisper to Sophie something that had come to her during her sleepless hours. "Do you remember when I lost my phone last spring?"

Sophie looked at her blankly, before memory dawned in her eyes. "During the art walk?" Each May, Kitty coerced the residents of Raven Lane to join the citywide celebration of art by setting up tables on their street to showcase their talent. She had grudgingly allowed Esme to include a table with intricately made desserts. Though Esme had been the busiest of all their neighbors, she knew Kitty considered her baked goods lowbrow compared to Torn's signed novels and Miriam and Levi's autographed performance posters.

"Yes. My phone dropped out of my pocket at some point. When I realized it was missing, I walked around the whole neighborhood looking for it, but it was nowhere to be found."

Sophie looked at her curiously. "You think someone stole it?"

"That's the thing. Those photos . . . Torn and I took them with my phone."

"Oh my God," Sophie gasped. Her face turned dark. "Why, Esme? Why would you do that?"

"It was supposed to be . . . sexy," Esme said uncomfortably. Her friend took a deep breath.

"Oh, mon dieu. Okay, so, what do you think happened? Why would someone do that to Benedict?"

"Leaking those photos was what elevated the charge. What if someone had a grudge against him? Or thought they could gain something by framing him?" She turned her head toward Miriam, who still had her earphones on, though the movement made her headache deepen. "Neither Miriam nor Levi has said a word to me since Benedict was charged, and they are testifying for the prosecution. Benedict told me that Levi saw Torn and I together that night. Has he ever said anything to you? About us?"

Sophie turned to her and spoke softly. "No. Levi doesn't talk much to Ray or me. But Miriam told me once that Raven Lane needed to change."

"Why?"

"She said that we had all lost our faith."

"Assuming we had any to begin with. When did that conversation happen?"

"I can't remember exactly. It was after the art walk, definitely," Sophie said.

"She seemed so quiet. It's still so hard to imagine either of them trying to frame Benedict," said Esme, looking over to see if her friend agreed.

"Maybe it wasn't about framing. Maybe it was more of a moral crusade, a chance to get rid of the less-desirable people on the street."

"Then wouldn't she have started with Kitty?" Esme's joke fell flat as Sophie twisted her mouth before she answered.

"Kitty didn't take photos like that. And Levi didn't see Kitty kissing Torn."

Esme nodded dully. Even Sophie thought she was awful.

Sophie sat back against the wall, leaning her head onto it for support. A thin blue vein threaded its way down her throat. "I heard from Kitty that they asked her to let them know about any house that came up for sale in the neighborhood. Miriam wants her mother to move onto the street. What if they thought this kind of scandal would force you to move?"

"You think they would do this to get our house? That's crazy."

"Apparently, they put an offer on Torn and Aaron's house, quite a bit above asking, but the Graces' offer came in at the same time and it was even higher. Miriam was really upset when Kitty told her that the house was no longer available. I got the impression that she thought it was a done deal."

Esme was stunned at the unknown undercurrents of their street. She hadn't really believed that Miriam was plotting against them. Now it seemed more plausible.

"They were both at the art walk."

"Either of them could have found your phone."

"This is crazy, Sophie," Esme replied. They both looked down the bench at Miriam, whose eyes were still closed.

"So is the idea that Benedict killed Torn on purpose, but look where we are," Sophie said, waving a hand at their surroundings before laying it flat on Esme's leg. "I'm going to keep a close eye on both of them from now on, okay?" she said.

"I'll do the same."

"Esme, I'm here for you, remember?"

Esme let herself be pulled into her friend's warm arms. She felt Sophie's collarbone jutting into her chest. When the embrace ended, she told herself to bring her a box of pain au chocolat. The pastries were so delicious even Sophie couldn't forget to eat them.

"Thank you, Sophie."

"Always." Sophie wiped a tear from her eye before looking down at her leather laptop bag. "Is it horrible if I work a little? I need to finish this photo correction today."

"Of course," Esme said. "Go ahead. I brought a book." She pulled the novel from her bag, careful to keep its cover out of Sophie's sight, breathed deeply, then turned to the last page she had marked.

I couldn't wait until I got home to open it. Instead, I ripped the box apart with shaking hands as soon as I had closed the door of my car in the dank underground parking garage. A smudged, scrawled note on sloppily folded paper lay on top of a large lumpy rock. As I opened the thick paper, I saw fingerprints, so purple they were almost black, around the edges of the handwriting, as if someone had been frantically pinning down the paper as they dragged the pen over the page as quickly as possible.

I know what I am now. I cannot bear it.

Just ten words, inscribed in a hand unused to forming letters with anything but a keyboard. I held the paper up to the dim interior light to try to discern meaning from the bruise-colored fingerprints and the vague sentence. My hands grew cold with trepidation as I reached into the box to try to figure out if its contents would help decipher the meaning of the note. At first glance, I thought the lawyer had gone mad in the first round of the affected and shoved a piece of tarry asphalt into a box while under some delusion that he was executing part of my professor's will. As my fingers brushed against its rough surface, however, I realized that it was covered in precise marks too fine to be captured by the small light on my car's interior roof. I opened the door and walked to the bare bulb above the exit door.

In the orange glare, I saw the face of a monstrosity carved into the crude material, though I had been wrong about the stone's true nature. It was something like volcanic rock, though its surface felt oily and cool under my hands. The monstrous face combined the worst of squid, sea lamprey, and prehistoric shark and added hideous details unimagined until the moment of carving. In disgust, I dropped the stone. The thunk of it hitting the pavement echoed through the concrete tunnel, and I cursed myself as I reached to pick it up, certain I had broken the statue before I could properly assess it. I was shocked to see it sitting in a significant divot in the poured-concrete floor. Upon examination, I saw that the statue itself was undamaged. I was grateful it had landed facedown so I wouldn't have to see its beastly face as I picked it up. Its back was also marked by carvings but not so fine as those that defined the abnormality's face. The six lines were disorganized and deep, as if made in haste with a large, dull knife. After I brushed my thumb against the strange lines, the pad was stained purple-black, the same color as the marred surface of the lawyer's note.

Esme was so transfixed by the story of the student that time passed quickly. When Levi rushed out of the doors toward his wife, his face pale and sweating, she felt as if she had just begun to read. In contrast, Levi looked as if he had been granted a pardon from hell.

"The court is now in recess for one hour for lunch," the bailiff said.

Esme stood up at the same time as Sophie, feeling unnerved by the abrupt shift from Torn's monstrous world to her own.

CHAPTER
TWENTY-ONE

Despite the brevity of the lunch break, Esme and Sophie were back on the bench early since neither of them could stomach more than a coffee. As the prosecutor passed them on her way back into the courtroom, Esme noticed that Ms. Wong's raw silk suit was impeccably unwrinkled. Esme wondered absurdly if she ate standing up. Ten minutes later, when the bailiff opened the doors to usher Miriam in, tension rippled along Esme's hairline.

Sophie stared into the space in front of her. "It's hard to imagine Miriam doing all this, but she's wound so tight. If anyone was going to snap on Raven Lane, my dollars would be on her."

"Do you think people really do snap like that?"

Sophie breathed out of her nose. "Definitely."

"Do you think they can snap back again later?" Esme said quietly.

"Who knows?" Sophie said. "I never got a good feeling from Miriam. If she really did something this awful, I think it was in her all along, just waiting to come out."

Esme tried not to let her friend see how much the words affected her. "So one of them found my phone, figured out how to unlock it, uncovered the photos, and waited until it made sense to use them? It's pretty complicated."

"I know it sounds crazy to say." Sophie pursed her lips. "But your password was your house number, Esme. Even I knew it. And neither of us was paying close attention at that art walk. We were too busy worrying about Benedict and Ray."

Esme sighed as she remembered. "As usual."

Despite Kitty's disdain, Esme had decided to sell pastries at the art walk after her experimental dessert selection at Dix-Neuf had sold out in hours the week before. At the time, she had been toying with the idea to incorporate more pastries into her restaurant's menu, perhaps even create a retail space for them to be purchased. Not only would it diversify her income, it would also give her a place to channel the seemingly endless creative energy that Torn inspired in her.

The night before, her excitement about the possibility of a patisserie had grown as she rolled the delicate layers of dough into intricate shapes in her kitchen. The mix of marzipan and icing sugar made her feel just as happy as her sweet, stolen afternoons with Torn. Besides, Anthony had been hinting at wanting more responsibility in the kitchen, and, selfishly, Esme knew that giving him a larger role would free up more of her time for Torn. As she looked up the street at Torn carefully stacking his books on the table, she felt excited for what the day would bring. Aaron was away. Maybe she and Torn could sneak away for an hour after the art walk was done.

She had been wrong to have any hope of a good outcome for the event. The art walk had been a disaster, largely due to Ray's decision to pour a healthy dollop of whiskey into the coffees he prepared for himself and Benedict. By ten thirty, both men were slurring their words, and Ray's eyes were full of fire.

"What's going on with Ray?" Esme had asked Sophie under her breath after they'd gently guided their husbands far from the crowd, asking them to check to make sure the promotional signs on Main Street hadn't been vandalized.

"He met with an agent yesterday who told him that he wasn't talented enough to be published. He actually used the words 'don't quit your day job,'" Sophie said. Her light-pink lipstick contrasted with her frown. As they returned to her table, Esme noticed that several of her friend's small figurines had been knocked over, making the scene look like the site of a tragic accident.

"That's awful," Esme said, straightening a tiny Helen of Troy.

"Oh God. What now?" Sophie said, distracted by Ray and Benedict's quick return. Sophie's husband was stumbling toward Torn's table, where the author was autographing books.

"Maybe he's just going to say hello."

Sophie turned to her with apprehension in her eyes. "It was Torn's agent. He set up the meeting as a favor to Ray."

Esme and Sophie watched Ray clumsily bump a young man in a T-shirt with the cover of Torn's book cover printed on it as he neared the table. Ray seemed not to notice the boy's yelp. Instead, he gripped the edge of the table and faced Torn, breathing heavily. Esme felt a pulse of pain in her forehead at the sight of Benedict approaching from the other side, closing in on the two men.

"We need to stop him," Sophie said, hurrying to Torn's booth with Esme on her heels. When they arrived, Ray was addressing Torn, brandishing a copy of *The Call*.

"I want to get my book signed by a famous author with an amazing agent. Right, Torn? Your agent is the goddamn authority on art."

Esme saw flecks of spit rain from Ray's mouth onto Torn's books on the table. Ray noticed it too, and his sloppiness seemed to anger him, as if it was additional proof that he was lesser than the handsome, successful man standing before him. He looked down at drops of spittle on the table, then angrily swept a pile of books onto the ground. Sophie's eyes were wide with panic as she touched her husband's arm.

"Ray, please, this is not the time," she said.

Esme didn't dare meet Torn's eyes, for fear of conveying too intimate of a message. Instead, she too placed a hand on Ray's forearm, hoping to bring him back to his senses.

"Let's get you some food," she murmured.

Torn's voice was calm as he casually shifted the rest of the books away from Ray. "Ray, I'm sorry it didn't work out. I know there's someone out there that will understand your work. All you need is one person."

"Come on, Ray," Benedict said.

All their words fell on deaf ears. Ray's chest rose and fell rapidly as he stared at Torn. His face reddened as the breath heated him like a steam engine. Ray pulled his elbow back, hand curled into a fist. Benedict realized what was happening before anyone else. When Ray tried to complete the punch, Benedict grabbed his shoulder and spun him around. Ray's heel caught on the leg of the folding table, and piles of books crashed to the ground. Esme stumbled to get out of the way and knocked into the boy seeking the autograph. The two of them landed on the sidewalk.

"Are you okay, Esme?" Torn said as he stepped around his table to help.

"I'm fine," she said, standing up and rubbing her aching hip.

She saw Miriam Stein staring at her from across the street, her pile of posters flapping in the warm breeze. Esme smiled weakly, and after a long beat, Miriam looked away.

"Let's have another drink," Esme heard Benedict saying to Ray, who was still panting as Benedict steered him toward their house. Sophie followed, her shoulders stiff with fury. Esme caught Torn's eyes briefly and mouthed an apology. He smiled, and she smiled back. She felt incongruently happy as she walked back to Zoe, who had been staffing the table full of cookies and croissants.

"Is Dad okay?" Zoe asked.

"I think he and Ray both got a little too much sun," Esme said.

"Yeah, the whiskey probably isn't helping either," Zoe said. Esme laughed in spite of herself.

A familiar man appeared, and Esme smiled and greeted him.

"Everything looks so good. I might just have to buy the whole table," José said.

"You should do that, José!" Zoe laughed before her attention was caught by a group of teenagers walking up the street. "Mom, my friends are here. Is it okay if I go say hi? Just call if you need me."

"Definitely. Thanks for your help, Zoe."

José looked up from the baked goods. "Is Benedict inside? I thought you'd have him working the table today."

Esme shook her head. "Benedict is definitely not in any condition to be out here."

José's face turned serious. "Yes, I've noticed that Benedict has been in a difficult condition quite often lately."

"What do you mean?"

"Esme, let's just say that we both need to be aware of his, um, choices. We've seen Benedict go through this once before. I don't want him in the hospital again. Or worse."

Esme swallowed and thanked José for letting her know. Was it true that Benedict had slipped back into his old ways without her noticing? She knew he had used cocaine at Kitty's party. She had assumed it had been just like the handful of other times when Benedict was tempted, a lapse in judgment that he swiftly overcame. Then again, she had not been paying as much attention to him as she used to.

The crowd swelled around her table, and it was several hours before she realized that, somewhere along the way, she had lost her phone. After a thorough search, she and Sophie had given up, assuming that a sticky-fingered art lover had picked it up during the busiest period of sales. When she saw the phone on her doorstep the next day, Esme had considered it nothing more than an annoyance, albeit slightly creepy. Until now.

~

"Ray was such a mess that day," Sophie said. "If he had been the one who hit Torn, he would probably have been charged too."

Esme looked at her friend in surprise, her response dying on her lips as the courtroom doors opened once again. Miriam walked out with her head high. Shortly afterward, Benedict and Jack appeared. Esme was surprised when Benedict opened his arms, and she stepped into them reflexively.

"What a day," he said into her hair. "It's good to see you."

"Tell me in the car," she replied. She felt strangely exposed being embraced by the echoing hallway, as if every one of their actions was being judged. They walked Sophie to her car, then entered theirs. Once the doors were shut, she turned to him.

"How did Levi do?"

"Man, I hate that guy, but watching him on the stand was almost enough to make me feel sorry for him." Benedict nearly smiled but then seemed to remember himself. "It didn't make it any easier to hear what he had to say."

Esme stiffened.

"He testified about how 'passionate' the two of you were," Benedict said. "That was his word. He sounded like he learned it from Miriam."

Esme let him trail off.

Benedict pressed the heel of his hand against his jawline. "Anyway, Miriam was worse. It was just like the deposition. She described Raven Lane and you and me specifically as 'immoral.' She testified that I used cocaine regularly, which is obviously bullshit, and that I grabbed your arm so hard at Kitty's party it looked 'close enough to break it.'"

"Jack is planning to get Sophie to refute that. It's ridiculous," Esme said. "You were careless but not angry."

Benedict looked at her, and Esme saw something she hadn't seen in his eyes for a long time. Compassion. "Hearing her on the stand . . . it made me realize that I've been treating you like shit for months. I was high that night, Esme. I know I acted like an asshole. If I had been able to keep my self-control, if I hadn't let myself get so carried away at that party, maybe you wouldn't have felt the need to be with Torn. I keep blaming you for what you did because it's hard to be honest with myself."

The lines on Benedict's face looked like a map of all the places they had been.

"Oh, Benedict," she said. She could tell by the light in his eyes that the kindness in her voice surprised them both.

"Only you can tell them who I really am. A selfish idiot, too focused on himself to see that he was about to hurt someone."

"I'll try," she replied.

"I'm sorry I hurt you, Esme."

She didn't know how to respond. After a moment, Benedict started the car and pulled out of the underground lot. As they exited, Esme stared at the rain washing the color away from the group of people still gathered on the courthouse steps.

CHAPTER
TWENTY-TWO

Esme and Benedict arrived home shortly before Zoe rushed in the door, breathless and red-faced from running home from school to meet them.

"How did it go?" she said.

Benedict shrugged slowly, as if his shoulders were nearly too heavy to lift. "It was only the second day, Zo. They got through the testimony of the officer, Miriam, and Levi."

"So Kitty and Sophie are next?"

"Yes."

"What did Jack say about today? Did he think it went well?"

"He seemed to."

"Didn't you ask him?" Zoe's frustration burst out of her like juice from a rotting fruit.

"There wasn't time. We'll meet again tomorrow morning. I'll know more then."

"Let's talk about it over dinner," Esme said, hearing the deep fatigue in her husband's voice. His apology in the car had stirred a tenderness in her toward him that she hadn't felt in a long time.

Zoe looked at her mother as if she had just suggested they all paint their faces blue and go stand out on the street asking for spare change.

"I'm not hungry, Mom." She turned and left the room as quickly as she had raced into it.

"Sorry. I don't have much of an appetite either," Benedict said before following her upstairs. As Esme prepared sandwiches to try to tempt them anyway, she tried to shake her nerves about what Sophie and Kitty would say on the stand the next day. Sophie knew the most about her of anyone on Raven Lane, which could be dangerous in the hands of a skilled lawyer like Selena Wong.

When dinner was ready, Esme walked up the stairs, letting her fingers trail along the wall where they hung family photos. Even before the trial had begun, Esme and Benedict never seemed able to find time to print and frame new photographs. As a result, the shots were so hopelessly out of date that a stranger viewing the wall would think that Zoe was still the ten-year-old grinning with rosy apple cheeks into the camera. Esme's stomach sank at the thought that she might never hang a new shot of her daughter on the wall. Jack's fees were rapidly eating up their savings. She knew she would soon have to apply for a line of credit to cover the bills yet to come. Selling the house might be the next step if the loan was not enough. She knocked on Zoe's door softly, opening it at the same time.

"I made dinner, sweetheart. Time to eat."

Zoe was sitting on her bed cross-legged with piles of books around her, but she was focused on the screen of her phone. Esme's eyes were drawn to her daughter's bookshelf, where she had found Torn's novel. One textbook leaned into another to fill the empty gap where the novel had been. The tension in Zoe's body made it clear that she was reading about her father's case, despite Esme begging her not to do so.

"Have you seen this?" She lifted her phone to face Esme, who gasped at the sight of a photo of Benedict and Torn on social media. Her husband's arm was slung over Torn's shoulders. It was another shot from her phone, taken after the two of them had come home from a fifteen-mile run, the longest they'd ever managed. Someone had superimposed a ghoulish face where Benedict's smile had been. The caption read: *He heard The Call.*

"That's awful, Zoe. Please stop looking at this stuff," Esme admonished.

"Is it better to pretend it's not happening, like you and Dad?"

"Zoe, that's not what—"

"Torn was loved, Mom. You can't just pretend his death didn't matter. It mattered to me." Tears ran down Zoe's cheek, and Esme instinctively reached to hug her. "Don't touch me. I want to be alone."

Esme faltered at her daughter's anger, closed the door, then walked down the hall to the guest room. Her hands were shaking as she tried to blink away the sight of the demon looking through her husband's eyes. She prayed Benedict would never see it, and she felt sick at the thought of Zoe still staring at the pixelated image of hate, but her daughter was too old for Esme to protect her from the things she was seeking. She stopped at the open door of the guest room. Inside she saw Benedict looking out at the garden she had abandoned at the peak of its growth. Tomatoes that had not been harvested lay wrinkled on the ground, pecked by birds until they were little more than wasted skin. Their withered stalks still curled around the wire baskets beside them, as if they didn't realize there was nothing left to protect.

"Are you hungry?" she asked Benedict. Like Zoe, he didn't turn at her voice.

"No."

"Zoe and I are going to eat downstairs, if you are interested."

He turned, met her eyes, and shook his head again. "I'm too exhausted to eat, Esme. I'm just going to go to bed."

"In here?"

Benedict looked morose but resolute. "Yes."

Esme waited downstairs at the table set for three with brie and apple baguettes on each plate, nervously anticipating Zoe. After fifteen minutes, she realized her daughter wasn't coming. She gathered up the plates, took them to the kitchen, and then wrapped up all three untouched sandwiches. She slipped the plates on top of a crooked pile of others in the sink. The dirty dishes filled her with despair, like a problem that could never be solved, so she left them where they were and retreated up the stairs.

As she entered the master bedroom, she was stunned to see that she had forgotten to make her bed that morning. Her grandmother had taught her the simple joy of climbing into a freshly made bed at the end of the day, and it was a habit that had stuck with her since childhood. She never forgot, often coming into the room later if Benedict had slept in to make sure the chore was done. Tonight, the white duvet crumpled across the king-size bed looked soiled and unwashed. Outside the white paned windows, the black, spindly branches of the cherry blossom trees seemed sinister as the wind whipped them to and fro.

Instead of pulling the disheveled covers smooth, she slipped under them with her clothes on, then laid her head on the pillow. It wasn't even 7:00 p.m., but the room was dark and cold. She realized that she had forgotten to adjust the thermostat when the temperature dove that morning, and now she was too tired to walk downstairs again. The events of the day flipped through her mind like a bad movie. Jack's sharp-edged expression. The fear in Sophie's eyes. The new creases etched around Benedict's mouth.

Esme's body grew heavy. As her eyes closed, she thought she heard the sound of a bedroom door opening. Her daughter must have been hungry after all. She hoped that Zoe would see the sandwich she had made for her.

CHAPTER TWENTY-THREE

When Esme woke at 6:00 a.m., she still felt exhausted. The house was quiet, and she decided to check in at Dix-Neuf. She left a plate of Zoe's favorite breakfast pastries on the table, noticing that the sandwiches in the fridge remained untouched. Then she wrote a note for Benedict to tell him she would catch a ride with Sophie to the courthouse.

When she arrived, the restaurant was dark and peaceful. After the trial had begun, most of the press, bloggers, and gawkers had abandoned the site for the courthouse steps. She walked into the kitchen to ensure that the bread delivery had arrived. On the shelf above Anthony's station, she saw a dog-eared copy of *The Call*, its broken spine making it seem vulnerable. Her heart hurt knowing that, just like her, Anthony was seeking comfort for his loss in Torn's words. She left the kitchen, then prepared an espresso for herself behind the bar before sitting down.

Once again, the padded stools made her think of Zoe as a toddler, clambering on top of them to spin and shout with glee. It had taken Esme more than the usual time to love Zoe, but when she was finally able to see her daughter for who she really was, not who her father could be, her adoration had known no bounds. They had so few years of pure joy. Now she feared her transgressions had made Zoe as reserved in her love for her mother as Esme had been when Zoe was an infant.

Sophie arrived at half past eight, pulling up to the curb as Esme locked the restaurant doors.

"Everything okay at Dix-Neuf?" Sophie asked, cradling the warm café au lait that Esme handed to her as she slid into the passenger seat.

"Yes, Anthony is fantastic. Really, I mostly get in his way now."

Sophie smiled, but it couldn't hide the worry on her face. "This is so strange, Esme."

Esme reached over and patted her friend's leg. "Just answer the questions. Nothing you say could ever come between us."

"Thank you," Sophie said with tears in her eyes.

The two women rode in silence the rest of the way. Then Esme walked with her friend as far as the bench. They hugged, and Sophie made a small sound in the back of her throat before turning and walking inside the court. Esme's mouth tasted bitter from too much coffee. *Everything is going to be fine*, she told herself. Sophie had already gone through a deposition. Both she and Esme knew what to expect. Esme settled herself on the now familiar-feeling bench as people began to trickle into the courtroom. Jack nodded at her as he and Benedict walked past side by side. As expected, Aaron and Torn's parents didn't glance in her direction.

She could smell Kitty's perfume even before the woman sat down on the end of the bench. The sweet scent needled Esme in the tender spot right above her eyebrows, and she reached into the pocket of her purse for a migraine tablet and her novel. She looked at Kitty only when she rose in response to the bailiff's invitation. The other woman held her eyes, and Esme felt a ripple of understanding pass between them. In that moment, she seemed to know everything that Esme was thinking. Kitty looked polished and sophisticated in a muted blue Chanel suit. Her hair was gleaming in a simple updo. Everything about her seemed trustworthy, in sharp contrast to what everyone seemed to believe about Esme. She knew that if trolls online were making memes of her husband's face, there were surely hundreds of her as well: the failed actress who had tempted her lover into death. After Kitty crossed the hall to the courtroom, Esme stared at the ornate design on the cover of her book before turning to the only thing that could take her mind from what her life had become: Torn's words.

The call came shortly after that, as I was driving north on the isolated road to the cabin I was temporarily renting from an anthropology professor on sabbatical. I had placed the primitive statue in the trunk before leaving the parking garage. For some reason, I couldn't bear the thought of it in the cab with me as I traveled along the long, dark road. At first, I thought the high-pitched hum was emanating from the black lump in the back of the car. Then the sound increased so much that I felt as if it was coming from all around me, popping my ears even though I didn't realize they had been plugged. I heard once that the northern lights crackled and hummed as they rolled across the sky. I was a southerner, and before moving to the small northern town to pursue my degree, I had never even heard of the ghostly dance. I pulled over, but the dark late-winter sky was choked with thick layers of cloud, like it had been every night since the ides had ended. The sound grew louder and louder until I didn't just hear it anymore, but instead, I felt it throbbing in my chest and sinuses. My hands and feet grew cold, as if the vibrations were so great that they had stopped my blood from flowing.

The next day, I told the other students who wept around me that it had hurt me as it had them. I was lying to them. The truth was, the pain was exquisite. I realized as they looked at me with watering eyes that only some could hear the call for what it was. Hours later, my adviser inquired about the statue that had been left to me. It was only later that I realized I had never mentioned the bequest. Her eyes blazed as she fired question after question at me about its origin and composition. She was different from the others. She wasn't scared about what had happened the night before. She heard it the same way I did. The call wasn't meant for the weak. It was meant for her, me, and others like us. And the statue was part of it. Perhaps the most important part of all.

In the hours that followed, people went on with their work and studies around me, some mewing tears into their open books and others darting fierce looks around the library, like predators learning how to stalk their prey. I felt the call inside me as well and it shone like a terrible, beautiful beacon, but I fixated on my notes, not daring to give in to the urges that were growing.

I couldn't wholly accept my freedom. Not at first. Something human in me still bucked at the idea that what I wanted was now permissible, that morality had been fiction all along. That night, I told myself that I wasn't like them as the knives flashed in the street and the screams shattered the black stillness that we used to believe was our right. I thought I was better than them, that the statue gave me strength beyond the rest of the pack. I was right about the statue but wrong about myself. I wanted it just as badly. As I drove through the darkened streets, the raw violence made me thirsty beyond measure and hungry beyond words. I forced myself home and shot the dead bolt in the heavy wooden door to keep myself in. I twisted the sheets around my body as the forest around me echoed with agony. Even the animals had changed.

I couldn't sleep. I couldn't think straight. I knew what
I had to do, even as every part of me that was still human
fought against it. It was time to kill.

Torn's words were horrifying enough to engulf Esme in an icy fear
that felt welcome after the months of plodding anxiety. The world he
had created was too monstrous to be true, which made it the perfect
escape. The real horror of life was in the mundane, like sitting outside a
closed door where the court decided the fate of a man you loved.

Sophie was standing in front of her before she could hide what she
was reading, but she didn't seem to notice.

"We have an hour. Selena Wong just finished with Kitty."

Esme followed her friend's quick steps out of the courtroom and into
a small café. She ordered their coffees while Sophie went to the washroom.
Once seated, Sophie blew across the wide cup, sending a waft of warm,
milky coffee in Esme's direction. At another time it would have been comforting, but Esme felt too jittery waiting for Sophie to tell her if anything
unexpected had happened on the stand. Sophie's phone pinged with a text,
which she glanced at. Her face was different when she looked up again.

"Was Benedict with you last night?" Sophie said, high spots of color
rising on her cheekbones.

"Yes," Esme responded.

"All night?"

"I . . . I think so. I went to bed early, but he was in his bedroom
when I came up. Why?"

Sophie took a deep breath. "The text was from Kitty. She told me that
Benedict was at her house last night. She said he accused her of planting the
photos."

Esme suddenly remembered the opening and closing of a door that
she had thought was Zoe. "Why would Benedict do that? Why would

Kitty have anything to do with it?" Esme asked, anxious to see if Sophie suspected that Kitty might have a motive to ensure Benedict received the longest sentence possible.

Sophie looked at her with a face etched with confusion. "I don't know. You'll have to ask Benedict."

"I will," she said, hoping her friend couldn't hear the relief in her voice.

CHAPTER
TWENTY-FOUR

One week before Torn's death was the last time that all the residents of Raven Lane gathered to celebrate a happy occasion. The day had been sweltering; though it was the end of the month, the dog days of August were still refusing to step aside for the cooler nights of September. Torn was sweating as he shouldered a heavy wooden lectern into place at the front of the dining room in Dix-Neuf.

"I thought famous authors didn't have to do manual labor anymore," she joked as she walked to the other side to help him.

"That's assuming that famous authors ever did any in the first place," Aaron called from the front door. She and Torn slid the lectern into place; then she turned and smiled at Aaron, who was lugging a huge box of books.

"You're a rugged doctor," Torn said. "Surely you can carry a box or two?"

"I'm starting to think he married me just for my muscles," Aaron said. Esme chuckled, surprised at how easy it was to laugh at Aaron's jokes two hours after she had slept with his husband.

"Put it down over there; that's where Torn is going to sign books." She pointed to a table at the back of the room, and Aaron set the box down beneath it.

"Um, did you see me move that huge lectern by myself?" Torn said. Aaron tossed his head back in laughter.

"I seem to recall helping you, Torn," Esme said.

Torn grinned. "Where should I set up the speakers?"

She bit her lip. "I'm not really a sound person."

"I can help with that." Aaron crossed the room.

"I'll be in the back if you need me," she called, leaving her lover and his husband to finish the seating arrangements. She needed to get back to the trays of amuse-bouche that had to be prepared before the reading began in four hours.

In the kitchen, Anthony's face was bright red as he pulled prawns from a pot of boiling water. "You okay to finish the crudités?" he called.

Esme tried to welcome the new feeling of taking orders from him. "Yes, Chef," she agreed and headed to her station.

A few moments later, he strode up to her, wiping his hands on his apron. "Need a hand?"

She smiled and passed him a colander full of lightly blanched green beans. "That would be great."

He set it on the counter and began arranging the beans on a platter. "Do you mind if I stay and listen to the reading?"

"Of course not, Anthony. Torn would be thrilled. He told me last night that you are his favorite fan. I had no idea that you were so skilled with graphic design." Torn had proudly shown her a rendering Anthony had sent him of him and H. P. Lovecraft standing side by side, with a tangle of ghoulish but elegantly drawn tentacles wiggling behind them.

Anthony ducked his head. "Yes. I've read *The Call* three times, and every time I finish it, I feel like I'm going to wake up to a world of monsters. Or, worse, become one myself. As a writer, he captured something incredible. I can't wait for the next one." Anthony smiled shyly. "He's also a really nice guy."

"That he is," Esme said with a smile.

The two finished the starters with time for them both to go home and change. As Esme walked through the golden evening, she hoped Benedict and Zoe would be ready to leave in a few minutes. She still had to go through the night's plan with the servers. Although she was primarily hosting the event as a favor to Torn, it wasn't lost on her that it would draw a huge crowd of literati and critics who might need a venue of their own at some time. She wanted the night to be perfect.

"I'm here," she called up the stairs.

Benedict's voice rained down on her. "I need fifteen minutes. I just got home."

"Me too!" Zoe called.

"Great." She climbed the stairs and entered their room to find Benedict ironing a shirt. "I'm going to take a quick shower."

She rinsed off the cooking scents from the restaurant and toweled dry as quickly as she could. Esme had planned her outfit weeks ago. It was hanging on a hook on the back of the door, where she had left it that morning. She slipped the fabric of the sleek blue dress over her hips. It looked just as sexy here as it had when she and Sophie picked it out. She pulled on a pair of dangling gold earrings and applied her favorite dark-red lipstick.

As she stepped out of the foggy bathroom, Benedict looked her up and down.

"You look fantastic."

"Can you zip me up?"

She wasn't wearing a bra, and she heard him suck in his breath as he registered the fact.

"How much time do we have?" His voice was rough.

"Not enough." She thought about Torn's hands as her husband ran his finger down the length of her spine.

"Later, then."

She knew that tonight Torn would be going home with Aaron. She couldn't remember the last time she and Benedict had slept together.

Suddenly, she found the idea of being with him oddly dangerous, as if he were the one who was forbidden.

"Later," she promised, holding her thumb up to his bottom lip as she lightly kissed his mouth.

"Ready?" Zoe's head popped through their bedroom door. "Ew. Were you kissing? Hurry up!"

Esme and Benedict laughed awkwardly as they made a move toward the door.

"I think this is the first time that you have ever been ready before us, so don't get too high on that horse," Benedict called to Zoe's retreating figure.

Esme walked with her husband and daughter to the restaurant. Dix-Neuf used to host a monthly music night, but she had decided to end it when she began planning the patisserie. For the first time, she realized that the monthly occasion had been more than a chance for the neighbors to dance and relax. It had been an important time for her family to connect with each other. They had never missed a night, and she wondered if it had been disappointing when she had ended them. She'd been so distracted that she hadn't even thought to ask.

The sky was turning a dark shade of pink as they crossed the street to the restaurant, which glowed as the rise and fall of music and laughter spilled onto the street from the open windows. Once inside, Esme was pleased to see that the dining room looked soft and inviting as the sun set. Torn's agent had hired a decorator, who had filled the room with white candles in thick rose-gold candelabras. The restaurant was crowded with familiar and new faces alike, all there to celebrate Torn's success. *The Call* had just sold its five hundred thousandth copy.

"We have about twenty minutes before Torn reads. Are you both okay on your own? I need to check on the food."

"We're good," Benedict said with a light touch on her arm.

She watched as Zoe and Benedict made their way across the crowd toward a waving Ray and Sophie. She saw Zoe glance over at Torn, surrounded by fans, and beam. He looked striking in a white linen shirt and bright-blue pants, and as she moved through the crowded room, she felt his eyes on her.

In the kitchen, she helped Anthony organize the trays for service, making last-minute adjustments as needed before returning to the front of the house. Anthony followed her and she pointed to the first row, where she had reserved a seat for him. As he walked toward it, Esme scanned the room before taking her seat. She had rented one hundred folding chairs, and she didn't see an empty spot, except the three her daughter was saving in the second row. Torn's agent had said the event sold out in less than a day. He hoped to schedule another reading in October. She slid into the chair beside Zoe, patting her daughter's leg. Torn approached the microphone just as Kitty and Julia arrived and joined them, Kitty beside her and Julia beside Benedict, who always insisted on the aisle seat.

"Thanks for joining us," he laughed as he adjusted the mike. "You know, I should be used to this by now, but I'm always scared these things are going to start shrieking at me like a banshee. I see monsters everywhere. Occupational hazard, I guess."

The crowd chuckled lightly.

"I wish I could tempt you with new pages, but I'm still frantically typing away at those, so I'm going to read from a chapter in *The Call*. My agent is going to kill me for not starting at the beginning. Apparently, that's the part that sells books." He paused and then pointed to the side of the room. "On a related note, I'll be selling books after I read at that table over there."

People laughed again.

"I'll even sign them." Torn grinned again, then turned to the pages in front of him. She knew from thumbing through his reading copy at an earlier lunch together that they were covered in scribbles and lines, as if Torn needed to see something new every time he opened his book. *Writers would make the worst criminals*, she thought wryly. *They never stop changing their stories.* She saw Anthony in the front row, leaning forward eagerly. Torn put his lips close to the mike. Esme was struck by the depth of his voice when he spoke. After two words, the crowd was in his hands.

I had no interest in attending class the next day. Not after the echoes of the call had rung through my head all night. Instead, I found the home address of the lawyer who had shot himself minutes before I arrived at his office. As I drove through the desolate streets, evidence of the chaos of the night before was everywhere. Bodies lay lifeless on the sidewalks. More windows were broken than intact, and I heard the crunch of shattered glass beneath my tires.

The lawyer's home was unsurprisingly impressive, located in the town's most prestigious neighborhood, perched on the edge of the granite cliff that loomed over the valley where the rest of the town had been built. The front door was open, as if I were expected. I walked through the high-ceilinged foyer and up the stairs to the master bedroom, my steps tapping hollowly on the hardwood floor. Despite the home's enormous size, it seemed as if the lawyer had lived alone. Once inside the darkly painted bedroom, I felt myself pulled toward the top drawer of a black nightstand. I yanked it open and saw six pairs of women's underwear positioned carefully in the otherwise empty drawer. Three were lacy, and two were functional, utilitarian cotton briefs. The last pair was made of an ivory silk. It seemed almost elegant that they were the only pair stained with blood.

Had the statue turned him even before the call? Perhaps he hadn't been able to accept it, and so the statue had come to me. I wondered about my professor's true reason for taking his own life and who he had become in the days leading up to his death.

I slid the drawer closed on the nightstand and followed my path back home. Once there, I placed the statue on the sticky kitchen table and focused my burning eyes on the lumpy, grotesque gift from my professor. Its bulging cheeks and tentacle-laden mouth grew familiar, even comforting, as I made my decision.

On the second night, I began. I started with the home of my adviser. Her hair was the color of corn syrup. Watching her brush it from her face used to make my breath catch in my throat. It looked just as beautiful spread out on the pillow. Air moved in and out of her lungs in a fragile rhythm. She was almost too perfect to die. Then her eyes opened and I could tell I had been right to come, if wrong about the reason. She was a hunter, not a weak piece of prey.

"Are you ready now?"

"Yes," I answered.

Torn stopped reading, and the room was silent. Then it filled with applause. Benedict stood.

"I need another drink," he said as he rubbed his jaw. He looked disturbed by Torn's words.

Esme nodded distractedly. She felt lost in the story and told herself to find her missing copy so she could pick up where she had left off. From the interviews she had seen, she knew the rest of the book followed the protagonist as he transformed from an unassuming student to a murderer, attributing his newfound freedom to kill to the call. For some, discovering the monster within them forced their hand to suicide. For others, it liberated them to kill. It was ludicrous, of course, to think that a demonic signal could remove culpability from humans for murder, but something about the way Torn wrote about killing made it seem understandable. Even erotic.

"I wonder what the face looked like."

Esme startled at how much her daughter's pragmatism differed from her own line of thinking.

"Doesn't the monster look exactly like the face you see in the mirror?" Esme said without considering the effect her words could have on her daughter. Was Zoe too young to understand that Torn's book was suggesting something monstrous existed in all people? She was relieved to find nothing more than impatience washing over her daughter's features.

Zoe sighed. "No, Mom. The face of the statue."

"Oh."

"I'm going to ask Torn."

"Okay."

As Zoe wove through the crowd, Esme saw Sophie holding up a bottle of champagne at her from the bar, surrounded by their neighbors. Benedict was standing beside her with a nearly empty glass. Miriam and Levi looked up as she approached. Their hands were empty, and, as always, they looked as if they were trying to find an appropriate time to exit. Esme smiled at Miriam as she joined the group. She lifted her lips slightly in return, as if it required effort.

"You know, we would be happy to provide music at events like this," Miriam said quietly.

Esme was pleasantly surprised at her offer. "What a lovely idea."

"Something like, um, a string quartet . . . ," Levi began. He was cut off by the loud popping of another cork. Sophie had opened a second bottle of champagne. Esme smiled at her friend and accepted the glass. Benedict proffered his empty glass, and Sophie filled it as well.

"This is beautiful, Esme." Sophie waved a hand to indicate the decor.

"I wish I could take credit, but Torn's agent put it together. I was thinking I might hire him—"

"Have you read *The Call*?" Benedict interrupted. His voice was loud, and his question was undirected. Esme was surprised to see him downing his second drink as quickly as the first.

"I have. It was fascinating how—" Miriam started.

"Sex on the beach, please, and a soda water for Julia," Kitty called in the general direction of the bartender as she joined them. The attractive blonde woman was dressed in a boldly printed dress that hugged her curves.

"Can I have a mimosa?" asked Julia. In spite of his bad temper, Benedict grinned, and Julia returned the smile. Her bold request wasn't enough to lift his mood, however. Esme noticed him looking away sharply, as if refusing to be anything but miserable.

"Absolutely not." Kitty's tone was clipped, but it changed when she looked over the group. "Hi, Levi," she purred. Miriam's eyes narrowed.

"Hello, Kitty," she said.

"Hello," Kitty responded with a bright smile, as if she hadn't just been blatantly flirting with the woman's husband.

"I haven't read it yet," Sophie responded to Benedict, ignoring Kitty's interruption. "I am not a monster person. I get scared watching *E.T.*"

Esme laughed, and Miriam smiled tightly as Julia spoke.

"I've read it, Benedict. I think you'd really like it."

He met her eyes, then turned back to Sophie. "I think I'd hate it. According to Torn, there is a monster in us all. That's what the call means, right? It releases the monster in our minds." Benedict poured the remains of the glass into his mouth and wiped his lips with the back of his hand. "There is no escaping it."

"You don't seem so monstrous to me," Julia said.

Benedict ignored her and held up his glass to Sophie. Sophie tipped the bottle into his glass despite the slight shake of Esme's head. As Benedict took another large sip, Zoe and Torn joined their group.

"Orange juice, Zoe?"

"Coke?" Zoe bargained with her mother.

"Aw, why would you drink that garbage?" Sophie chided Zoe as Ray joined them.

"It's a party, Sophie. Jeez. Esme, come on." Ray winked at Zoe, who smiled gratefully.

"Fine, fine." Esme laughed and waved the bartender over as he delivered Kitty's drinks. The group began calling out their orders, beginning with Zoe's soda. Benedict set his empty champagne glass down and asked for a double whiskey. When Esme turned back from the bar, Torn flashed a smile at her as Zoe began speaking excitedly and nervously.

"Torn, I saw something that might inspire you. I mean . . . it might not work, but it's really cool. Have you heard of the creature they just discovered off the coast of Portugal? It has the head of a snake and more teeth than a shark."

Torn turned to her eagerly.

"Seriously?" he asked. "I can't resist a monster story. Especially if it's true."

Zoe spoke with enthusiasm as she detailed the creature.

Julia rolled her eyes at something Kitty was saying to her while staring fixedly at Benedict, who tossed back his drink. Esme heard the ice click against his teeth. She saw Miriam looking warily at Benedict out of the corner of her eye.

"Benedict, slow down." Esme touched his hand as he slid the glass on the bar for another. He jerked his hand away and knocked the heavy tumbler onto the floor. It shattered, and the sound of glass breaking, coupled with Sophie's surprised cries, caught the attention of a group of people close by.

"What the hell, Esme?" He turned to her in anger, and Kitty tsked. Anthony joined their group, squaring his shoulders as he faced Benedict while speaking to Esme.

"Is everything okay here?"

"It's fine, Anthony. Could you ask Clara to grab a broom?" Esme pitched her voice low to avoid a scene. Anthony spoke quietly as well.

"He's drunk. Again. Do you want me to get him out of here?"

Esme looked at Anthony, confused by his intervention. "No, it's fine."

"Okay. Just remember, I'm here if you need me. For anything." Her chef looked grim as he stepped away to find a server who could clean up the mess. Her husband turned to Zoe, who was still speaking animatedly to Torn. Neither of them seemed to have noticed Benedict's accident.

"Zoe, are you in the mood for ice cream?" Benedict cast glazed eyes toward their daughter as Esme gently herded the group away from the broken glass. Miriam whispered into Levi's ear, and the two of them headed for the exit without a goodbye.

"Sure. Just let me finish—"

"Let's get out of here," Benedict said, folding Zoe roughly under his arm.

"Okay, cool. Bye, Torn. We can talk later."

They shared a smile that was warm enough to make Esme feel uncomfortable. She told herself that she was just shaken by Benedict's abrasive exit. There was nothing going on between Torn and Zoe besides an adolescent crush. Dismissing her own jealousy made her realize that perhaps the same emotion had been fueling Benedict's outburst. *Does he suspect something between me and Torn?* she wondered as she took another sip of champagne.

Aaron came to stand beside Torn.

"Hey, everyone." He looked flushed. "I have a little announcement. Torn, before you begin signing, would you mind if I made a toast? I have a surprise for you."

"Are you finally buying me a sports car?"

The group laughed as Sophie expertly popped another bottle of champagne and filled flutes.

Aaron raised his. "As you all know, I am so proud of my husband and all he has done. We have been so lucky in our lives, and he's asked me for a long time to open my heart and share what we have."

Esme's hand faltered, and the cold glass slipped an inch in her fingers. She gripped it tightly. She was grateful that she was able to hold on without making a scene as Benedict had.

"For years, I have worked in a country that has very little opportunity for children. Today I received a phone call from a colleague. They have just found a newborn in desperate need of a home."

Aaron swallowed hard, and his eyes shone.

"If my husband agrees, I would like to begin the process of adoption. I would like to make you a father, Torn. I want us to have a baby."

Torn fell into Aaron's arms before the group's cheer ended. The two men cried as they embraced fiercely. Esme locked arms with Sophie, and Julia let out a two-fingered whistle that drew the eyes of others in the crowd. Esme noticed Ray stepping back from the group, and her stomach sank. Once again, Torn had achieved one of Ray's unrealized dreams.

Torn pulled away from Aaron and clinked his glass on each of theirs, whooping loudly. "I'm going to be a dad!"

The group cheered again. Esme drank more champagne, hoping it would dissolve the lump in her throat.

"Now how am I supposed to sign books?" Torn laughed as he swiped at his eyes.

"I'd like to get on a flight tomorrow and stay for a while to get the papers in order," Esme heard Aaron say softly. "It might take some time."

"Of course. Whatever you need. I'll be waiting here. Painting the nursery!"

Torn and Aaron embraced again; then Torn walked to the table where many people were already gathered.

The party lasted several more hours, but Esme felt too dazed to enjoy it. Raven Lane residents lingered, chatting about the new baby coming to their street and watching Torn speak with his fans. Ray and Sophie were the first to leave; both had to work the next day. Kitty and

Julia stood in line and ostentatiously purchased copies, then drifted into the dark summer night. Aaron tried to stick it out, but his yawns eventually overcame him when Torn asked for one last round. Finally, it was just the two of them.

"Can I walk you home?" Torn asked while waving to his assistant, who was packing up the few remaining books.

"Of course." Esme reminded the staff to set the alarm as they walked out of the restaurant.

The walk back to Raven Lane was full of Torn's excited questions about newborns, formula, and diapers. Esme tried to seem interested, but the days of crying babies and sleepless nights felt as far away to her as Syria. She knew how consuming a newborn was, and she tried to push down a pang of jealousy at how distracted Torn would be, with Aaron, for years. As they approached Esme's house, she looked over at Torn with half-lidded eyes. All the lights in her own home were off. Zoe and Benedict likely had been asleep for hours. The champagne made her feel bold, and she leaned close to steal a kiss.

Then she saw it. The flicker of hesitation, even contempt, at her advance. She pulled back as if stung.

"Esme, I'm sorry. My life's about to change so much. It just feels . . . complicated. I have a lot to process. And a lot to do."

Esme nodded, even though her face was as numb as if she'd been slapped. "Of course. Let me know if you need anything. I kept a lot of Zoe's baby things in storage."

"Thanks, Esme. You've always been such a good friend."

Esme smiled despite his use of past tense and emphasis on the word "friend," trying not to notice the forlorn look in Torn's eyes. It reminded her of how Zoe used to gaze at her old toys on Christmas morning, just before she began putting the new ones on the shelf.

CHAPTER TWENTY-FIVE

Benedict was nursing a beer at the dining room table when she walked into the room. She had stopped at Dix-Neuf after her conversation with Sophie, and her blood was boiling even before she saw Benedict drinking at three in the afternoon.

"Where's Zoe?" she asked.

"Upstairs. As usual," Benedict said. His loose enunciation suggested that the drink was not his first.

"Did you talk to Anthony today?"

"Yes. He saw me grabbing a couple cases of beer from the bar fridge. He told me he needed you to confirm by text the loss of inventory. He's getting a bit uppity, if you ask me."

"He's exactly right. Dix-Neuf is not your private stock. We discussed this last time you did this."

"Jesus, Esme, I'm on trial for murder. I can't walk into a store right now. I needed a drink and we own a restaurant."

She willed herself to stay calm. Benedict's petty theft was the least of her concerns. "Did you tell Anthony that we are selling Dix-Neuf?" Despite the effort, her voice rose, and she checked the doorway, hoping that Zoe wasn't coming downstairs to investigate.

"We might have to." Benedict grimaced. "Jack's legal fees are going to be astronomical. He wants to bring in some more forensic experts, and they are not cheap."

Red danced in front of Esme's eyes as she realized he thought he had every right to take what she had worked so hard to build. Her rage choked her. She didn't trust herself to say another word.

He took a large swig, finishing what was left in his glass. "Want one?"

She shook her head as he fetched another bottle, keeping silent as he poured it into the tall glass. Benedict took another drink before he put it down and stared at her across the table.

"I asked Kitty if she planted the photos," Benedict said.

Fire turned to ice in her mind. "Why would you think that?"

"Esme, she's been trying to sleep with me for nearly twenty years. I've always said no. Someone here on the street has it out for me. I thought it might be her."

She kept her eyes steady as if Benedict were telling her about the weather. He took another swig. Esme could smell the tang of the hops as the liquid moved.

"And what did she say?"

"She denied it. But it seemed like she was lying. I think it was her, Esme. I think she's trying to frame me. Tomorrow, I'm going to tell Jack to bring her back on the stand and pressure her to admit it."

The numbness leaked from her body like antifreeze from a broken engine, and the sickening anger returned.

"How can you accuse one of our best friends of doing this to you?"

"That night in May, the evening after the art walk when Ray was on the piss, Kitty invited us all over for pizza, remember? You told me that you didn't want to come because you couldn't handle being around me when I was 'so drunk.'"

Benedict wiggled his fingers in the air in an imitation of quotation marks. Esme swallowed hard. She remembered how the day had ended. Ray and Benedict had not stopped drinking after Benedict had coaxed

Ray away from Torn. By the time the tables had been taken down and the crowd had dispersed, both men had hardly been able to stand. Her annoyance was legitimate, but it had also provided the perfect excuse for Esme to decline Kitty's invitation. She had spent the rest of the afternoon in Torn's bed.

"I remember."

"Ray passed out early, but Kitty and I kept drinking. I went to the bathroom, and when I came out, she was looking at a phone. When she heard me coming, she acted really weird, like she'd been caught, and shoved the phone between two cushions. I think it was yours. I think she texted herself those images. It's the only thing that makes sense."

"Benedict, you are acting crazy. Kitty has done everything she can to protect you during this trial. Jack told us she was one of the strongest witnesses for your innocence. Why would she try to pin this on you and then backpedal so hard?"

"But then who did it? Who planted those photos?"

"I don't know. Miriam wants us as far away from this street as possible, and we both know Levi would do anything she says. Maybe it was Aaron? He could have found out about my affair and been trying to out me." She knew she was grasping at straws, trying to answer an unanswerable question.

Benedict slammed down his glass. "So, basically, it could have been anyone on Raven Lane?"

"That's exactly what I'm saying."

Benedict picked at the corner of the label of his beer as he considered the idea that the people closest to them were also the ones most likely to have betrayed them. When he looked up again, Esme could see pain in his eyes.

"Why did you take those pictures, Esme?"

She flushed uncomfortably. "I already said. It was stupid. There was no reason for it."

"Did it turn you on?"

"Benedict—"

"Just tell me. The least you can do is tell me why you'd do that with him and not with me."

She blanched. "It wasn't like that—"

"Of course it was. You were having sex with our neighbor. My friend. You did things with him that I wouldn't have dreamed possible for you. I thought sex made you uncomfortable. Nine times out of ten, you'd tell me you were too tired. It happened so often that I just stopped asking. But as it turns out, you were just too tired for me. So why, Esme, my darling wife? Why him and not me?"

The two of them locked eyes across the table like gunfighters in a dusty street, waiting to see who would draw first. When Benedict breathed deeply, Esme prepared herself to be berated again. But he didn't speak. Instead, the air in his lungs was released in a shuddering sob that shocked her more than any accusation ever could. Benedict had never cried in front of her. Not even when his father had died. Not even when he emerged from his near-death overdose.

"I know what he did to you," he said.

Esme's mind raced. She sank back into the dining room chair. How could Benedict know how cruelly Torn had discarded her? She tried to buy time.

"What do you mean?"

Benedict raked his hands through his hair. "How could I not know? I went to Jed's parties, Esme. I saw the way the women looked when they walked out of his private room. I knew what kinds of roles they landed after those nights. Everyone knew what you had to do to get in his good graces. Then there were the others who couldn't handle what had happened, like you. I saw the ones who quit his movies too. They all looked the way you looked when I came out of rehab. Broken. And no one did anything. Including me."

Esme felt the familiar pain tighten her head. Benedict wasn't talking about Torn. "If you knew, why didn't you ask me what happened?"

"I was a mess back then, Esme. I was high so often, then I was going through treatment, and then my career crashed, and you came into all that money and I just . . . it was easier to follow your lead. I've never forgiven myself for not warning you about Jed Matheson. I wish I had asked you where the money really came from. I was going to, I swear. When you told me you were pregnant, I just didn't want to talk about it, in case . . . the baby wasn't mine. I wanted to be her father so badly. To be the husband you needed me to be."

Esme's head ached at the realization that Benedict thought he had acted heroically throughout Zoe's life. His version of himself overlooked the general disinterest in Zoe that his self-involvement and doubts about his paternity had bred.

"No matter what created her, she was always your daughter," Esme said, realizing suddenly that she had said the words so many times over the years that she had made them true.

"And I've always loved you both, Esme. You stuck by me through everything. I wanted to be a better man for you, to make a life with you outside of all the fame and the money and the stupid shit. I was so astonished you would want to be my wife, the mother of my child. We built so much together. We have worked so hard."

Esme blinked hard at his certainty of his own merits.

"All I ever wanted was to be your husband," he said. "All I have ever done is love you with all of my heart." He brushed the tears from his eyes with the back of his hand.

She knew her heart should be full of sympathy, guilt, maybe even forgiveness. But all she could feel was rage.

"If that's true, then how could you?"

"What?"

"How could you sleep with Julia?"

CHAPTER
TWENTY-SIX

Their due dates were only days apart. During the final stages of their pregnancy, she and Kitty saw each other every day, sharing pots of raspberry tea along with their shared terror and wonder about carrying and caring for a baby. Esme had been relieved to have a friend who understood part of her worries—or at least as many of them as she could admit out loud. She had never been able to confide that, sometimes, she feared her baby would tear her into pieces during labor, like the recurring nightmare she had every time she thought about Jed before she fell asleep.

Julia had been born first. When she came home from the hospital, Kitty had been standing unsteadily on the sidewalk as her soon-to-be ex-husband fumbled with the latches and belts of Julia's first car seat when Esme burst out of her house to greet them. Kitty had looked exhausted, but her face brightened at the sight of Esme.

"Congratulations!" Esme thrust a huge basket full of diapers, wine, and prepared dinners at her friend. Kitty threw her arms around Esme, nearly weeping with joy. Her husband stepped back as the two women peered at the tiny baby in the car seat. Esme had marveled at the sight of Kitty's newborn, trying to comprehend the impossibility of fingernails smaller than a peppercorn.

"Her name is Julia. Like the movie star," Kitty whispered in awe before her face fell. "Is that stupid?"

"Oh, Kitty. It's not stupid. It's perfect. She's perfect."

Esme had reached a hand out to the soft, fuzzy head, marveling at the creature's tiny fingers and wide eyes. She had never seen a newborn in real life before, so it was surreal to imagine she was carrying one inside her that she would soon meet. She hoped that her child would be just as beautiful and innocent. She hoped that her little one would not have to carry the sins of her father, whoever that might be. After Zoe was born, Kitty had been the only one she could confide in about the long, black nights when the baby's cries were so loud it felt like Esme's rib cage was shaking. When Julia's father left them, Esme was the only person to hear how broken Kitty was, how she had been forced to wean Julia early to ensure she wouldn't be damaged by the two bottles of wine her mother was drinking every night. Julia and Zoe had also been inseparable, back when they had no one else but each other. For years, she had felt like Julia's second mother. Even now it was hard for her not to act maternal around her.

The day after Torn's reading, Esme had been pleased to see Kitty and Julia had reserved a table for lunch. After the rush ended, she had joined them.

"Did you enjoy everything?" Esme asked.

"So good," Julia said.

"As always," Kitty added.

"Excellent. Anthony is off today. It's been a while since I've been alone in the kitchen. Nice to know I've still got the touch." She winked as she gathered up their plates, trying not to judge the huge portion still left on Julia's. She hated the idea of the young girl vying for the emaciation that seemed to be required of clients at the Padillo-Werner Modeling Agency. Her own stomach had ached for the entirety of her struggle to be an actress. The only feeling Esme remembered hating more than hunger was her guilt when the pain stopped, because it meant she'd been too weak to maintain her discipline.

"Dessert?"

"We can never ever resist your crème brûlée, Esme."

"One each? Or one to share?"

"Definitely to share," Julia said quickly. Esme nodded, even though her heart felt heavy. As she prepared their order, she added six vanilla truffles to the plate, hoping that Julia's most beloved chocolates would coax her into eating a few more calories.

"One crème brûlée, two spoons." She slid the plate between the two women and felt proud when Julia eagerly reached for a chocolate. Esme was surprised to see a dark-red string tied around her slender wrist.

"What's that?" she asked, pointing to the makeshift bracelet. It looked like a cross between a friendship bracelet that kids made at summer camp and a ragged piece of yarn.

"Nothing," Julia said, popping the chocolate into her mouth and returning her hand, out of view, under the table.

"Julia seems entranced by the mysticism of kabbalah these days." Kitty rolled her eyes toward Esme before tapping the crust on top of the creamy custard in front of her.

"Wow. That's an interesting road to travel," she replied.

She smiled at both women before making an excuse to return to the kitchen. As the doors swung shut behind her, she shook her head to rid herself of a nagging and ridiculous feeling that, over the last months, Kitty was not the one she should have been worried about.

CHAPTER
TWENTY-SEVEN

The day before Torn died, Esme walked to the big house at the top of Raven Lane to visit him with a hopeful heart. She hadn't heard from him since his reading the week before, and each day that passed had made her more worried that she really was something he could cast off easily. When he had sent a text the previous night saying the adoption was "stressing him out," she had hurried to tell him that she would come as soon as she could, grateful for another chance to show him how much he needed her. As she knocked on his door, she thought that perhaps he had come back to his senses about what they had and would be eager to make love to her as soon as she arrived. Instead, Torn seemed distracted.

"Hello."

"Hello, Torn." The rest of Esme's enthusiastic greeting died in her mouth when he didn't lean forward for a kiss.

"Is everything all right?" she asked as he stepped back unceremoniously to let her in. The house was dark after the bright glare of the early-September sunshine.

"I just . . . I need more time to write. This whole adoption thing has been a nightmare. Aaron was in Turkey trying to secure the visas, but it seems like he's getting more and more mired in bureaucracy and bribes. He ended up back in Syria yesterday to try and sort it out. He wants to talk it through endlessly, but he doesn't understand that I've got to meet my deadline or my editor is going to kill me."

"Maybe I can help."

Torn rolled his eyes at her suggestion, and she stifled her irritation by reminding herself that he was under tremendous pressure.

"What I really need is your daughter," he said.

"Zoe? What does she have to do with this?"

"She is just so full of life and creativity. That whole monster conversation at the reading was the best talk I've had in months. It really sparked something in me, but I feel like I've lost it again."

"She's heading to a high school conference this afternoon, but I'll give her your regards when she gets back," Esme said curtly. "I should go."

"No, no. Don't leave." Suddenly, Torn looked as frustrated as a toddler trying to ask for something he didn't know the words for, and Esme's heart melted. "I'm sorry. This is all falling down around me, but it's not your fault."

"Look, why don't you keep writing? I'll fix you something to eat, and then maybe we can talk about it together."

"Okay."

Torn turned back to his desk without another word, and Esme wondered if she should go through with her real reason for being there. She took a deep breath to convince herself that Torn would be cheered up once she put her plan into action. Torn began typing rapidly, and she knew he wouldn't notice that, instead of heading to the kitchen, she'd walked up the stairs to the bedroom he shared with Aaron.

Torn had never minded bringing her into this space, so she didn't feel like she was betraying him by opening his closet. She riffled through it and chose a button-down shirt, a hat, and a red striped tie. For some people, a lover dressing in their partner's clothing might seem distasteful, but she knew Torn wouldn't see it like that. This was the perfect way to make him realize that she was, and always would be, indispensable.

She set up the tripod for her phone in the corner, checking to make sure that its field of vision captured the bed. The thought of taking these photos made her feel nervous, but Torn was an exhibitionist. His publicist did so little on his social media pages that she wondered why Torn even kept her on the payroll. Every image and every post was all Torn. She knew he loved it when people paid attention to him and admired what he looked like in public. It seemed logical that he would be excited by it in private as well. When everything was ready, she lay on the bed to wait. She knew Torn could never write for more than an hour at a time without a break.

"Esme?" he called just as she was starting to wonder if she had been wrong.

"I'm up here."

She felt herself warming as his footsteps came closer and closer, up the stairs and down the hallway to the master bedroom. Like her own, it took up the entire front half of the second floor. Esme had pulled the shades on the floor-to-ceiling window. The room was dark.

"What are you doing up here?" He stepped into the room, then stopped to allow his eyes to adjust to the dim light. When he saw her on the bed, his eyes lit up.

"Come here." She knelt on the bed, lifting the man's button-down shirt that hung loosely on her body so he could see the lacy panties she was wearing underneath. She didn't have to ask again. He crawled onto the bed, and his mouth was on hers in seconds.

"What's all this?" he murmured as he stopped to catch his breath.

"I wanted to give you a surprise. It's been a long time."

She pressed the remote trigger she had bought the day before for the phone's camera as he kissed her stomach, and the flash filled the room. He turned his head to see where the light had come from.

"Why are you taking my picture?" He kissed her again, then broke away to whisper, "That doesn't seem fair. Don't I get to take one of you?"

"Be my guest."

She handed him the trigger, then slid off his belt and his pants and leaned forward. As she took him into her mouth, he snapped another shot. She wished the photo could capture his moans.

"Esme," he breathed.

She released him, then pushed him gently by the shoulders so he was lying on the bed, taking the trigger from his hand once again. "You need a break to help your creativity flow, Torn. Lie back."

As he did, she slipped the silky tie out from her collar and wound it around his eyes, then took him back into her warm mouth. His hips bucked against her, but she didn't stop, snapping photos as he writhed under her touch, as he shuddered into her mouth.

With a half smile, he pulled her up so she straddled his chest.

"Your turn," he demanded, yanking the tie from his face and placing it in her hands. She wrapped the silky material across her eyes.

In the sudden blackness, she felt free. He gripped her hips. She rocked against him, clicking the camera before she was overcome by the force of his body against hers. Then she rolled off and wrapped her legs around his, slinging her arm across his chest. Their breath came in gasps, then calmed. Only a crack of light at the edge of the curtains showed them that the real world still existed.

"What's it like?" Torn asked. His voice was quiet, and for a moment, Esme thought he was asking her about sex.

"What's what like?"

"Having a daughter."

Esme's heart swelled as she thought of Zoe's tiny fists wrapped around her hair, the sparkle in her eyes whenever she saw the ocean, and the flick of her pink tongue as she tried her first ice cream cone.

"It's wonderful."

"And hard?"

Esme remembered the sleepless nights, the ceaseless chatter, and the feeling that she was failing. The endless need and the constant worry. The certainty that her baby was an intruder.

"Yes, it can be excruciating. It does get easier as they get older, though. They become so independent that they almost don't need you anymore at all."

"I don't think I'll be able to do it, Esme. To be a dad."

"Of course you will. It's what you want."

Torn sighed, and Esme felt his chest rise and fall beneath her arm. "I need to be able to focus if I'm going to do it right. I need to finish this book. If I can stop distracting myself, I can do this."

Esme spoke fast. There was a finality in Torn's words that she didn't want to hear. "I'll do anything I can to help you."

He sighed heavily and rolled onto his side. The worry had left his voice, and she felt assured that he needed her after all. "Thank you."

His soft snores began almost immediately, but she was too wired to sleep. She had nearly won him back. There was only one last thing she had to do. If Torn needed help with his work, she was going to give it to him. She slipped from the covers and pulled on the men's shirt again before padding across the floor, down the stairs, and to his laptop. When she got downstairs, Professor didn't even raise his head from his large bed.

The draft of his next novel was open on the computer, and she began to read. Her horror at what he had done to her grew with every word.

For months, nearly a year, it fed on her, emptying her of everything good she had left. At night, it would toss and turn inside of her, jerking her abdomen from side to side with its violent movements. Twice, she screamed when its sharp heel struck her hard enough to damage her unguarded vital organs. She ached from the battle happening constantly within her, but she dreaded its bloody arrival even more than its greedy war with her body.

She didn't love it. When he was there, she called it by the name he chose to make it seem less monstrous, but she knew what it was. After all, it had grown inside of her, making her stomach distend and her mind wince at the memory of the ugly force that had planted the seed for its creation.

Once on the outside, its endless hunger for her grew. As it fed, she had to turn her head to keep her nausea at bay. She could feel it leaching every single nutrient from her body. Every moment of motherhood weakened her as it took what it needed with no care for the effect on her body.

Its helplessness inspired no instinct in her. As it cried, her husband slept through it as if the air were still. She too lay in bed, as if she couldn't hear the screams ripping through their once peaceful home, but she could. She listened to it with fascination, feeling no urgency to stop its wails, though her breasts swelled uncomfortably with milk as its cries increased. It was as if her mind and body had finally been separated by the repulsion she felt for it. She kept her hate secret. She had always been skilled at hiding who she really was.

Bile rose in her throat as she read the next line. Her head pounded with shame, anger, and fear. *What had made her trust him? How could he have done this to her? Would Zoe know what this really meant?*

"What do you think?" he asked from the doorway behind her. The hope in his voice made it seem as if he thought she would like it.

Her shoulders tightened with tension as she turned her head away from the computer. The sunlight seemed to be trying to creep around the edges of Torn's body in the doorframe.

"Is this supposed to be about me?"

Even though he was backlit, Esme could see Torn's face change.

"Of course not."

"Is this your next book?"

"Yes." He ran his hands through his thick black hair. The gesture reminded her so much of her husband that her heart started to pound. She had done it again. She had trusted someone, and she had been betrayed.

"What is the title?"

Torn rubbed the back of his neck and wouldn't meet her eyes.

"I don't have a real title yet. Just a working one."

"Torn, what it is called?"

He wouldn't look at her. "*The Purpose*. It's good, Esme. It's a feminist retelling of motherhood and rape. It will change lives."

"You bastard."

At her words, his eyes became colder than she had ever seen them. "Esme, I don't have time for this. Any of this. You should go."

"How could you do this to me? If you publish this, you will ruin my life. If there's more in there about the assault, Jed could come after me for violating the NDA. Everyone will know. And not the truth. The horrible, warped version that you've created."

"I've ruined your life?" he said, his words iced with anger. "What was there left to ruin?"

"What do you mean?"

"I never wanted to tell you this, Esme. But you forced me. Remember that."

"Torn! What are you talking about?"

"I came to your house once, in April. I got my days confused; I thought you were home alone, and the windows were open. I heard the sound of sex, and I stopped behind the hedge. I wanted to hear how you sounded when your husband was with you. I wanted to know if it was the same as with me."

"What are you talking about?"

Esme told herself to stand and fling the computer onto the floor, to destroy as much of Torn as she could before he ruined her. But it was too late. His mouth was moving. His words were coming, and she was still sitting on the padded desk chair.

"It was quick. Maybe that's why he didn't think about closing the windows, but it was stupid. Anyone could have heard her. Anyone could have seen her face when she walked back out onto the sidewalk. Flushed and a little bit happy and a little bit scared. Really, I should have taken a photo for reference. She looked like you used to. When you were Esme Lee."

"Whose face? What are you talking about?"

"Julia Dagostino."

Esme dug her nails into her own hands to stop herself from scratching his passive, smug face. He was wrong about her. She didn't hate her daughter. She hated him and Benedict and Jed and all the men who thought they could get away with anything. The men who hurt her. She rushed to the bathroom to vomit, as if her body was trying to purge the thought of her husband's hands on Julia's body. It hadn't been Kitty's perfume she had smelled. Julia must have been wearing it that night to cover up the smell of her cigarettes, just as she had at the back-to-school barbecue the year before. Esme got to her feet, shaking as she ran up the stairs to gather her clothes, nearly ripping the button-down shirt as she yanked it off her body.

"Are you okay?" he asked as he followed her into the room. It still sounded as if he cared, which made her stomach turn again.

"Of course I'm not okay. How could you keep quiet about this? Why wouldn't you tell me? Tell Kitty? Jesus, Torn. She's seventeen years old."

Torn breathed in deeply as he raised his shoulders in a show of powerlessness. "Who am I to judge someone else's sexuality?"

"Who are you to sit by and let my husband hurt a young girl?"

"Esme, I'm sorry I didn't tell you, but it wasn't my place to get involved."

Esme turned to him and spat out the words. "Funny, Torn. You had no problem getting involved in other aspects of my life. Or taking the worst secret of mine and making it the basis of your next novel."

"You are angry. Take a minute to calm down before you rush out of here."

She didn't answer. Her mind was racing. As she walked past him, he tried to pull her into his arms.

"Oh, Esme Lee."

"That is *not* my name."

She ran down the stairs and through the front door, not even noticing that Professor had slipped out behind her until she felt his wet nose nudge the back of her hand. She knew she should coax him back to his home, but she had little desire to do Torn any favors. Instead, she let him keep pace with her. The bright light felt like an assault on her eyes, and she blinked hard to try to adjust to the world. As she walked down the street, Kitty was stepping out of her car. She pasted a smile on her face as she waved.

"Hi, Esme. Beautiful day, isn't it?"

"Hi, Kitty. Do you have a minute to talk?" She was amazed that her voice sounded as bright as the yellow sunshine that surrounded them. If anyone had overheard her, they wouldn't have given the nature of their conversation a second thought. They could never have guessed that something awful had happened and something even worse was yet to come. She beckoned Torn's dog to accompany her into Kitty's house.

CHAPTER
TWENTY-EIGHT

Esme knew she had made a mistake as soon as she opened the door to the stuffy hotel room painted an unpleasantly deep shade of peach-tinted beige. Benedict should have been the one to leave their home on Raven Lane after he had drunkenly, unconvincingly, denied her allegation about Julia. She should have insisted that he pack his bags after she'd realized that she couldn't bear to spend another night under the same roof as him, even in separate rooms. Instead of demanding his exit, however, she had stuffed an overnight bag for herself and her daughter, then ushered Zoe out the door by telling her that their carbon monoxide alarm had gone off and Benedict needed to stay behind so he could help the repair person. Zoe had been skeptical but compliant, for which Esme was grateful. Her mind was too consumed by the thought of being on the stand tomorrow, testifying about the innocence of a man she knew to be guilty, though not of the crime of which he had been accused.

"This looks great," Esme said.

The trill in her voice was too much, but Zoe either didn't notice or pretended that the stale air and stained carpet were just as nice as her mother believed them to be. Calls to several of the higher-end Fraser City hotels had all come back with answers of no vacancies. They had been forced to accept a room at a place that boasted economy prices and a free continental breakfast contained in large plastic dispensers with dials that crushed the cereal to dust during the course of its delivery.

"Is it okay if I watch TV?" Zoe asked.

"Sure," Esme said. "Sophie and Ray are bringing us pizza in about half an hour. I'm just going to make a quick phone call."

"To Dad?" Zoe said hopefully.

"No. To Grandma." Her mother had left a message the day before to tell her that the remote breeding program she had been managing for the last six months had been successful. She was back home now, in the small town two hours away from Fraser City. Esme knew her mother would be seeking praise for another job well done. It was the only reason she ever reached out to her, but Esme couldn't ignore the call. It was time to let her know what was going on.

"Oh. Tell her I said hi."

"I will." Esme heard the false musicality in her voice again as she slid the glass door open to a tiny balcony that overlooked one of Fraser City's busiest streets. She hoped the background noise would keep the conversation brief.

The phone rang three times, and Esme thought she might be lucky enough to reach her mother's voice mail until the connection abruptly became live.

"Esme! Hi!"

"Hello, Mom."

"You sound awful. What's wrong?"

Esme fought the irrational urge to not tell her what was going on and punish her for her lack of interest in her life, but she clung to the hope that her mother would offer words of advice. Esme knew her too well to hope for comfort.

"Benedict was in a car crash at the end of summer."

"What? Is he okay? Why did you wait so long to tell me?"

Esme rolled her eyes but kept her voice level. "It's difficult to get in touch with you during the breeding season."

"Esme, for God's sake. You could have left a message with the switchboard operators. They are very reliable." Her mother sighed with disapproval, and Esme bit back a response that it wasn't exactly the kind of news she wanted passed on by a stranger.

"We are in the middle of a trial. His trial."

"You're kidding." Her mother's disapproval turned to shocked anger. "Esme, how could you not think this was important? How is Zoe handling all this? What happened?"

"Benedict's car hit our neighbor who was riding by on a bicycle as Benedict was backing out of the driveway."

"What is the charge?"

"Second-degree murder."

"How can that be? From what you described, this was an accident, plain and simple."

"Oh, Mom. It's all gotten so complicated."

Esme was stunned to feel her eyes fill with tears. She worked hard never to show her vulnerability to her mother.

"Honey. It sounds awful." Her mother's voice was warm enough to make Esme forget who she was talking to.

"Mom, is there any way you could come here? To help me?"

The silence on the line made Esme cringe at her stupidity.

"I mean, after this all settles, maybe we could come for a visit?" Esme's words were rushed, and her mother replied just as quickly.

"Oh, of course. I would come now but I've just gotten back, and I need to get a few papers written before next term begins. You understand."

"Yes, definitely."

"Esme, I'm feeling a bit overwhelmed with all this. Look, why don't I catch my breath and call you back in a few days. I can read over the transcripts and get a sense of what's going on."

"Transcripts?"

"Yes, I can request the court record as soon as the trial concludes. I'll be able to read over the specifics so I can speak about this more knowledgeably next time we talk."

Esme's heart sank, but she tried to keep her tone light. "That sounds great."

As they said their goodbyes, Esme wondered if her mother would ever speak to her again after finding out the role she'd played in all this. She'd probably count it as further proof that she'd given birth to a failure who wasn't worth her time and feel justified for the years she'd spent away.

As Esme slid open the door and reentered the room, she was relieved to see her two closest friends sitting on the bed with Zoe. The musty smell in the room had been replaced by the scent of roasted tomatoes and warm dough.

Sophie jumped from the bed, nearly catapulting a box of pizza onto the floor. Ray caught the box with his left hand but dropped the slice of pizza in his right. Zoe laughed as it plopped softly on the bed, and Ray joined in.

"Sacrifice the few to save the many, right?" he laughed.

Always, Esme thought as Sophie wrapped her arms around her. Ray's words seemed like permission to show the jury the truth about her husband, even if it meant telling lies.

"Oh, Esme. We were just telling Zoe that no matter what you need, we will be here. For both of you. You will always have us."

Sophie pulled away and noticed the red splotch on the bedspread. "Ray! What a mess. Come on, let's help Esme clean this up."

He raised an eyebrow. Esme walked over and yanked the dusty-rose comforter off the bed.

"Honestly, I think it's an improvement."

As they all laughed, Esme felt like she was loved enough to be forgiven for anything, even for what she might say on the stand tomorrow. It would be easier to do what she needed to do without Sophie and Ray, neither of whom was able to miss another day of work to attend the hearing. Esme was happy for their company. They stayed until Zoe's eyes grew heavy enough to prompt their exit. Esme told them not to worry about their absence in court and embraced them tightly as they assured her that Benedict could borrow their car the next day to get to the courthouse. She kissed Zoe good night once she was nestled into the bed two feet from her own.

Despite her conflicted thoughts about the day to come, Esme felt a sense of peace at being so close to her daughter as Zoe drifted off. It reminded her of the nights she had fallen asleep with her tiny baby lying in the small space between her and Benedict—the few moments in Zoe's early life when her love for her daughter had been pure. She waited until she heard Zoe's breath slip into the slow rhythm of sleep before she pulled out her book to finish the final chapter.

The rain ended the moment we closed her front door. My skin pricked with the leftover moisture in the air. I stared down streets that shone like marble. Everything was ours. Why had it taken me so long to realize it? Her smile made my body stiffen with anticipated pleasure. I would have followed her into the sea. Instead, we walked up the driveway of her next-door neighbor.

"Steve Patterson," she whispered as she tested the windows. "I've always hated him."

In the back of the garage, a small window creaked under her strength and opened a reluctant inch. The layer of mud that coated it suggested that it hadn't moved in years, yet she was able to coax it far enough to let in our two bodies. The wet dirt coated my hands as I slid through after her. It was as thick as blood.

The moon pushed through the clouds and shone in the window, making a path for us between the crumpled beer cans and discarded hockey gear. Steve was a slob. It made what we were about to do even more appealing. She walked up the wooden stairs to the door that connected the garage to the house. It was unlocked. Steve was also careless. We passed through the dark kitchen, pausing only to slide two butcher knives from the block. Mine seemed to sing in my hand as we crept through the living room, also full of beer cans, with the addition of take-out containers and an ashtray full of putrid-smelling roaches. A beam from a streetlight in the front window caught her hair, and I felt as if the world had never been more perfect.

At the top of the stairs, I took a deep breath to allow myself one last moment to savor the world we had been called to create. As I filled my lungs, the scent of something weaker than I filled my nose.

"This way," I said, then grinned as I saw her already advancing toward the bedroom door to the left. She was always one step ahead of me.

As she gracefully swung open the door, a waft of alcohol sweat came out. An immense disgust for Steve filled me. It took only seven steps to reach the side of the large bed, where Steve lay on his back wheezing drunken snores. My adviser raised her blade above Steve's neck. The moonlight made it sparkle like a diamond as it descended.

The call rendered us monsters. That's what they say, as if it's an insult. The weak are still looking for reasons why and codes by which to live. What they don't understand and never will is that the call released us from the search for meaning entirely. It made us free. This is not a suicide note. It is an erasure of everything that I used to call a soul.

There is something inside me that morality will no longer contain. I used to think the killers of the past were an aberration. Now I understand that they simply heard the call earlier than the rest of us. They evolved. And so have we.

The lawyer's note had been incomplete and wrongly worded. What he should have written was:

I know what I am now, and you cannot bear it.
But you must.

Esme closed the book and turned off the light of her phone. Torn had given her the answer she needed. She knew what she would say on the stand tomorrow. The certainty calmed her into a deep, restful sleep.

CHAPTER
TWENTY-NINE

The knock on the door came at 7:30 a.m. The sharp rap registered as an unsettling part of a dream where Esme was walking through the home she grew up in, but it was crowded with strangers telling her she was no longer welcome. Every door she tried to exit opened to another stranger pushing past her so hard that she was forced back in.

"Mom," Zoe said blearily, "there's someone at the door."

"Okay," Esme said, pushing herself up to standing as she gathered her sleep-matted curls into a bun. The elastic snapped back on her wrist painfully before she could contain her hair, and she gave up on looking presentable. As she peered through the foggy peephole, the blurry shape of a tall blond man came into view. Benedict.

"It's your father," she said. No matter what happened between her and Benedict, she hoped her daughter would never stop believing that fact was true.

"Did they fix the gas?" Zoe's voice was muffled by the pillow she had put over her face to block out the harsh light Esme had flipped on.

"What?" Esme said, confused, before remembering why Zoe thought they were staying in the hotel in the first place. She slid open the chain and opened the door instead of answering.

"Hello, Esme."

"Hello."

"I'm here to pick you up."

"No," Esme said in a low tone. "I'll meet you there."

"We need to talk."

"Not now."

"Mom? Is Dad coming in?" Zoe called.

"No, he can't stay. He has an early-morning meeting with Jack." Esme's tone warned Benedict not to disagree. Though he frowned, she could see that he understood what the cost would be of going against her. Zoe would never forgive her father if she found out the truth about Julia. After all, she had learned how to hold grudges from him.

"Can I at least say good morning to our daughter?" He pitched his voice so only Esme could hear him.

"Dad?" Zoe called in a clearer, seemingly pillow-free, voice. "Is the house okay?"

"The technician is coming today," he said over Esme's shoulder. "Everything should be fine by this afternoon."

Esme rolled her eyes angrily at the imposed time frame for their return. He pitched his voice so Zoe couldn't hear again. "She's going to think it's weird for me to yell at her from the hallway."

"Fine. I need to shower anyway. Make it quick. I don't want you to be here when I get out." She turned and ducked into the small bathroom to the left. Through the thin door, she could hear Zoe and Benedict speaking warmly. She turned the water on full force to dampen the sound, then stepped into the chipped enamel tub and let the hot water course over her, protecting her with its silence. As she had demanded, Benedict was gone when she came out of the bathroom, and Zoe was dressed in a black hoodie and jeans.

"You don't want to shower?"

"I'll wait until tonight, when we get home. A hotel bathroom? Gross," Zoe said, smoothing her hair back into a ponytail.

Esme closed her eyes at Zoe's assumed timetable. "I'm not sure the leak will be fixed by then."

"Dad said it should be pretty straightforward," Zoe said as she slung her backpack over her shoulder. "Zach is coming to give me a ride. I'll see you at home. Good luck today." She leaned in to give Esme a kiss, and Esme smiled in spite of the tightness in her jaw at Benedict's manipulation.

"Okay, love you, Zo."

She walked toward the door, then turned back as she remembered something. "Dad said to tell you to meet him outside on the steps so you can walk in together."

"Thanks, hon." She waited until her daughter's back was turned before she let her annoyance show on her face.

After the door closed behind her daughter, Esme dressed in the dark-red pantsuit Jack had encouraged her to purchase for her testimony. *It's important to look credible*, Jack had said. *Attractive but not sexy. Juries like it when you make an effort.* The echo in his words of her agent's advice before her appointment with Jed was not lost on Esme, but she knew that this day had nothing as horrific in store for her. She smoothed the fabric over her hips before applying mascara to her eyelashes and blush to her cheeks. She collected the few items she and Zoe had left around the room and walked to her car.

The hotel was just down the street from the courthouse, and she arrived early. She had hoped that the message from Zoe was a ruse to distract their daughter from the tension between them and that Benedict wouldn't be waiting for her, but as she pulled onto the street, she saw him seated in the car he had borrowed from Sophie and Ray. His golden hair was shining in the sunshine bathing the driver's seat. Rather than pull into the parking garage, he had found a spot on the street where he could wait for her. Despite herself, she felt touched that he had noticed that she had forgotten to grab the pass card for the underground parking lot.

He stepped out to greet her. She could sense the crowd stirring on the steps at the sight of him, so she let him take her hand as they crossed the street together. She knew the television cameras were rolling. He had told her months before that he would never forgive her if he was found guilty. She didn't want any video footage of their estrangement to add to his grievances against her. His touch didn't bother her as much as she thought it would. She had spent her life pretending, first with the help of scripted words and then with her own. Why stop now?

He gripped her hand and turned his body toward her as they walked up the stone steps together, shielding her from the raucous crowd. Voices and people clamored around them, still calling the name she had abandoned when she took his. In his eyes, she searched for an explanation for what he had done. The reason he had been willing to sleep with Julia and put himself first above all of them. An explanation for the fact that he had never been capable of seeing the needs of others before his own. But instead of the remorse she was seeking, she saw something that looked oddly like pride, as if despite the circumstances, a part of him was glad to be back in the spotlight with her at his side. Later, she realized that had they not been so focused on each other, they might have seen him coming.

The gunshot was loud enough to startle the pigeons from the top of the roof of the courthouse. She looked up, not comprehending why she couldn't hear their frantic wings hammering the air. The sounds of the world had become a dull, sucking hum. As it had once before, time slowed into still frames. The silent silhouette of the cloud of birds. Her gaze turned back. Light left Benedict's eyes. The flaw became more pronounced than ever before. Red blossomed on his chest like a monstrous rose. His hand went limp in hers. Blurs of bodies reached, grabbed, tore her away as he fell hard on the cold steps. The gray concrete slammed against her cheek. Blood. Everywhere. From her face, from his heart. She fought against the hands keeping her from raising her head, finally freeing herself from the people who thought they were protecting her. A blur of faces. She was looking for Benedict. Instead she saw him.

Anthony was being restrained by six or seven men, one in uniform. As the damage to her eardrums eased, she heard the roar of individual voices rendered impossible to understand by their fear. She turned to stare at her husband crumpled impossibly on the stairs, a black handgun beside him, but Anthony was shouting something that he wanted her to know, looking at her, yelling over and over until she wanted to scream for silence. Instead, she faced him and absorbed the blow of his words.

"Now you are free."

PART THREE

She hid her hatred so well that it looked like love: a singular devotion to a secret that would destroy them all. The man who had been deceived into raising a child that was not his own. The woman who needed to be lauded by all. The child who had been fooled into thinking she was good.

—*Torn Grace,* The Purpose, *unpublished manuscript*

CHAPTER
THIRTY

She hired caterers for his wake. It was the first event on Raven Lane in fifteen years where nothing served was prepared by her or delivered from the kitchen of Dix-Neuf, but she couldn't bring herself to care about where the steaming food in the chafing dishes in the dining room had come from. Her head chef was in prison for murdering her husband. Her husband was a box of ashes at the crematorium. Her restaurant was closed for now, perhaps for good. Food no longer mattered to Esme. Nothing did except Zoe.

The family room was crowded with people, though the only person Esme focused on was her daughter, Zoe, huddled on the sofa with Julia beside her. Both girls had dark circles under their eyes. Their knuckles were whitened by the tightness of their grip as they clasped hands. Benedict's mother and her own huddled on either side, like aged bookends. Kitty was tucked into the space beside Julia, close enough to touch her daughter's hip. She was speaking softly, and Esme knew that of all people, she was the most likely source of comfort for the two devastated girls. After all, if Kitty could convince an author on deadline to rush away from his laptop to save his missing dog from harm on the highly trafficked Main Street, she had a chance of helping Julia and Zoe work through their grief.

Miriam and Levi had come and gone, dropping off a store-bought tray of vegetables and a card with no inscription, just their names. On another day, Esme would have laughed at Levi's unusually long embrace of Kitty, who returned it with the same enthusiasm as she had for Benedict's handsy uncle. Apparently, Kitty hadn't been the only one who had enjoyed their flirtation.

The closest Esme had come to shedding the feeling of being encased in glass was when Aaron had arrived with the same dish she had brought to his house for Torn's wake. It was full of eggplant parmesan.

"I can't believe I'm returning it like this," he said. There was no emotion in his voice either. Months after the shell shock of losing his husband, he wasn't the same man he had been. She knew he never would be.

Sophie had graciously taken the dish from his hands.

"How are you, Aaron?" Ray had asked as he shook his hand.

Aaron looked at him as if unsure how to answer. When Ray released his hand, he jammed it into his pocket. "Busy. Planning to sell the house. Working through a deal for the estate."

"What kind of deal?" Ray asked.

Aaron stared at Esme. "There's been a lot of interest in *The Call* since Torn's death. His agent just sold the movie rights. I had to be involved. Next of kin."

"That's . . . great," Ray said, taking a deep swallow of his whiskey.

"Yeah, I hope so. It's what Torn always wanted. I just hope the production company, MirrorMirror, can do it justice. The company certainly helped launch your career, right, Esme? We might even hire a ghostwriter to finish his last book."

Aaron's words were intended to be cutting, but Esme felt nothing as she excused herself. The dining room was empty, save for the pile of uneaten food that would become garbage if no one else took it home. She walked into the kitchen and sat on a stool instead of telling someone that the remainders should be taken away.

"Can I fix you something?" Sophie said, following her into the room. Her eyes were rimmed with the same pink shade as the tip of her nose, where the skin had been rubbed raw.

"No, thanks," she said.

"Esme. You need to eat."

Esme knew there was something funny about her friend pushing food on her after so many years of Esme doing the same, but she didn't smile. Ray sat down beside her while Sophie left to fix her a plate of food she knew she wouldn't be able to look at. The black dress Sophie had selected for her that morning felt uncomfortably baggy where the pleats ballooned out from her hips. Sophie was right that she should force herself to eat more. In the week since Benedict's death, she had been slowly disappearing.

"Sophie told me not to show you this today, but I thought you should know," Ray whispered, holding up his phone, which was queued to a frozen frame of a video clip. "Take it in the bathroom. I'll tell her you'll be right back."

Esme numbly followed his instructions. Once she'd shut herself in the powder room, the voices outside became little more than a hum as she activated the screen and saw the unmade-up face of a local news blogger. The woman's warm voice reminded her of Kitty.

"In the days since the public killing of Benedict Werner, on trial for the murder of famed author Torn Grace, the accused Anthony King has remained silent from his holding cell in county jail. Hours ago, we received an audio recording from the alleged killer, recorded by a family member in the visiting room of the prison. We have verified its veracity to the best of our ability, and we play it now for you, uncut and unedited. Here are the words of Anthony King."

Esme leaned against the door for support as Anthony's voice came from the small speaker in her hand. He sounded stuffed up, as if he had a cold or had just been crying. The recording was tinny, full of background conversations and chairs scraping.

This is a message for Esme Werner. Some of us were made monsters when we heard the call. Others were made angels. I am yours. I always knew what was best for you, even when you didn't. I know you wanted this. Now he is gone. You are free. We are safe. Never a wasted step. Please come. I miss you.

The video ended with the same black screen with which it had begun. Esme set the phone down on the edge of the sink. She knew Anthony's words should make her feel something or do something, but her mind and movements were robotic, as they had been since he had shot Benedict. The only thing she felt was that she would never feel anything again. She had not slept in seven nights. Instead, she passed the dark hours sitting on the bed she used to share with her husband and now shared with her daughter, watching the streetlight shine on Zoe's form.

Sometimes she thought about what she had said to Anthony the night before he killed her husband, when Benedict had once again assumed it was his right to take everything. The evening she had stopped at Dix-Neuf and Anthony had relayed the conversation, Esme had grown more furious. Dix-Neuf was not his to sell. Julia was not his to sleep with. Esme was not his to use. Not anymore. Esme had spoken to Anthony without realizing what she was saying. She had been angry, angrier than she had ever been before. Too angry to control herself.

It would be so much easier if he were gone.

She had been wrong to say that. She had been wrong to think it. It wasn't easier now, and she wasn't sure anything ever would be. Esme stared at her face in the mirror. Then she walked out of the powder room and into the rise and fall of voices in the entryway. People were leaving. She stood in the hallway and said things as they passed. When the rooms were empty and both grandmothers were resting in their beds, one in Zoe's room and one in the guest room where Esme's husband had spent the last nights of his life, she climbed the stairs, touching the half dozen new photographs she had framed and hung since her husband's death. When she got to her bedroom, Zoe was lying on the bed.

"Too much?" Esme sat beside her daughter, brushing away a strand of hair that had escaped her ponytail.

"I'm just so tired," Zoe said.

"It's over now. We got through it."

"What do you mean 'we got through it,' Mom? That's not how it feels to me at all."

Esme leaned over to embrace her daughter, then carefully cradled her as Zoe sank back onto the pillow. Once Zoe was settled, Esme stood to get a pad of paper from the drawer where she kept stationery. As she pulled it out, she saw an open package of full-size envelopes. For a moment, she was taken aback by her own carelessness. Had he opened the drawer to find a pen, Benedict would have realized that the single missing envelope had been used to hold the photographs that were placed carefully under the seat of their SUV. Esme hadn't lied to Jack. She had not been trying to hide anything. She had put them in a place where she knew they would be found. Her daughter's voice interrupted her thoughts.

"What are you doing, Mom?"

Esme closed the drawer gently, like the cover of a book that had been resolved to her satisfaction. She carried the notepad back to her daughter on the bed and settled beside her.

"I need to tell you how it came to this, Zoe. But first, I have to write it down."

She began writing immediately. Finally, she knew exactly what she had to say. She began with the title.

The Things They Thought I Wanted
By Esme

ACKNOWLEDGMENTS

Thank you to my incredible, astonishing team of talent. Thank you to Alison Dasho, a mother warrior and elite editor who has a genius beyond measure that gave me a killer ending and a vicious path to get there. Alicia Clancy, an amazing leader and potential muse for a new novel about twin sisters and Italian voyages. Sarah Murphy, for giving me a wealth of ideas, insight, and inspiration and a much-needed intelligent perspective on the words I have written. To Jon Ford, for an enjoyable, inventive, and incisive review of all my grammatical errors and creative style choices. To Kellie and Robin for polishing up the final pieces. Thank you to the amazing tactical coordinator, Nicole Pomeroy, for organizing the million bits and pieces. And finally to Gordon Warnock, my fantastic agent and consigliore. There are so many bad agents in this book, but I am lucky beyond belief to have an incredible one.

It's going to be a very long time before my children can read the books I write, but that's no reason not to thank them for the drive they have given me to be a real live writer, as well as the daily comic relief that their crazy kookiness gives me. Eve and Thompson, you are the reason that I do this. I hope, someday, my words (even the scandalous ones) will make you proud and will inspire you to be exactly what you want to be when you grow up.

Thank you to my husband, Ben Greenberg, my one, my only, my all. Thank you for helping me build this fake empire, and thank you for believing in me.

Thank you to my sister, Morgan Cowie, for chipping away at the ugly doubts and reading every single word (no matter how god-awful) that I send you. I am, and always have been, so proud to be your twin.

Marc, Jasper, and Emmerich, you are all rad dudes. Your joy and enthusiasm about me being a writer makes me feel proud enough to keep going even when the days are early and the nights are long.

Linda and Ulrich Hollin, thank you for bringing kindness to my life and work every time we speak about it.

Thank you to Kim Slater, Nate Nash, and Miss Olivia, for showing me how to make dreams come true in the most beautiful place on earth.

Thank you to my super-supportive, skillful, and inspiring beta readers. Your willingness to plow through the rough patches and lend your insight is deeply appreciated.

I have a super amazing group of friends that bring me cookies when I am sad and toast me with champagne when I am happy. Thank you to Chantelle Simpson, Julie and James Babiy, Jane Boles and Hugh Stimson, Don and Connie Nguyen, Julia and Erin Young, the Guelph guys, Heather and Given Davies, Jan and Jenne Pratschke, Christine Lee, Tasha Gallagher, Kate Rose, Jon Bennett, Megan Hetherington, Justin Ford, Chris Berry, Anne-Marie Belanger, Kate Leslie, Paul Johnston, Alex Merrick, Nicholas Scapillati, Kas Shield, Alison West, Grant Matzen, and Bridget Ku.

Thank you to my awesome writing group, Deborah Wade and Tatiana Lee, who worked on so many parts of this with me. Meeting with you makes me happy, productive, and full of joy that there are other incredible voices soon to come into the public realm.

Thank you to Karen Dodd, for being so full of kindness, love, and joy in my darkest days.

Thank you to the founding members of the Secret Club, especially Lee Carney, who sped through my book the way I always hoped someone would read it. I am so excited to share all the ups and downs of making books with you and very grateful for your early support in this wild journey of being a novelist.

Thank you to my parents, Ava Perraton and Deryl Cowie, and to my stepmother, Darlene Cowie, for your eagle eyes and support. Thank you to my grandmother, Joan Jacobsen, and my uncle Chris Cowie and my aunt Donna Cowie for believing in me. Thank you to my grandmother and grandfather, Helen and Myron Smith, for supporting this crazy dream. Thank you to my fabulous auntie Lynda, uncle Dale, and cousin Sherri, who have been such ardent, loving champions of my work! Thank you.

A note of appreciation for my lovely neighbors on the small cul-de-sac on which I live. I wrote the first draft of this book months before I moved onto our beautiful street, and the goings-on of Raven Lane are in no way a reflection of the amazing community we have!

Thank you to the unwavering, hilarious, astonishing, and deeply relied-upon support of my talented fellow Lake Union authors. The group is a touchstone for me and has gotten me through some sad moments. The deepest of thank-yous for reviews from A. J. Banner, Emily Carpenter, Imogen Clark, Amber Collins Carter, Jo Furniss, Kerry Lonsdale, Catherine McKenzie, Karen McQuestion, D. M. Pulley, and Patricia Sands. I am so humbled and honored to call you my colleagues and my friends.

Finally, thank you to the creators of *Octonauts* and *PAW Patrol*. Without you, this book could never have been completed.

READER GROUP QUESTIONS FOR AMBER COWIE'S *RAVEN LANE*

1. What benefits do Esme and Benedict each get from their marriage? Do you think they were ever truly in love, or was it always a relationship of convenience/need? What about Torn and Aaron's marriage? Are the other relationships (i.e., Sophie and Ray, Miriam and Levi) based on something different?

2. Why was Esme tempted by Torn? Why was Torn so drawn to her? What did he offer her that was worth risking her marriage? Would she have slept with him without the "push" from Kitty's key party?

3. Esme was the keeper of secrets in her marriage (e.g., Jed's rape and the ensuing fallout, the question of Zoe's paternity, her affair with Torn). Is she a sympathetic character despite her withholdings, or could she be considered a master manipulator? Alternately, do you think Benedict acted nobly in pretending that he didn't suspect Jed's

transgressions against Esme, or in raising Zoe without questioning her parentage?

4. How do the culture and exclusivity of Raven Lane both limit and inform the perspectives of its residents? Are the characters' actions a product of their inherent natures or of their unique, hot pot of an environment? Where is the line between intimacy and intrusion in a close-knit community?

5. Do you feel sympathy for any of the characters? Are there any who are redeemable/good, in your eyes? Why or why not? Were the residents of Raven Lane drawn into something beyond their control, or did they create the poisonous dynamics of their neighborhood?

6. Many of the characters are artists who create beautiful work (e.g., Sophie and her miniatures, Torn and his novels, Esme and her cooking). How do the ugly aspects of their personalities and actions feed their art? Would their work be as profound without the shadowy side behind it? Or in some cases, did the characters' failures (e.g., Ray's manuscript rejections, Benedict's stalled modeling career, Esme's decision to leave acting) make them monstrous in turn?

7. Why would Ray surround himself with successful artists while he struggled to achieve his own dreams? Does the proximity of their achievements inspire or damage him? Do other people on Raven Lane feel similar animosity and admiration for the things their neighbors have achieved?

8. Do you think the incident with Benedict and Torn was truly an accident? How did the author set up the various pieces to create that tragedy? Are any characters implicated, in your opinion? What might have happened to them had Benedict not been killed? Do you believe Esme was preparing to testify for or against Benedict on the morning of his murder?

9. What do you think motivated Anthony to kill Benedict? Were you surprised? Do you think any part of Esme was grateful to Anthony for what he did? Do you think she is culpable in any way?

10. Did Torn and Benedict both deserve what they got in the end? Do you think either of them accepted responsibility for their shortcomings, or ever truly acknowledged them, before their premature deaths? Was it necessary for them to die?

11. Has Esme successfully earned the love she so desperately craved in response to her mother's cold and distant treatment, whether in her relationships or her pursuits? Do you think she was a good mother to Zoe? Oppositely, did she fail Julia as a maternal figure? As fathers, how do Benedict and Torn compare? Do you think they are both selfish in their desires to be parents, or do they have the capacity to love?

12. How does Torn's novel *The Call* reflect the themes, events, and characters in *Raven Lane*?

13. How does reading about monstrous people make you feel? Does the damage that has been done to people in

the past excuse their actions in the present? Is it comforting to read about characters' bad choices, knowing you would never make the same mistakes? Does it help alleviate guilt over mistakes of your past to see you're not alone? Or something else?

14. "I know what I am now, and you cannot bear it. But you must." How does that quote resonate with the real world? Who must bear the monstrosities of today, and how do they survive?

15. How did the interpretation of Esme by others in her life differ from the way she saw herself? Did her past trauma cloud her own self-perception? Or make her shield herself so well that no one was able to truly know her?

16. Esme seeks solace in her restaurant and the secret space of her kitchen after her assault, shying away from the public eye. How does Jed's abuse of power affect her, even when she believes herself to be safe? Did she bring the echoes of violence into her newly created life without realizing it? Why does it bother her that Torn cannot let go of Esme Lee?

17. Is Esme in control of her own destiny, or have the men in her life dictated her fate? Considering that these men asserted their power and/or robbed her of her own autonomy in one way or another, does she ever get ahead of that trend? Based on your interpretation, is the ending a hopeful one? Do you perceive Esme's vow to write her story as the potential for her to redirect the future? How will telling Zoe the truth as she sees it influence the next generation?

ABOUT THE AUTHOR

Photo © 2018 Benjamin Greenberg

Amber Cowie is a graduate of the University of Victoria and was short-listed for the 2017 Whistler Independent Book Awards. She has also served burgers at a frontier-themed diner, hot chocolate at the only ski resort in Scotland, and pints at a bar in downtown Dublin. She planted trees in northern Canada and staffed the front desk of a hotel on a remote island between France and England. She has also been a reporter for a small-town newspaper, in-house writer for a snowmobile magazine, and freelance pattern designer for knitwear companies. Now she is a mother of two, wife of one, reader of many, and the author of the acclaimed debut novel *Rapid Falls*. She continues to write books that make her browser search history highly suspicious. For more information, visit her at www.ambercowie.com.